For the Rest of Forever

BECCA NEIL

Cover design and formatting by Destined Publishing

Cover art by @angki.s_

Interior art by Elise LaValle

Edited by Sara Onstine of Mild-Mannered Editors

Published by Destined Publishing

Content Warning

This novel includes the following sensitive topics that may trigger reactions in some readers:

- References to past trauma, including parental neglect and physical/emotional abuse

- Instances of homophobia

- Depictions of severe anxiety and depression

- Depictions of suicidal ideation

- Food aversion/eating disorder

- Refusal of medication for mental illness (*please see Note From the Author for further explanation and a statement)

To my grandparents,
who showed me what real, deep,
unconditional love looks like.

Chapter One

Greg

"I'M GETTING TOO OLD for this, you know."

Greg Westin grinned as he set down the last print to be packed. "Well, if you're getting too old, what does that make me? Ancient?" He twisted his head around and glanced over his shoulder, reaching up to shield his eyes from the sunlight streaming in through the open doors of the small cargo trailer. His husband, Allen, stopped just at the entrance of the trailer and set down the box he'd been carrying, grunting slightly as he straightened back up.

"I believe the correct terminology is 'old geezer.' Or at least, that's what Tina's daughter called you last time we visited."

Greg laughed and ran his hand through his graying hair. "I thought 'old geezers' had to be at least sixty. I've still got four years to go." He shook his head, still grinning, then motioned to the box Allen had set down. "That the last one?"

"Yeah," Allen said. "Faye and Ron asked if we'd be staying for dinner, but I told them we were probably going to try to catch the late ferry since that storm's supposed to be coming in tomorrow. I'd rather be home than trying to drive through it."

With a nod, Greg turned and stepped over to the edge of the trailer, peeking out and up at the early evening sky—still clear and blue and sunny. It was beautiful, as late August days tended to be in Friday Harbor. But Allen was right—a huge storm was supposed to pass through tomorrow, and he'd much rather be snugly at home in North Bend, with everything safely unpacked into his studio, than worrying about the weather.

Greg hopped off the back of the trailer, and Allen leaned against him and closed his eyes. "Sorry it was such a long day," Greg said quietly. He pressed a light kiss to Allen's forehead. "And I'm sorry for the quick up and back. It's much more fun when we get to spend a few days up here."

The wrinkles around Allen's eyes creased as he smiled. "Next time. And we should come for vacation, not work. Maybe I'll even make you leave your camera at home."

"Oooh, what a threat!" Greg laughed, wrapping his arms around his husband's waist, and Allen lifted his head up, his gray-blue eyes now sparkling with silliness.

"Think about it. When's the last time you've gone anywhere just to go? When's the last time *we've* gone anywhere not for one of your work things?" Allen's smile faded into a frown, and he shook his head. "I didn't mean for that to come out how it did. I meant it as a joke."

Greg had known that, but he still had to swallow back his guilt. It was true. They traveled for him to photograph places. They traveled together, that is, or he traveled alone, since Allen worked five or sometimes six days a week at the North Bend Library. In fact, the last time they'd gone on a vacation that wasn't for his work or for a wedding or funeral had been over five years ago, when they'd celebrated their fifth wedding anniversary.

He loved photography, which was good, because he'd made a very successful career out of it, but it was much too easy to get caught up in trying to capture just the right view at just the right moment or trying to find the most impressive landscape in the most difficult-to-reach location, nearly always somewhere off the beaten path. It could sometimes make him forget everything else, become a bit obsessed, neglect his other obligations. Including his husband.

Allen had always been infinitely supportive, of course. In the thirty-three years that they'd known each other, Allen had never once complained about the extra time Greg always packed into their trips so he could explore and find the next great place he wanted to photograph. Just like he hadn't complained when Greg had renovated their garage into his photography studio, and when Greg had needed to spend large amounts of their money on new equipment—cameras, lenses, printers. Allen had even helped design and build the modifications to their cargo trailer to make packing and unpacking for trade and art shows easier. And he had accompanied Greg every time, to every show.

It wasn't a one-way street. Greg had been equally as supportive of Allen's passions and career as well. They wouldn't have made it this long and still have the incredible relationship they did otherwise. But sometimes—like now—Greg was reminded of just how much his career had taken over their lives.

Greg vowed silently that he'd make it up to Allen as soon as possible and worked a careful smile onto his face. Then he bent down to press a light kiss to his husband's lips.

"You're right. We should come up here *just* for a vacation. Maybe later in the year?" When Allen nodded a quiet agreement,

Greg looked back into the trailer briefly. Everything was in its place but not secured yet, so he still had some work to do.

"Why don't I finish packing, and you go see if Darryl's got any more of those boxes of strawberries left?" he suggested. "Then we can get going and hopefully catch that ferry. It leaves at seven thirty, right?"

With a nod, Allen stepped away from Greg, scratching his beard. "Seven thirty, yeah," he said. He glanced back toward where the other booths from the Friday Harbor Farmers' Market were still being packed up and then grinned. "Darryl's still here, good. Those strawberries—so sweet this year!"

Greg bent over and picked up the box Allen had set down a few minutes ago, and when he straightened back up, Allen was watching him with a gentle expression. "What is it, darling?"

But Allen just shook his head, smiled softly, and leaned in to kiss Greg again. "Nothing at all. You're just looking quite handsome in your old age," Allen teased. He planted another kiss on Greg's lips and then turned and headed off toward Darryl's red pickup truck, which was parked on the other side of the small courtyard where their booth had been.

Laughing to himself, Greg hefted the box into the trailer, hopped back in, and continued packing up.

The drive to the wharf was short, and Greg listened as Allen talked quietly about his final preparations for the event he was hosting at the library on Sunday—the last in a series of open-library summer literacy events where children from North Bend and other surrounding communities were invited to come share and exchange books, read aloud to the group, and participate in games and activities.

Thankfully, they managed a spot on the next ferry back to Anacortes, and about an hour and a half later, Greg pulled their small SUV out onto the highway, headed east toward I-5. The roads were clear, and all the light from the day had just finished disappearing below the horizon.

He glanced over at his passenger and grinned. Allen's eyes were closed, his head tilted back against the headrest, and his mouth parted slightly in his sleep. Greg had to resist the urge to reach over and push Allen's hair back off his forehead—those few strands that always wanted to fall down almost over his eyes. But he didn't want to wake his husband, and so he kept both hands on the steering wheel and focused his attention on the road ahead again.

The drive wasn't terribly long, and he pulled up in front of their house just after ten thirty. The slight jostle of the SUV as he stopped woke up Allen, who groaned and stretched.

"Home already? Aw, shoot, I slept the whole way? You should have woken me up."

Greg just laughed lightly. "You looked like you needed the rest," he said, and Allen grimaced but then shrugged.

"I'll let Beans out in the back and then open the garage door," Allen suggested, unbuckling his seat belt. "Shouldn't take us too long to unload—"

"I'll handle it tonight, darling," Greg cut in. Normally they would work together to unload all of Greg's prints and equipment, and it would only take them about fifteen minutes or so. But he'd seen Allen's exhaustion earlier, and tonight, it just didn't feel right to ask more of his husband.

Allen looked poised to argue, his eyes narrowed slightly as he seemed to study Greg. His expression tightened before he nodded in agreement. "Okay, but you'll come straight to bed, right? No . . .

getting distracted by something in your studio or sitting down at your computer to edit some of those photos you took Thursday night or—or anything?"

"Of course," Greg promised, though his stomach clenched at the immediate relief he saw in his husband's eyes.

"Good." Allen smiled, and then, as though he could tell the direction of Greg's thoughts and wanted to redirect him, Allen leaned in until his lips were just about half an inch from Greg's. "Because I want to cuddle with you tonight," he whispered, his voice low and husky.

The familiar tug of desire made Greg groan, and he reached up to cup Allen's cheek, then closed the rest of the distance between them so their lips met. It was a deeper kiss than the quick, light ones they'd shared earlier, and when Allen's hand settled high on Greg's thigh, he groaned again and pulled back, breathing heavily.

"Give me a minute to put Beans out back," Allen said, slightly breathless himself, and Greg just nodded. Allen's hand then left his thigh, and Greg leaned his head back against the headrest for a moment as he listened to Allen open the door and exit the SUV.

When the passenger door shut, he opened his eyes and watched his husband tread stiffly up the driveway and along the front walkway and then disappear into the house a moment later. He sat there for just another minute or two, tracking Allen's path through the house as windows lit up one by one. Muffled barking, followed by the sound of the back door opening and closing called him to action, and Greg blinked to reset himself and put the SUV back into drive. He pulled forward a bit and then expertly backed the trailer up into the driveway, stopping with the rear of the trailer only a foot or so from the garage door just as it began to rise.

By the time he parked and hopped out, Allen was at the back of the trailer, unlocking it and starting to open up the rear doors. Greg almost laughed, almost made some teasing comment about

Allen being a stubborn old man. But when he saw his husband's tired eyes, he just shook his head.

"You go rest. Please," he said, setting his hand lightly over Allen's on the handle. "I'll only be a few minutes."

Despite Allen's obvious exhaustion, Greg still expected push-back. They *always* did this part together, after all. So he was quite surprised when Allen just nodded.

"Okay, okay. I'll text Joe and let him know we're home so he doesn't come over to check on Beanie in the morning. And you'll be up soon?"

"I promise," Greg said, and he leaned over and brushed a gentle kiss on Allen's cheek.

The next half hour or so went by slowly as Greg unpacked the trailer, putting everything away carefully and setting aside the pieces that had sold so he could pack them up to ship or deliver them the following week. All the while, he heard noises from the house—Allen's voice calling their dog, Beans, in from the back-yard; some noises from the kitchen; then the creaking overhead from their second-floor bedroom and telltale sounds of the shower turning on and then off a little bit later.

By the time he was all finished and the trailer was parked back in its spot along the side of the house, it was well after eleven, and the house had been quiet for some time. He shut the garage door behind himself and glanced at his small studio. His eyes were immediately drawn to his camera case, which he'd set in its place on his desk.

The sunset Thursday evening. That was what he'd pho-tographed when they'd arrived in Friday Harbor. There had been just enough wisps of clouds in the sky, tinted orange and pink, and the light had reflected off the water. It was a view he'd seen often enough, but for whatever reason, on Thursday evening, it had held some sort of enchantment to it, and he hadn't been able to resist.

Just like he couldn't quite resist now. A quick look, just two minutes. Just to remind him of the beauty. Then he'd edit the photos tomorrow.

He stepped over to his desk, but as he reached out for the camera case, his eyes drifted to the framed photo sitting next to his computer, and his hand paused. Allen's kind gray-blue eyes smiled back at him, and Greg inhaled sharply.

"My love," he whispered, and he reached out and ran his fingers along the edge of the frame. It was really nothing fancy—just a selfie of the two of them at the top of Shriner Peak in Mount Rainier National Park. He'd taken it with his cell phone nearly three years ago. The view behind them wasn't even great—fog and clouds obstructed what should have been a phenomenal view of Mount Rainier itself off in the distance. But in all of the more than thirty years he'd been hiking and photographing people and places and landscapes, it was his favorite photo.

His arm was looped loosely around Allen's shoulders, and his head was tilted sideways just enough so it touched Allen's. Allen's smile was bright and carefree.

Greg's heart stuttered, and he closed his eyes for a moment. Then he blew out a short breath, turned, and headed inside, flipping off the light switch behind him.

The photos would wait until morning.

Chapter Two

Allen

"GO ON NOW," ALLEN said, shooing Beans off the bed for the third time. The little brown terrier almost seemed to grumble, but he jumped down and plodded over to his bed in the corner of the room. Allen shook his head. "Every night it's the same thing."

Beans curled up and rested his head on his paws, then looked up at Allen with what Allen could only interpret as a sad, soulful look.

Allen sighed. "Don't look at me like that. You know the rules."

The dog's eyes closed, and Allen settled back on the bed again, letting his body relax into the soft mattress.

He was tired. And that was an understatement, really. If not for the short nap he'd gotten on the drive home from Anacortes, he might already be asleep. If he had to guess, he'd say his current state of exhaustion was probably because Thursday night had been less than restful for him. It had been one of *those* nights, his sleep plagued by bad dreams that had left him more than anxious when he'd woken up and unable to relax and fall asleep again.

It was silly. Silly and frustrating, actually. He'd handled lack of sleep a lot better when he was in his teens and twenties and even in his thirties. But now that he was in his mid-fifties—having just turned fifty-four earlier this year—the restless nights seemed to hit him much harder.

They didn't come that often, thankfully, and he wasn't entirely sure what had triggered this one. He felt like he was in a good place now. In fact, he'd been in a good place for a long time, and it had been years, probably, since he'd experienced the level of anxiety he'd woken up with in the middle of the night last night.

There had been a time, decades ago now, when the dreams had been much more frequent and when he'd still remembered them as he awoke—dreams filled with impossible darkness and intense loneliness, dreams where he'd been running down an endless hallway, desperately trying to get away from whatever monstrosity had been chasing him. They'd been particularly disruptive when his relationship with Greg had been new and exciting, which had at least made sense to him. And now, although they were few and far between, they were no less disorienting and tended to stick with him longer—or at least the exhaustion did.

From downstairs, Allen heard the door to the garage shut, and a second later, Beans jumped up from his spot in the corner and rushed out of the room, barking his little head off. Allen sighed and sat up again, switching on the light next to him.

"Did you miss me? You did, didn't you, you silly dog. Silly little dog. Ha. I missed you too, buddy." Greg's voice carried up from the bottom of the stairs, deep but happy and enthusiastic.

Allen ran a hand roughly through his hair and then pushed himself up to stand as he heard Beans bounding up the stairs. In a sudden burst of wiry brown fur, the dog sprinted into the room, zoomed to the far end, spun around and leapt up onto the bed, and then ran, still going as fast as his little legs would carry him, back out and down the hallway.

Greg's laughter echoed along with Beans's barking. "Shh, now, you're gonna wake up the whole neighborhood, you little rascal."

Beans sped back through the room once more, circling around Allen three times before he jumped up on the bed again and plopped down right in Allen's spot, now panting hard.

With another sigh, Allen shook his head at the dog. "Off now, Beans. Go to bed." He didn't really like using his stern voice with the dog, but at the same time, Beans's antics were just not amusing right now, and—

Allen frowned and clenched his jaw. He recognized the particular evolution of emotions he'd been having, culminating in this short-fused intolerance of things he usually found silliness and joy and amusement in, and he didn't like it.

From behind him, Greg's light laughter continued as Greg entered the room. "Sorry. You know how excited he gets to see us after we've been gone," Greg said.

Gentle hands slipped around Allen's waist, and he closed his eyes and tried to let his tension go. He leaned back into his husband and tilted his head as Greg's lips found the side of his neck. Light kisses trailed down to the collar of his T-shirt. Allen let out a short, shuddering breath and reined in his irritation with the dog, but not before Greg seemed to sense that something wasn't quite right.

"What is it?" Greg asked, his hand now rubbing gently up and down Allen's arm. "Are you feeling okay, darling?"

"Yeah. Yeah, I think so. I'm just tired, and the dog"—Allen motioned to where Beans still lay, sprawled out on top of the comforter—"he's . . ." Allen just trailed off and shook his head. "It's fine. I'm just . . . I'm tired."

Greg's hand stopped just above Allen's elbow, and he squeezed gently. "Beans, bed. Now."

The dog immediately jumped to attention at Greg's firm command, and he hopped down from the bed, trotted over to his place in the corner, and lay back down. The minor annoyance Allen felt at the fact that the dog appeared to go out of his way to ignore Allen and listen to Greg quickly faded when Greg laughed lightly and kissed Allen's neck again.

"Don't be mad at him. He means well," Greg said. There was another kiss low on his neck, this one lingering a tad longer. "You can be mad at me if you want. Sorry I took so long. And I've still gotta take a shower. Give me ten more minutes?"

Allen felt himself pulling away—not physically, but emotionally—and even though he recognized it, he seemed powerless to stop it. His mind raced through all the words he knew to be true: Greg loved him; there was no real reason to be upset; he wasn't really upset anyway; Greg would be quick; unloading the trailer alone was a lot of work, and Greg hadn't taken a long time on purpose; he was probably just as tired as Allen. Yet, even though Allen knew the words to be true, other, more negative thoughts—thoughts he hadn't had in quite a while—swirled around, drowning out all the truth.

Unworthy. Unloved. Needy. Disruptive. Burden. Burden. Burden.

An intense emotional numbness seemed to suck all the air from his lungs. He shook his head, not in response to Greg's question, but to try and rid his brain of the intrusive thoughts.

"Allen?" Greg stepped around in front of him, paused very briefly, and then wrapped him up in a gentle embrace. "Where are you right now, darling?"

"Not where I want to be," he said quietly, knowing Greg would understand.

"What can I do?" There was another light kiss on his cheek, and Allen leaned against his husband. When he didn't answer—because he didn't really know the answer—Greg's arms tightened around him. "I'll be quick, and then, let me hold you while you sleep tonight."

Allen gave a short nod, and Greg released him, brushed a light kiss on his lips, and tilted his head toward the bathroom. "Five minutes," he promised.

"Yeah, yeah. It's okay. I'm fine. Don't rush. I'm . . . fine." Allen exhaled and looked down, shaking his head again.

Liar. Burden.

Greg's arms were around him almost immediately, and he let his husband's embrace surround him. It was warm and familiar, and he buried his head into Greg's chest and closed his eyes.

"Don't let your brain trick you, Allen," Greg said softly. Then there was a small huff, not quite laughter. "Oh, boy, it's been a while. It can hit at any time, huh? I'm so sorry, Allen. I love you. You know that, right? You're loved. So much."

"I know."

"Five minutes. Or less."

Allen nodded, and this time, when Greg let him go, they kissed briefly, and it felt just a tiny bit better. He pulled away and looked up at his husband. Greg was watching him with concern, his kind eyes studying Allen's face.

Allen let himself smile, even though it was a bit strained, and then he reached up and touched Greg's temple. "I'm giving you a few more gray hairs, aren't I?"

Greg laughed lightly. "They make me look distinguished."

"A distinguished old geezer."

"Indeed."

Allen closed his eyes again as Greg leaned forward and gently kissed his forehead.

"Make yourself comfortable, and I'll be right back," Greg reassured him, and when Allen nodded, Greg seemed to pull away with reluctance. Then he disappeared into the bathroom.

From his spot in the corner, Beans whimpered a little, and Allen glanced over his shoulder at the dog, frowning. His irritation was *still* there, even though the poor pup hadn't done anything wrong. And he hated that.

Allen sat heavily on the edge of the bed and then patted his lap. "Beanie buddy, come here," he called quietly.

The dog lifted his head, his eyes wide and bright. Then he jumped to his feet, bounded across the room, and hopped up onto the bed, plopping down so his head rested on Allen's thigh. Allen sat there for several minutes, stroking Beans's fur. From the bathroom, he heard the shower turn on and then shut off, and when Greg stepped back out, still toweling his hair dry, Allen looked up, his hand pausing on Beans's back.

There was a subtle shift in Greg's expression, a faint hint of guilt flickering in his eyes. But it was gone before Allen could really be sure he saw it. Still, he couldn't help the negative thoughts coming back yet again, echoes of a past he was sure he'd left behind when he'd moved to Seattle some thirty-five years ago.

Stop bothering him with this. You're too much work. He won't love you anymore. Burden. You're a burden.

Allen blew out a sharp breath, and as though the dog knew their cuddle time was up, Beans jumped off the bed and shuffled over to his corner. Greg tossed his towel into the hamper next to their dresser and quickly took the spot where Beans had been. Then he wrapped both arms around Allen. Again.

"Don't listen to it," Greg murmured. "Listen to me instead. I love you. You're worthy, you're loved and valued, and you deserve all the love and all the happiness."

Allen heard the familiar words and clung to them, just as he clung to his husband. "Hold me?" he asked after another moment.

"Of course."

Together, they crawled under the covers and settled in bed, and Allen let his husband's warm embrace surround him and chase away all that other rotten stuff.

It seemed to work. Mostly.

Chapter Three
Greg

GREG WOKE UP HOURS before the sun rose, drawn by a familiar longing to be out on the trail, to experience the very beginning of the new day at the top of a mountain peak somewhere, surrounded by the soft quiet of the forest. He felt the pull strongly that morning, despite the pouring rain and howling winds already battering the windows from outside.

The storm had arrived early, and that was probably a good thing, really. He wouldn't have left anyway, not with Allen still clinging to him in a restful but fragile sleep. But he did have to consciously make that decision, especially since another part of him was just dying for the opportunity to test out the new custom-fitted rain cover he'd purchased for his Nikon.

There was a quiet whimper from over by the bedroom door, and Greg pushed himself up onto one elbow, careful to not wake Allen. Beans sat squarely in the center of the doorway, his tail thumping on the ground. He whimpered again and then barked. Loudly.

Greg groaned inwardly and gave the dog a stern look, but Beans just barked again and then turned and bounded off down the hallway. Frowning, Greg looked down at Allen, and he was relieved to see his husband was still sound asleep, still curled up right next to Greg, still breathing slowly and deeply.

His frown turned into a soft smile, and he bent down and brushed his lips lightly against Allen's forehead. The gesture was something he did several times a day, and yet it felt as full of love as it always had, even after thirty-three years.

"I love you, Allen, my darling," he murmured, and then he carefully eased himself out from under his husband's arms and scooted off the bed. Allen shifted but didn't wake, and Greg smiled, then hurried to let Beans out into the monsoon outside before the silly dog decided he'd waited too long and did his business right in front of the back door.

Jogging down the stairs, Greg heard Beans ahead of him, whining and pawing at the sliding patio door. He let Beans out, then took a short detour to the laundry room to grab a towel, since the dog would no doubt be soaking wet and muddy when he was finished outside. By the time Greg returned, Beans was already back at the door, scratching to be let back in. Greg dried the dog, tossed the dirty towel into the washing machine for a later load, and then climbed back up the stairs, Beans following at his heels.

He paused in the doorway, leaning against the doorframe as Beans ambled on past him and toward the bed where Allen still slept soundly.

"Nuh-uh, Beans. Bed. Now," Greg warned, his voice firm but quiet. The dog stopped and gave Greg a look over his shoulder. "Now," he repeated. Beans stared at him for another long second, and Greg thought the dog was seriously considering whether to obey or not. With what seemed to be a resigned sigh, if a dog could sigh or act resigned, Beans turned and headed to his bed to curl up and go back to sleep.

Greg shook his head. "Silly dog," he muttered under his breath. After a quick trip to the bathroom to relieve himself and wash his hands, Greg returned to the bed, settling under the covers and then shimmying over until he was about in the middle of the bed. Allen seemed to sense him, and he turned over and cuddled up against Greg's chest, still not waking up.

It was good, really. Allen needed the sleep. In fact, given how tired Allen had been the night before and how much and how quickly he'd started to struggle just after they'd gotten home last night, Greg knew that what Allen needed the most was rest, affection, and reassurance.

Experience told him that. Thirty-three years of experience helping his boyfriend and then husband work through extreme anxiety and depression caused by years and years of emotional abuse from his parents.

It had been a long time since he'd seen that expression in Allen's eyes and felt the tension in Allen's embrace. Years maybe. They'd been in a really good place for years, and as Greg replayed the last few days in his mind, he couldn't immediately identify anything that might have triggered his husband's spiral. And when he thought harder about it, he realized it had been more of a plummet than a spiral since he hadn't noticed any signs or anything until Allen had gotten upset with Beans the night before.

Although it was possible he hadn't really been paying close enough attention.

At fifty-six, he was well aware of most of his own personality flaws by now, and he knew that one of them—maybe the most intrusive one at this point in his life—was his tendency to get fixated on things. Generally, it was his work—he'd just *have* to get a certain photo, even if it meant extra days out on the trail or at a certain location, waiting for the perfect weather or the perfect lighting. And he really *had* been distracted the last few weeks.

In fact, just before their Friday Harbor trip, Greg had been gone for three days, wandering around Olympic National Forest, searching for the exact location for a photoshoot he wanted to do in October, when the deciduous trees would start to change colors. And the week before that, he'd been holed up in his studio for hours on end, editing a set of photos he'd gotten months ago but hadn't had time to sort through and process. He'd been so distracted by it that he'd lost track of time more than once and not made it up to bed until after three or four in the morning several days in a row.

He frowned as he realized that yes, with how distracted he'd been the last few weeks, he probably wouldn't have recognized any early signs that Allen was feeling low. They could be difficult to see and easy to miss, even if he wasn't as distracted.

And he should know better. After thirty-three years, he should know better.

He closed his eyes and swallowed hard, telling himself to try and not worry so much. Experience also told him that wouldn't really get him anywhere. No, what he needed to do right now was be present and reassuring. And make sure he was *not* distracted so he didn't miss anything else.

From next to him, Allen let out a long sigh, his hand coming to rest right in the center of Greg's chest. "You're up so early, dear," Allen said, his voice muffled as he buried his head deeper into Greg's shoulder. "Don't tell me you're going out in this weather? You know, even a super-specialized, custom-fit rain cover for your camera can't keep rain out when it's flying at you horizontally because of the wind."

Greg chuckled and covered his husband's hand with his own. Then he lightly kissed Allen's forehead again.

"Beans needed to go out," he explained. "And I wasn't going to go anywhere this morning. I want to be here with you."

"Hmm, don't tell me the forest wasn't calling you. I know you better than that." Allen's hand pressed into his chest. "But I'm glad you're here. I didn't want to wake up alone today."

Greg's stomach clenched, and he shook his head and kissed Allen's forehead one more time. "It called. It always calls," Greg admitted. "But I wouldn't have gone. Not today. Today, I'm drawing you a bath and making you breakfast in bed and"—his hand shifted to Allen's chin, and he gently tilted his husband's head back and pressed a brief kiss to Allen's lips—"then whatever *you* want today."

"You don't have to—"

"I *want* to," Greg reassured him. He cupped his husband's cheek and kissed him again, and it was still short and chaste but just as loving, just as warm.

"I—I don't . . ." Allen trailed off, and Greg's heart ached for his husband. He knew the words Allen was thinking but trying valiantly not to say out loud. He'd heard them often enough and countered them often enough.

He was happy now that Allen had stopped himself from speaking them, but at the same time, he could see them etched clearly on Allen's face.

I don't want to be a burden.

Gently, Greg shook his head, and he let his hand slide down Allen's arm to rest at his elbow. "You're not," he murmured. "I'm not thinking that, I promise. I love being with you. I love taking care of you, just as I love when you take care of me. I'm more in love with you than I ever have been, and I want nothing more than to show you that, every day."

They weren't just rote words. Sure, he'd said them before. Many, many times before. But he meant them. Always. And he knew Allen felt his love and commitment. Sometimes, though, Allen's brain just wouldn't quite let him believe it, wouldn't quite let him forget his childhood and all the berating and neglect and negativity he'd experienced.

"It's still quite early though," Greg added, and he let his fingers caress down Allen's forearm the rest of the way and back up again. "Maybe you should get some more rest. I love just lying here with you, holding you. Can we do that, darling?"

Allen took two long, slow breaths and then nodded. "I'm still tired," he admitted.

Outside, the wind howled, and there was some not-too-distant crack, followed by a pop and a flash of light through the shutters on the windows. They both groaned in unison.

"I'll go turn on the generator," Greg said, fighting not to grumble as he pushed back the blanket and grabbed a flashlight out of the nightstand next to the bed. "I'll be right back."

Beans jumped up and met him at the foot of the bed, bouncing up and down on his hind legs. Greg just shook his head and glanced back at Allen, who was now sitting up with his back against the headboard.

Power outages were a fact of life in their slightly rural-ish neighborhood, although they were much more common in winter, when snow and ice could accumulate on the power lines. They'd invested in a top-of-the-line generator some years ago, and Greg was thankful for it. But that did mean going outside to switch it on, which meant braving the weather and leaving Allen alone for several minutes.

After reassuring himself Allen would be okay, Greg continued out of the room, down the stairs, and into the garage. He stopped for a moment at the back door to tug on his rain boots and coat, then he pulled the hood up over his head, switched the flash-light on, and opened the door. Beans rushed out ahead of him, zooming off across the yard. Greg quickly scanned the fence line to make sure it was still intact so Beans couldn't take off and go terrorize the neighborhood or something, and when he was satisfied the dog would be safely confined to the yard, he trudged over to switch the generator on.

Five minutes and another dirty-dog-drying towel later, Greg re-entered the bedroom to see Allen still sitting up in the bed, his reading glasses now on and his cell phone out. He glanced up at Greg and then back down at his phone.

"So, Jocelyn and Tad in our group chat both said it was the transformer between their houses that blew. Joe said he's out of propane and had meant to fill up, so his generator won't work, but he's headed over to his aunt's house in Gig Harbor later today anyway. And I offered for Marcia to bring the twins over, but she said her brother is coming to pick them up in an hour and they'll stay at his place until the power is back on." Allen slipped his glasses off and set them down on his nightstand just as Greg climbed back underneath the covers.

"Glad Marcia has somewhere to go," he said, settling on his side to face his husband.

Allen nodded in agreement, hit a few more buttons on his phone, and put it back on the nightstand next to his glasses before lying down again.

"Where were we?" Greg scooted over the last bit to close the distance between them, and Allen cuddled up against him, wrapping one arm around his waist.

"I was going back to sleep," Allen mumbled, and Greg laughed quietly and kissed the top of Allen's head.

"That's right."

"I love you." The words were muffled against his chest, but Greg heard them easily enough, and he smiled and closed his eyes.

"I love you too, darling."

Chapter Four

Allen

"HI, FRIENDS! WHO'S READY to read?"

Allen's voice carried easily across the room, and the group of about twenty-five children collectively hushed as they settled on the colorful carpet in front of him. He smiled as he surveyed the group. He knew most of the children, but there were a few new faces, too, and that made his heart happy.

"We've got a very special treat for you all today," Allen told them, and he could see as their little eyes widened with curiosity. He grinned again and then winked at them conspiratorially. "And by treat, I actually mean"—he leaned forward a bit as though he were telling them a secret and lowered his voice to a whisper—"*ice cream.*"

On cue, Sandra and Hank Belford, who owned a small ice cream shop in town, popped out from behind the bookshelves to Allen's left. Both of them were wearing giant colorful ice cream cone costumes—where they'd managed to find them, Allen had *no* idea—and excited whispers and clapping and even a couple of barely contained squeals broke out around the room. Allen gave the kids a moment to express their excitement and then held up both hands, still smiling.

"Now, friends, listen carefully, okay? Our guests here today are going to read you a book. It's a story called *Ice Cream For Breakfast*. Oh, my! Raise your hand if you've ever eaten ice cream for breakfast," Allen said, pretending to hold back his smile for a moment as he lifted up his own hand. Several of the children laughed. "I hope you'll love the story. It's one of my favorites! And then, when they're finished, we've got a fun activity for you to complete so you can earn a coupon for a *free* ice cream cone. Do you want to hear about the activity?"

All the children nodded, and Allen continued. "Excellent! Here's what you're going to have to do—and remember, your grown-up or any of the other grown-ups here at the library can help you if you need it! So . . ."

He loved watching all of their little faces light up as he explained the rest of the activity he had planned, which involved a scavenger hunt of sorts around the library. When he was finished, he re-introduced Sandra and Hank and then stepped off the makeshift "stage" to find his way to the other side of the room.

Greg had his tripod set up just off to one side, and he was snapping photos of the group, which he'd edit and offer free to all the attendees. He straightened up and grinned as Allen stopped next to him.

"Ice cream for breakfast, eh, darling?" Greg whispered.

"Once," Allen answered, keeping his voice low. "My first day in the dorms at UDub. My only huge act of rebellion, you know. Chocolate and vanilla swirl in a waffle cone."

There was a light laugh next to him. "After thirty-three years, I'm still learning things about you," Greg said quietly, and when

Allen glanced at him again, he was back to his camera, the shutter going again as he took more photos.

The familiar fullness in his chest took Allen's breath away, and he moved just a little closer to his husband, who reached out to take his hand with a gentle squeeze.

The next two hours passed uneventfully, and by the time the last of the attendees and volunteers had left, it was just after 4:00 p.m. Allen texted Greg to let him know he'd be home in about thirty minutes and then spent a little bit more time tidying up.

Just as he was pushing in the last chair, there was a loud, rough knock on the door. Startled, he turned around and was about to call out "One minute!" to whomever the late visitor was when a crash erupted near the front of the library. The sound of glass shattering and cascading to the ground was followed by two male voices shouting.

There was a sharp pain in Allen's chest as his brain registered the words—a mix of profanities, threats, and homophobic slurs. His hand automatically flew to his pocket, and he pulled out his phone as he backed up toward the corner of the room. From his angle, he couldn't see the men, and their voices didn't seem to be coming any closer, but his heart raced, pounding hard in his chest.

Shaking and fighting an odd, panicky lightheadedness, he unlocked his phone and managed somehow to dial 9-1-1. He continued backing up until he was behind the bookshelves where Sandra and Hank had come out in their costumes earlier in the day, and he closed his eyes and held his breath. An operator answered after just one ring.

"9-1-1. What's your emergency?"

"Hi, I-I'm at the North Bend Library, and—and—" Allen sunk down to the ground as another wave of lightheadedness rushed him, and his chest tightened painfully, forcing the air from his lungs.

"Sir, are you okay? Is there an emergency?"

He started to answer but then heard crunching glass near the front of the library.

"Allen? Holy shit, what happened here? Allen?!" Joe Walsh's voice echoed through the room, and a few seconds later, Allen felt his neighbor's hand on his shoulder. "Allen, are you okay? Holy shit."

A haze clouded his vision, and he tried to nod—because he was okay, or at least he thought he was. But he didn't know if Joe saw or not. The phone was taken from his hand, and he heard Joe's voice again, maybe speaking with the 9-1-1 operator? He wasn't sure. The next thing he knew, Joe was pulling him to his feet, firing questions at him, helping him over to a nearby chair so he could sit.

"The police'll be here any minute. I'm gonna call Greg, alright, Allen?" Joe asked, his voice quieter now.

"Yeah, yeah, thanks, I—" His heart still pounded, and some strange mixture of nausea and dizziness made him lower his head to rest on his knees as he tried to steady his breathing.

"You just sit tight. You're okay, man," Joe said, and Allen felt him move away just a few feet, muttering some choice words under his breath. To Allen's ears, it sounded something like "Fuckin' teens. Dammit. Greg's gonna be pissed." Although, knowing Joe, there were probably several more curses tossed in there as well.

Allen closed his eyes and tried again to stabilize his breathing as he heard sirens not too far away. Everything was fine. Nothing had happened to him, and it was all fine. He was okay.

He was okay. He was okay. Really.

Around him, though, the room became a blur of voices and people and noise, and he wasn't able to keep track.

"Allen? Hey, man, Greg's on his way, okay? Shit, shit, shit."

"Mr. Westin, I'm Officer Jackson. Can you tell us what happened?"

"Joe, what did you see?"

"Two kids—teens—running off. They went that way . . . Yeah, down Third Street . . ."

"Mr. Westin, was anyone else here?"

"Mr. Westin?"

"Jake, maybe he'll talk to you."

"Has he been like this the whole time, Joe? . . . Well, shit."

"Allen?! Allen? Excuse me, please. Let me through. Please, everyone please get back, leave him alone, he needs space."

Two familiar hands settled on his knees, and he finally lifted his head and blinked his eyes open. His husband's kind brown eyes stared back at him, soft but full of concern. Some immediate sense of relief seemed to chase away a tiny bit of the panic.

"Greg . . ."

"Hi, darling. I'm here. I'm here. You're okay."

He managed some sort of a nod, even though Greg's words hadn't been a question.

"I'm okay," he repeated, and for the first time, he looked up at the mess of activity around him. It looked like half the town was there. There were several police officers, and his neighbor Joe stood off to one side, talking to Annabeth, the other librarian. Sandra from the ice cream shop was talking with Eleanor from the antique store near the entrance. Some man Allen didn't recognize was taking pictures of the broken window, and groups of others milled about, talking in hushed voices, sneaking occasional glances his direction.

"Allen," Greg said, his hands squeezing Allen's knees gently. "*Are* you okay?"

This time it was a question, and Allen tried to refocus on his husband, even as he noticed a police officer step closer again. Still kneeling, Greg looked up at the officer.

"Jake, what happened?"

"Joe said—"

"I know what Joe said. But how could this have happened? How could—dammit. Did you catch the kids who did this yet? Do you have anyone out looking for them? Did Joe recognize them?"

"Greg, easy, man. We've got Cheryl and Mike out looking for them right now. Trish is following up another lead. Unfortunately, Joe didn't have enough of a description for any identification. They were on foot, wearing nondescript clothing, and—"

"That's not good enough," Greg cut in. "You should—"

"Don't, Greg. They're doing the best they can, I'm sure," Allen said, and he leaned forward and let out a short breath. "And I haven't exactly been helping much. Sorry, Jake. I didn't see anything, though. I was finishing up here, about to head out. I was back by the—the children's table here, and I heard a loud knock on the door and then a crash, like the window shattered. And . . ."

He trailed off, not sure how much more he wanted to say. Greg stood up but shifted one hand to Allen's shoulder, and he heard Jake scribbling something in a notepad. He tried to ignore the hushed whispers from the other people at the library.

"Did you happen to get a look at them? See anything at all? Even the smallest detail could help," Jake said, but Allen just shook his head.

"No."

"Did they say anything? Joe said he heard some yelling, but he couldn't make out the words."

Allen hesitated again, and Greg squeezed his shoulder. "Allen?"

He couldn't repeat their words. He wouldn't. He lowered his eyes to his hands, which now rested in his lap.

"I-I heard them," he stuttered. "Their words were . . . not kind." There was an almost palpable thickness to the air around him now, and he closed his eyes again as he felt Greg tense up. He shook his head. "They were just kids. They don't—"

"All the more reason they learn this behavior isn't okay," Jake said gently but firmly. "What did they say, Allen?"

But Allen just shook his head. "I'd rather not repeat it."

There was a pause, and Allen's jaw clenched as he felt Greg's tension again. He knew Greg would be upset, angry even. Not angry at Allen, of course, but angry at the perpetrators and the situation. And Allen understood. Maybe he'd be upset enough himself in a day or two, when the lightheadedness and shakiness were gone. But for now, he couldn't do it.

"I-I'm sorry," Allen said, his voice sounding rough, even to his own ears.

Greg knelt down next to him. "You're okay, right, darling?" he asked quietly, and Allen managed a nod. Greg's lips pressed lightly against his forehead, and then Allen felt Greg stand up again. His voice seemed a bit farther away and hushed, though Allen could still feel the warmth of his presence. "Jake, maybe . . . well, can I just take him home now? And we'll call later if he remembers anything else."

"Of course, sure, Greg. Allen, take it easy, okay?"

"Thank you, Jake," Allen said.

Jake's heavy footsteps moved away, and Allen slowly opened his eyes and lifted his head again, blinking as the light from the room sent a sharp pain through his skull. He took a deep breath and tried to ignore it. It was probably just a stress-induced headache, not a migraine or something else.

Greg's hand covered his, and Allen let his husband help him to his feet. He felt everyone's eyes on him as they started toward the entrance, Greg's arm looped through Allen's to support him.

He wanted to be stronger, to brush it off, to be able to reassure everyone that he was okay.

Because he was.

Nothing had even happened.

But when he got closer to the front entrance and saw the mess for the first time—one of the front windows shattered, a large brick on the ground only a few feet from the main desk where he usually sat to work, shards of glass everywhere—his stomach dropped. His hand holding Greg's tightened as he leaned heavily on his husband.

"They threw a-a brick?" he rasped.

"Come on. Let's get out of here." Greg sounded solid and in control next to him, and Allen just nodded again and let Greg lead him around the debris, out into the warmth of the late afternoon. There were more people gathered outside, and he heard the murmurs of the crowd fade into a tense silence as Greg supported him, leading them toward the SUV.

His eyes landed on his own car, parked down at the end of the short row of parking spots, and Allen stopped suddenly, his legs nearly giving out. The windshield and windows were smashed in, the tires were slashed, and several derogatory and threatening words had been carved into the hood.

Greg tried gently to steer him away, down the last of the front steps of the library. "Allen, let's just go, okay? The police will handle it."

But he couldn't move; his legs physically wouldn't carry him, and instead, he grabbed ahold of the railing next to him, barely keeping himself from slumping to the ground. "Why?" he breathed. "Wh-what reason would they have for—for . . ."

Around him, the crowd was still silent, and Allen was suddenly overwhelmed by the feeling that he wasn't safe. He scanned the crowd; he knew everyone there, and they all watched him with sympathy. But standing there, his ruined car not more than forty feet away, unable to move of his own accord, without his husband's support, Allen felt more exposed and vulnerable than he'd ever felt in his life.

"Get me home, please," he begged quietly, letting go of the railing and leaning on Greg again. "Please."

"Of course, darling. Of course."

Chapter Five

Greg

GREG WAS FRETTING. OF course he was fretting. Anyone in his position would be. Only, he knew it wasn't helping his husband, who seemed to still be in shock after having seen the damage to his car.

Allen was resting upstairs now and had been for some time. And Greg had been fielding all of his calls. He'd spoken multiple times with the sheriff and other local law enforcement, but the last call . . . that had been the toughest yet.

It had been the sheriff, Mike Foster, calling to let Greg know that they'd found the kids.

Apparently, with social media being what it was, it hadn't been too difficult of a task. The idiots had filmed themselves doing it—using some heavy-duty utility knife to slash the tires on Allen's Toyota and etch several horrible words into the hood; smashing the windshield and windows with a brick; and then joking and laughing as they chucked another large brick into the front window of the library. They'd filmed it and then posted the damn video to social media, along with some more obscene and derogatory comments indicating they'd specifically targeted Allen. The thought made him sick to his stomach—that his kind, caring, compassionate husband who had never, ever done anything to hurt anyone had been the target of such maliciousness.

And the two boys *were* teenagers, both of them just sixteen years old.

But maybe the worst part, Greg thought, was that he and Allen knew them and their parents. The kids went to the local high school and had attended several of the community events where Allen and Greg had volunteered. One of them worked as a bagger at the grocery store just down the street from the library. They both lived only a few blocks away.

Greg's phone buzzed again, just as it had been doing for the last two hours since they'd been home. It was probably another text message from another neighbor, wanting to express their support. He'd gotten dozens of those by now. Their community was behind them, he knew. Yet he'd never felt so isolated.

All the supportive messages in the world wouldn't change what had happened.

They'd lived here for nearly thirty years. Allen had worked at the library in one capacity or another for just as long. And in that time, the community had evolved a lot and grown more accepting and tolerant, for the most part. It had been many years now since they'd had to be careful about being out and openly gay in their small community.

And this . . . this was beyond anything he'd ever expected to experience.

He powered his phone off, not wanting to take any more calls or texts for the time being. Then he double checked that the doors were locked, turned off all the downstairs lights, and headed up to the bedroom.

Just like a couple of nights before, he paused in the doorway, his eyes drawn to his husband's sleeping figure. Beans lay protectively on the floor right next to the bed, rather than in his spot in the corner, and the dog looked up at him briefly before settling his head back on his paws with a quiet whimper.

It was pretty telling—that the dog wouldn't even get up to greet Greg when he entered the room. The silly dog didn't move an inch as Greg made his way across to the bed. He knelt down and ran a hand over Beans's rough coat while studying Allen's features. Even in his sleep, there was tension—a tightness in the way his mouth was held closed, a slight irregularity to his breathing.

Greg's frown deepened as he straightened up, and his hand went back to his pocket. He should call Annabeth. Allen was scheduled to work tomorrow, but it was possible the library would just be closed or that Allen wouldn't feel like going in.

God.

It wasn't fair. It wasn't right—that the *one place* Allen had always considered safe for him now maybe wouldn't feel that way anymore.

"I've always felt at home here. In any library, I mean. When I'm surrounded by the quiet and the books, and I can get lost in another world—whatever's written on the page—I just feel . . . safe. God, I sound silly, don't I?"

"No, I don't think so. That's how I feel out on the trail—it's just me and the mountain, the forest. Quiet and peaceful and yet also alive and wild. I feel at home and safe. I think I understand perfectly."

The memory shattered, shards piercing Greg's heart as he shook his head. Allen had been through a lot as a child. His parents had been horrible—his father downright mean and occasionally

physically abusive, and his mother an angry, narcissistic, manip-
ulative woman who'd spent years humiliating Allen and telling
him he wasn't good enough, he wasn't worth her time, he was a
waste of space and a burden and all those other things that had
tanked Allen's sense of self-worth and self-esteem. So growing up,
Allen had ended up spending a substantial amount of time at the
local library rather than at home. He'd always called the library his
"safe space." A place where he felt comfortable, where he could
be himself, where he could get lost in other worlds and surround
himself with the joy books brought him.

Would Allen still be able to feel that now? Now that he'd essen-
tially been attacked in his "safe space"?

Greg pulled his hand out of his pocket, leaving the phone where
it was. He wanted to help, but he knew he really couldn't make any
decisions for his husband; they'd have to talk, and Greg would have
to let Allen decide for himself. What he hoped more than anything
was that this would all just be a small blip and that Allen would be
able to return to work without much fuss.

It was still early, just a little after seven, but they weren't going
anywhere else tonight. So Greg stepped away from the bed and
quietly changed into sweatpants and a T-shirt. Then he crawled
into bed and carefully gathered his husband up in his arms. Allen's
tension didn't really ease, which made Greg's heart ache even
more, but he did wrap an arm around Greg's waist and let out a
short, sharp sigh.

With a quiet whisper of "I love you" to his husband, Greg
closed his eyes and tried to let himself relax. But the weight of
everything—the last few days, his realization that he'd not been
present enough, and now . . . this whole mess—rattled him more
than he cared to admit.

It took him quite a while to fall asleep.

Greg awoke the next morning to Beans's quiet whimpering, and he was surprised to see weak sunlight streaming through the windows. He turned over, grumbling something to Beans to go back to sleep while reaching out to Allen's side of the bed. But his hand just landed on a cold pillow, and his stomach dropped. He sat up quickly.

"Allen?"

Beans whimpered again from the doorway and then turned and trotted off down the hallway. The house was otherwise quiet—there were no sounds from the bathroom or kitchen, no muted playing of the piano from the living room downstairs, no indistinct noises from the garage.

Greg ran a hand through his hair and let out a short breath, then pushed himself up out of bed. He resisted the urge to call out again, and instead, he made his way out of the bedroom and downstairs. He stopped at the bottom of the stairs, and his expression tightened as he saw Allen sitting at the kitchen table, staring blankly at the cup of coffee in his hands.

"Shane and Lily are donating a new window to the library, along with the installation. But it's still going to take at least a week because the window isn't a standard size, and it'll take some time." Allen's voice sounded oddly detached, and he didn't look up as he spoke. "At least the weather's supposed to be good for the next few days, so we can keep the library open in the meantime. But the preschool group that was supposed to visit on Wednesday canceled. And Tina said the homeschool group might cancel too. They're supposed to visit on Thursday. I haven't heard from—"

There was an odd sound that escaped Allen's throat—not quite a sob, but more of a strangled breath—and he dropped his chin.

Greg couldn't get his feet to move right away. When he saw his husband reach up and swipe at a tear on his cheek, however, that seemed to unstick him. He closed the distance between them, pulled a chair up next to Allen's, and sat, slipping his arm protectively around Allen's shoulders.

"Did you look outside yet?" Allen asked, his voice rough.

"No, what . . . ?" Greg trailed off, almost afraid to ask.

"It's the only reason I'm . . . sort of okay," Allen said, and he leaned his head against Greg's shoulder for a moment before straightening up slightly. He lifted his eyes to Greg's and gave his husband a gentle but strained smile. "Go look."

Reluctantly, because he didn't want to put any distance at all between them, Greg pushed back his chair and stood. Allen nodded weakly, his expression tired but hopeful, and Greg pursed his lips but turned and made his way out through the living room to the front door. He unlocked the deadbolt and slowly opened the door.

Just at the bottom of the front porch steps, the short walkway and small grassy lawn were blanketed with rainbow flags, handmade cards and notes, bouquets of colorful flowers, and other gifts. Dozens of small showings of support and love.

An older woman Greg recognized from several community events, though he wasn't sure they'd ever really met, had just set down a beautiful arrangement of pink and yellow flowers, and she straightened up, smiled at him, and waved.

"You are both loved and appreciated and such an important part of this community. We just want to make sure you know that," she said, her voice soft but also filled with optimism, and Greg felt a tug at his heart.

"Thank you," he managed.

And as though she knew that he didn't have words to express everything he was feeling, she just nodded and then leaned heavily on her cane as she turned and shuffled back down the walkway to her car, which was parked along the street at the edge of the lawn.

From at his side, Beans gave a low whine, and Greg bent down and stroked the dog's head. "Wow, right, buddy?"

He slowly closed the door and then turned around. Allen was watching him from the kitchen, his eyes still tired, still pained, and now also glistening with tears.

"I didn't expect that," Allen said quietly, shaking his head. "I mean, I . . . I think I expected some sort of a media circus, especially . . ." When he trailed off, Greg pushed himself away from the door and started back to the kitchen.

"Especially, what, darling?"

"When I turned on my phone this morning and scrolled through all the texts and—and everything, and when I saw who had done this and . . . and I-I never thought . . ." Allen shook his head. "But I'm glad we don't have reporters banging on the door or . . . or anything like that."

Greg stopped behind his husband's chair and set his hands on Allen's shoulders, letting his thumbs massage gently into Allen's stiff muscles. "I'd worried about that too," he admitted quietly.

They were both silent for a few minutes, and Greg continued his massage, his hands working their way up Allen's neck and then back down. He switched to longer strokes, then let his hands drift out to Allen's upper arms and downward. When he reached Allen's elbows, he leaned over and wrapped his husband into an embrace, brushing his lips against Allen's cheek.

"Can I make you something to eat?" he asked, squeezing Allen gently before straightening back up again. "I have a delivery scheduled today, and some consultation with a client who wanted—ah, it doesn't matter. I'm going to reschedule both, and—"

"Don't do that," Allen cut in, an edge to his voice. "Don't reschedule or cancel or—n-not for me. I'll probably be working all day anyway, and—and I don't want to . . ."

Greg's hands froze, now resting on Allen's shoulders again. "Allen . . ."

The words were familiar but also jarring, a reminder that just three days ago, Allen's mental state had been fragile enough already. He'd seemed to recover Saturday, after some good rest and relaxation, but Greg wasn't surprised to hear his stuttering dismissal. Sad, but not surprised.

"I have to work anyway," Allen argued again, though there was a hitch in his voice. "I have to . . . I mean, there's a lot to do, and . . ."

Greg took the seat next to Allen again, and when he reached out to take Allen's hands in his, he felt his husband trembling. He closed his eyes and started to speak, but Allen beat him to it.

"I can't stay home. I won't live in—in fear. Those boys, they . . . are misguided, and—and I'm going to work today. You—you should too." Allen pulled his hands away, and Greg looked up as Allen stood, picked up his mug, and turned so his back was to Greg. The tension in his shoulders was clear, and when he spoke again, his voice was unsteady. "And p-please don't argue with me, I'm not sure I could handle . . . that."

"I—" Greg shook his head. "Allen, I . . ."

He knew. He knew how much Allen was hurting, despite his words and despite the small smile he'd managed earlier and despite his attempt to brush off the fact that he was scared. And Greg also knew how difficult Allen's last sentence had been—standing up for his decision and admitting he'd struggle if Greg argued.

He pushed himself to his feet slowly and then moved up behind Allen and slipped his arms around Allen's waist. Leaning down, he pressed a light kiss to Allen's jaw, just below his ear, the short hairs of his beard tickling Greg's chin. "I won't argue," he said softly, and he kissed his husband again. "But will you let me walk you there? And pick you up at the end of the day?"

Because I am *scared.* Greg didn't say the words, but he knew they were true. He remembered the phone call from Joe the day before. He'd been just about to start cooking dinner when the phone had rung. Joe had been calm and collected, but his words had had an edge to them, a note of something more than just concern. And when Joe had said, "Allen's okay, but..." Greg's heart had plummeted. Even though Joe had warned him about the car, seeing it had brought an unexpected wave of nausea—a combination of anger, fear, and pain.

Allen's breath shuddered, but he nodded. "I'd appreciate that."

He didn't say anything more, and neither did Greg. Instead, they got started making breakfast—something mundane, simple, normal. Something they did nearly every day.

And that made things feel just a little bit better.

Chapter Six

Allen

THE SUN SHONE BRIGHTLY overhead by the time Allen and Greg left home at around a quarter to nine. It was a short walk—they only lived about half a mile from the library, and the weather was pleasant and warm, typical of a late August morning. The neighborhood was quiet, as it usually was, but to Allen, the silence felt unsettling in some way, almost as though something was lurking in the bushes, about to jump out at them.

He slipped his hand into Greg's and was rewarded with a comforting squeeze.

"Where's your delivery today? Is it local-ish?" Allen asked, hoping to distract himself.

"Renton. So, yeah, not too far. I should be back by noon if—"

"And those photos that you took yesterday—when will they be ready? In case anyone calls to ask?" Allen cut in, stopping what he assumed was going to be Greg's attempt to offer to meet him for lunch or something.

Burden. Don't make him do anything extra. It's disruptive. You're being too much.

It was bad today. Much worse than Friday. Much worse than he remembered it being in a long time, in fact. His internal monologue seemed to be running rampant, anxious and on edge. He was fighting it at every chance, trying to tell himself he should go about his day, not be scared, not feel unsafe and unsure and all the things. But his brain continued to drown him with intrusive thoughts, telling him everything he was doing wrong, everything that would annoy and burden his husband.

Like having to take time out of his day to check in on Allen.

"I-I'm sorry," Allen said quietly, when Greg didn't immediately respond to his question. "I didn't want you to feel . . ."

Greg's hand released his, and his arm looped around Allen's waist as they rounded a corner and the library came into view.

"I don't feel that way," Greg assured him. "I wouldn't. I never have. I love you, and I would love to meet you for lunch today, if you'll have a break." Greg paused for a moment and sighed—not a frustrated or upset sigh, but more of a sad sigh. Or maybe a worried sigh. He continued in a quiet voice. "Yes, it's partly because I do want to check on you midday. But I . . . I was also affected by yesterday, Allen."

Greg slowed and stopped, his arm tightening around Allen.

"Of course you were. I-I'm sorry, I—"

With a quick shake of his head, Greg cut Allen off again.

"No. No apologies, please darling. But I know what you're thinking, and I want you to understand. I need to see you later today—for me. For me, so I can know you're okay. Because I'm scared to be away from you right now, *not* because I think you're not capable of being on your own. Please, would you be okay if I stopped by around noon?"

The effect was immediate. Guilt and nausea hitting him in an unpleasant rush. "Yes, of course. I'm—" *Sorry. I'm sorry again. No, no, don't say it. He doesn't want you to say it. But, god . . .* Allen screwed his eyes shut, his train of thought unable to stop him from apologizing again. It was a damn compulsion that he couldn't control, and he hated it. "I'm sorry. I'm sorry. Yes, I'd love to see you at lunch."

Greg directed them to start walking again, though he was silent, and that just made Allen's anxiety tick up another notch. He shouldn't worry. But knowing he shouldn't worry didn't stop the worry from happening. And the closer they got to the library, the more everything just seemed to compound.

He stared straight ahead, but his heart began to thud in his chest, and when they got within view of the parking lot, little bits of leftover glass from the shattered windows of his car shimmered as they caught the bright sunlight. The car wasn't there; it had been towed to a repair shop in Issaquah. Yet a rush of emotions still hit him.

"I-I need—I need a minute," he said, forcing the words out as his feet rooted to the ground.

He saw it, even though it wasn't there—his broken car, with its slashed tires and shattered windows. Pain erupted in his chest, and he clung tightly to Greg, gasping for breath.

"I just need a minute. Just a minute. Just a—just a minute," he repeated, closing his eyes as Greg stepped in front of him. His husband's familiar embrace surrounded him, and he let out a soft sob as he buried his head in Greg's shoulder.

"Shh, shh, shh," Greg soothed, his hands rubbing up and down Allen's back. "Take all the time you need. You're—you're okay. You're okay."

The sound of Greg's voice cracking made everything hurt even more.

This time, however, Allen managed to not apologize, and that was partly because he couldn't speak anyway. They just stood there, holding each other, for what had to be several minutes. And when the aching in Allen's chest finally subsided, he took a deep breath and managed to straighten up. He hadn't actually cried, and he was grateful for it, though the tears were right there, ready to spill. It was already bad enough that he wasn't quite as presentable as he'd usually be, having opted to wear jeans and a simple black sweater rather than his typical slacks and dress shirt. Adding puffy red eyes to the mix would just make things worse.

He felt a light kiss press to his forehead, and he was still shaking, even as he nodded to Greg and cleared his throat.

"I-I'm ready now. I think."

Without a word, Greg took his hand, and they started walking again. Allen's eyes darted from the parking lot to the building. Plywood had been rigged up to block the broken window, and the sight made his stomach turn.

"It really happened," he rasped, without meaning to.

"Yeah," Greg said quietly, and they stopped again, this time right at the bottom of the steps. Greg's hand still held his tightly. "You can still decide to stay home today if you want. No one will fault you for it."

He should. He should go home. For maybe the first time in his entire decades-long career, he didn't want to be here. He could still hear the sounds of the glass shattering, the two voices shouting at him. He could still feel his heart racing, his breaths becoming unnaturally short.

And he didn't really know.

He didn't know what to do. He didn't know what was best or what *would be best* for his long-term mental well-being. But he also hated how he was feeling, and something inside of him *needed* for him to fight it.

"I . . . I know I can, but I—but I need to stay. I need to . . . not let them—"

"It's not letting them win," Greg corrected gently. "It's doing what you need to do for your own health and safety."

"You're right," Allen said, though his voice still shook with uncertainty. "And I . . . But I need to . . ." He closed his eyes. "If I don't do this today, I'm afraid, Greg. I'm afraid I won't ever come back."

He hadn't even known it was the truth until he said it out loud, and he expected all the pushback he probably deserved. After all, it sounded wrong. Illogical. Irrational, even. Yet his husband just shifted again to loop his arm around Allen's waist.

"I will support whatever decision you make. Always," Greg said.

With a nod, Allen gritted his teeth and started up the steps, Greg following him.

The morning was a blur. Greg stuck around for fifteen or twenty minutes, until Annabeth showed up, and although Greg hadn't said anything specific, Allen knew exactly why he'd stayed that long. He was thankful, really. He was glad he hadn't been left alone. Even the thought of being there alone again brought his heart slamming to a stop.

So he was also glad that there were a lot of visitors who stopped by, too. It was a bit unusual for a Monday morning, when they typically only had a few people who came in to drop off books, maybe one or two to use the computers. Many of the visitors that morning brought gifts of support—more flowers, handmade cards, even some baked goods. And thankfully, when Shane Whitman and his wife, Lily, showed up around eleven to discuss the installation of the new window, Annabeth handled that for him.

It wasn't until about noon when Greg showed up with lunch, ushered him off into the back office, and shut the door that Allen realized how badly his head was pounding and how fast his heart was racing.

He crossed his arms over his chest and forced himself to take slow, deep breaths as he watched Greg begin to unpack several containers of food from a small tote.

"I made that chicken salad you like—the one with the red grapes—and I stopped for some fresh croissants at Harvey's Bakery. Plus I've got—" Greg stopped suddenly and frowned. "Sorry, I want to ask you how you are and how your morning went, but I don't want to upset you, darling."

Allen understood. He closed his eyes and nodded, then he reached out. Greg's warm embrace was there immediately, and Allen felt his whole body relax for the first time that day.

"It wasn't bad, really. This morning, I mean," Allen started. Together, they moved to a small sofa pushed up against one wall of the office, their lunch momentarily forgotten. "There've been so many people who have shown up to drop off cards and flowers and make donations. We—we've received over twenty-six hundred dollars in donations just since yesterday. And three trays of brownies. I-I told Mrs. Gupta that it's—it's a really good thing you love chocolate so much. It's been . . . incredible, really. And, um, well, as long as I'm distracted, it's fine, I think. I've been fine. But it's . . . hard. It's really, really hard."

That was certainly much, much more than he'd intended to share, and Allen shook his head as he stopped talking. Greg kissed his temple and continued to rub his upper arm, as he'd been doing nearly the whole time they'd been sitting there together. With a long sigh, Allen leaned against his husband.

"I can imagine how difficult it is," Greg said quietly. There was a reluctance to his voice that Allen recognized well. And his next words seemed very carefully chosen. "You could take the afternoon off to rest, if you want."

The gentle reminder was just that—a gentle reminder that he didn't have to overcome *everything* today. He didn't have to pretend like today was just like any other day, or like being here at work today was a normal thing.

And again, he wondered whether Greg was right. He didn't feel well, either. There was a lightheadedness accompanying his nausea now, and his knees and back hurt, which didn't really seem to be related to the previous day's events or anything, but it certainly wasn't really helping.

"I've got so much to do though. I want . . . to . . ." There was something in the back of his mind that he couldn't quite put words to yet, but he tried. "I don't want . . . to—to let the community down—"

He felt Greg tense up next to him, and he shook his head.

"That's not it, I mean. I'm not finding the right words. What I don't want is for . . . That preschool group already canceled, and there's nothing I can do about that. But the homeschool group—I want them to be here. I don't want them to cancel. And I want . . . I want . . . the library to be here and open and accessible to anyone who needs it, whenever they need it. I don't want there to be any doubt about what type of place this is, whether it's . . ."

Something pulled at him, memories of when he was a kid, and he lifted his eyes to meet Greg's, which were filled with a deep understanding and softness.

". . . whether it's a safe place. Of course, darling," Greg murmured, his voice low and kind.

"So, I need to be here," Allen continued, "to show that."

Greg pulled him into another hug. "I understand. I do. Just don't forget"—Greg kissed his cheek, then lingered with his lips still just barely brushing Allen's skin—"that you need to think about yourself too."

Allen's chest tightened, and he closed his eyes and nodded a weak agreement. Then he settled his head on his husband's shoulder with a long sigh. "We should have lunch now."

"Sure, darling," Greg said quietly, and after another moment, they stood together and headed back to the table.

Chapter Seven

Greg

BEANS WHINED AND TUGGED at the end of his leash, but Greg gave him a stern look, and the dog barked indignantly before sitting down with obvious impatience.

"How that dog has so much energy at five thirty in the morning, I'll never understand," Allen huffed, stopping next to Greg as he wiped the sweat from his brow.

The Wednesday morning air was crisp but hinted of a later warmth. Darkness was just starting to give way to light, which peeked through the thick pine trees of the forest. The trail was quiet at this time of day, especially since it was a weekday, and Greg was thankful for that.

It had been a heavy, busy couple of days.

Monday had been rough, filled with too many intense emotions for both of them. And then, yesterday morning, just as they'd been walking out the door, Sheriff Mike had shown up.

The two teenagers apparently wanted to apologize to Allen in person.

That shock had been enough to send all of them back inside, where they'd talked for about a half hour. When the sheriff had left, Allen had admitted to Greg that he was terrified of what his reaction to seeing the boys might be. He wasn't sure he could handle it.

So they'd decided to "sleep on it."

Allen had still gone to work, although he'd been in late. And he'd come home early, nursing an awful headache.

They were supposed to talk today—this morning—and Allen had been the one who'd suggested they go on a sunrise hike to one of Greg's favorite local spots—Little Si, a much smaller companion peak to the extremely popular Mount Si. The peak wasn't as formidable, and it usually wasn't quite as crowded—especially on a weekday at five thirty in the morning. The trail up was mostly in the shelter of the forest rather than open along the mountain face, which suited Greg just fine. He loved the feeling of the forest surrounding him; it felt protective, soothing even, especially on days like today.

Greg smiled weakly as he handed Allen a bottle of water and then reached down to pat Beans's head. "He's in denial that he's turning nine this year, so he's gotta show us how much he's still a puppy at heart. Until later, that is, when he'll crawl upstairs and sleep all day."

"I might have to join him," Allen complained, frowning as he shifted on his feet a bit. "My knees just aren't terribly happy with elevation changes like this anymore. I'm not looking forward to the hike back down."

Greg's smile faded, and he straightened back up. "We can turn back if—"

"No, no, that's not what I meant." Allen closed the cap on the water bottle and shook his head. "I want to be out here with you. Just . . . it's a good thing we're only hiking Little Si. I don't think I could handle the whole mountain now."

There was a hint of something to Allen's tone, almost some sort of guilt. Greg looked off up the trail, unsure what to say, and he tried to push away his unease. He blinked and turned back to Allen. "There's an easier loop we could take that doesn't go all the way to the peak but should still give us a decent view of the sunrise. Would you like that, darling?"

Allen swallowed hard and looked down at the ground, and Greg cursed inwardly. Wrong thing to say. That had definitely been the wrong thing to say. He should know better by now.

But he'd been off kilter all week, and Allen's normal "tells" weren't really showing through as clearly either. There were too many other emotions. There was too much other pain.

Allen's hiking boot stubbed into the ground. "I-I'm sorry, I—"

Greg stepped up behind his husband and let his hands settle on Allen's upper arms. Then he pressed his body up against Allen's and leaned down to kiss Allen's cheek.

"You have absolutely nothing to apologize for, and I need you to know I only suggested the easier route because I don't want to see you hurting. I will not be disappointed either way. I'm extremely grateful to just be spending this time out here with you, whether we make it to the peak or whether we turn back now or whether we take the easier route. I didn't mean to imply otherwise."

Allen leaned back against him and let out a short breath. Greg could feel the heat of Allen's body and his slightly-too-fast breathing, and it worried him. They still had a good three-quarters of a mile up the mountain to get to the peak, and it was a steady, steep climb. If Allen was already so winded . . .

"I'm okay. We can keep going. I'm sorry, I—" Allen stopped, just like he had before, and he was trembling. Actually, physically shaking. Greg could feel it, and Beans seemed to sense it too. The pup sat himself right at Allen's feet and leaned against Allen's legs with a quiet whimper.

Greg's heart clenched, and he let his hands drift a little lower, down to Allen's elbows. He almost wished he didn't know everything that was probably running through Allen's head right now—all Allen's thoughts about how he wasn't good enough, or how he was a burden to Greg, or how he was just getting in the way of what Greg really wanted to do. *Nuisance. Disruptive. Burden.* Greg had heard it all throughout the years, and the last five days or so had been particularly bad in a way it hadn't been in a really long time.

He felt almost out of practice in dealing with it, awash with uncertainty. But he was sure of two things—Allen needed him and needed his reassurance, and he needed to let Allen make the decision. He bent down to kiss Allen's cheek again and then let out a long, slow breath.

"I love you," Greg said softly, and Allen's weight pressed back against his chest more.

"I know."

"Whatever you choose to do, I'll be okay with. I won't be upset or disappointed or unhappy in any way, because I'm here with you. That's what matters most to me."

It was the truth. One hundred percent, no question.

The forest called him, yes. The early mornings, watching the sunrise from a mountain peak, feeling as the light and warmth washed over his skin—those things also called him, and he yearned for them in a way that was deep, tugging at his soul.

But his love for Allen was deeper than all of that. This last week had reminded him of just how much he'd let himself become distracted by all those other things, when the only thing he really needed was his husband. The last week had also reminded him how much *he* was needed—how much Allen needed him to be there. Present. Attentive.

Allen stepped away from him but then glanced back over his shoulder and gifted Greg with a soft smile. "Let's keep going," he said, adding, "but I'll be sure to let you know if I need to turn around."

The tension in Greg's shoulders eased, and he returned his husband's smile. Beans jumped forward, whining, and Greg laughed.

"Alright, let's go, and you can tell me more about that new display you were hoping to put up at the library. A showcase for local authors?"

Allen nodded, and together, they started off on the trail again. Allen spoke quietly, telling Greg all about his plans to host a special event for local authors to share their work, hopefully in collaboration with the local bookstore.

They made slower progress than they had the first half of the hike, but Greg let Allen set the pace. By the time they reached the peak, Allen had been quiet for several minutes. They weaved through the pines to Greg's favorite ledge, and then Greg slipped his backpack off and pulled out a couple of lightweight foam pads for them to sit on.

After helping Allen settle, he sat down himself, scooting as close as he could and then wrapping his arm around his husband's shoulders. Silently, they watched as sunlight started to inch its way up over Mount Si to the east, bringing a gentle warmth with it.

He'd seen this same view probably a hundred times now. Yet it never got old. Next to him, Allen seemed to relax with a long sigh, and Greg turned his head slightly and pressed a kiss into Allen's hair.

"Do you remember the first time we came up here together?" Allen asked, his voice low.

Although the memory was over three decades old, Greg nodded. "Like it was yesterday," he said softly. "I remember every minute."

Allen's head tilted more to rest against Greg's, and there was a light laugh. "Even when I tripped over my own feet right at the start?"

"Especially that. I caught you, and it was . . ."

"What?" Allen's voice was low now, nearly a whisper.

Greg closed his eyes, letting the memory replay in his head. They hadn't even been dating at the time. In fact, it had been during a three-day hiatus Greg had taken while on the last stretch of his 2,600-mile-long hike of the Pacific Crest Trail, way back in the summer of 1990. He'd caught a ride from Snoqualmie, where an offshoot of the PCT had brought him into town. And then, he'd called up Allen, who had been surprised to hear from him after several months.

"I just still remember how it felt to hold you for the first time," Greg said, letting out a quiet huff.

Allen laughed, louder this time, and shook his head. "It was for all of two seconds before I got my bearings again. I was so embarrassed. You . . . actually remember that?"

"Your hand landed right in the center of my chest, and I could smell your shampoo. It was . . . citrusy. And I didn't want to let you go. That was the first time I'd ever had that feeling before." Greg felt heat in his cheeks at the admission, even after all these years, and he ducked his head. "I was so ready to ask you out right then. I thought maybe I'd do it when we got up here, to the peak. But then there were too many people, and the timing didn't feel quite right."

Allen's hand came to rest on Greg's leg. "I don't remember it being crowded."

"It was terrible," Greg said, shaking his head again. "I'm surprised you don't remember. It was the last weekend before school started again, I think. Any weekend day is packed, but this was worse. And the weather was perfect too, which was nice but didn't help."

"Ahh, you're right. That's right. I had an 8 a.m. class the next day."

"And this spot right here . . ."

"It was the only empty spot," Allen recalled.

Greg nodded. "And that was perfect for me because it was always my favorite spot on this little peak, and I was just so happy to get to share it with you, even if I didn't have the courage to ask you out then."

He loved the memory; it was something he thought about every time they came up here.

"I remember being so surprised you wanted to spend your time off the PCT hiking more." Allen chuckled lightly and squeezed Greg's leg. "That's you though. And . . ."

Greg frowned as he felt Allen tense up slightly. He turned his head to kiss Allen's temple. "What is it, darling?"

"I never told you this, but I almost said no. When you finally did ask me out, I mean." Allen twisted a bit to look up at him, and Greg was surprised to see amusement rather than anxiety in Allen's eyes. "After that day—when you actually called me just like you'd said you would, after you'd hiked over twenty-four hundred miles on the PCT, and you came in from Snoqualmie to see me, and—" Allen stopped and shook his head with a small smile. "I was so worried that you wouldn't be content with me because you . . . because I could tell you needed adventure. But *me*? I wanted to be a librarian. All my life, that's what I'd wanted. I seemed so . . . boring in comparison."

There was a pause, but it didn't feel uncomfortable, and Greg didn't even get the impression that Allen still believed his old self's words. And that was good. That was progress.

He did remember feeling Allen's reluctance at the very beginning, before he knew the depth of Allen's struggles with his self-worth and self-esteem. But what he remembered most was the vision he'd had of the two of them together—he'd wanted to surround himself with Allen's goodness and kindness, his empathy and heart, and he'd wanted to show Allen the same things in himself.

Allen sighed—to Greg's ears, it sounded like a happy sigh—and then straightened up a bit and turned until he was facing Greg. He reached up and touched Greg's cheek, and together, they leaned in for a brief kiss.

"We should get back," Allen said when they parted.

Greg nodded, stood up, and helped Allen to his feet, not missing the grimace that Allen tried to hide. Beans, who had been sitting quietly, jumped up as well, eager to get going again. After Greg packed up their foam mats and shouldered his backpack, he slipped his hand into Allen's, then brought Allen's hand up and kissed his knuckles softly.

"I probably don't need to tell you how happy I am that you said yes, but I'll tell you anyway." Allen's eyes dipped down, but Greg shook his head, reached up, and tilted Allen's chin back. "I'd already fallen for you, even just in the short time we'd known each other. And I loved your passion—yes, it was a different type of passion than mine, but"—Greg smiled gently and leaned in for another short kiss—"it was—and still is—beautiful. You are beautiful and kind and caring and compassionate. The best person

I know. And I love you so much. Thank you for giving me a chance to show you that."

Tears glistened at the corners of Allen's eyes, and rather than speak, he simply nodded some sort of acknowledgement. And together, the two of them—plus Beans—started back down the mountain trail.

Chapter Eight

Allen

"THERE YOU GO—YOUR VERY first library card! How neat is that? Are you ready to go pick out some books?"

The small child on the other side of the desk smiled and nodded, her bright blue eyes full of excitement. Allen's heart felt as full as ever, and he glanced briefly up at Tina, their neighbor and friend who also coordinated outings for a local homeschool group. Tina gave him a small, knowing grin and knelt down next to the girl.

"You said kittens and dragons, right?" Tina said, and when the girl nodded again, Tina looked back up at Allen.

"I know *just* the right books," Allen told her, and he stood up, ignoring the soreness in his muscles from the previous morning's hike. "Follow me, and we'll see what we can find."

The next fifteen minutes were spent ushering a few children around the library and directing them to find books that would interest them at their reading level. Kittens and dragons for Kiera, monster trucks for Dylan, unicorns for Sara and Silas, and superheroes for Finn. The group was smaller than normal, but no less enthusiastic, and Allen felt a mixture of relief and joy at seeing new faces—like Kiera, who was visiting the library for the first time.

When everyone had checked out their books, Allen handed out special bookmarks to each of them, and the children all gathered around, their arms loaded with books, happy and smiling. Allen let his gaze drift over the small group, and he felt a tightness in his chest.

They almost hadn't come today—the whole group. Allen and Annabeth had worked hard Tuesday and Wednesday to rally Tina to try and convince the parents to let their children come. It wasn't that there was doubt about the safety of the library. Not really. Just that many of the parents wanted to push the gathering back a week or two to sort of let the dust settle.

But Allen had needed this today as much as he knew the children did, and he'd been elated when Tina had called him yesterday evening to confirm the group's visit, especially know-ing what he still had going on later in the afternoon.

"Thank you for coming to visit, friends. I hope to see you all again next week!" Allen said cheerfully, pushing away his uneasy thoughts as he waved goodbye to the group. But once Tina had ushered them all out the door and the library was quiet again, Allen had to work a little harder to not struggle. He busied himself with tidying up, and Annabeth kept him company, as though she knew how tenuous his good mood was.

When three o'clock finally came, Allen said his goodbyes to Annabeth, pocketed his cell phone, and headed out. He wasn't surprised to find Greg already waiting for him at the bottom of the steps outside.

"How was your day, darling?" Greg asked as Allen came down the stairs to meet him.

Allen tried to speak, to tell Greg that he'd in fact had a pretty good day, but his words failed him at the moment. When he didn't respond, Greg just reached out and took his hand.

"You're strong and brave for doing this," Greg said, and he led them over to where his SUV was parked just a few feet away. "And remember, you don't have to do this. We can leave at any time. You don't have to say anything to them, and if it's too much, we can cancel, or—"

Allen stopped and shook his head. "Don't let me do that. I need to go, even if it's hard. Please, Greg. It'll be better for those boys if I let them say what they've planned, and . . ." He trailed off when he felt Greg squeeze his hand.

They'd talked about all of this the day before, and he'd explained his position to Greg then. And although Greg hadn't said anything, Allen could tell Greg didn't quite agree with his viewpoint. He didn't blame Greg—he knew his position left him vulnerable. But he felt strongly enough that he was doing the right thing, even though his husband didn't share his conviction.

"I want to show them kindness and forgiveness, Greg," Allen said quietly. "I really believe it's the only way this will have a positive impact on their lives."

"I know, darling . . . I just worry about you."

Greg reached out ahead of them to open the passenger side door, and Allen blinked and looked down at the ground again, trying to convince himself it was okay for Greg to worry about him. It was difficult though, not to let the guilt rise up like it wanted to so often lately. He took a deep breath and nodded.

"I know, and I'm trying really hard to just be strong because I really, really believe this. It's going to be very hard, but I'm the adult here, and they're just kids, and if adults can't show kindness to them, how are they going to learn to have more kindness themselves?"

These weren't new thoughts, but he had to repeat them now. He had to remind himself of why he'd made the decision so he could get through the next however long without completely breaking down.

"You're right. You're absolutely right, and I'm behind you one hundred percent," Greg said, his expression softening.

Allen just nodded weakly and let Greg help him into the SUV. A few minutes later, they were on the road, heading up Snoqualmie-North Bend Road toward the police station in neighboring Snoqualmie. The drive was short, only about ten minutes, but it felt much longer to Allen as he stared out the window and tried not to worry more. The sun shone brightly overhead, and outside looked peaceful as always, the mostly rural-ish area set in a low valley between the mountains.

Greg reached over and took his hand, and Allen pulled his gaze away from outside to turn to his husband. Greg was still watching the road ahead, but he lifted Allen's hand up to his mouth and placed a gentle kiss on Allen's knuckles.

"You'll be okay. And I'll be there with you the whole time, and if you need to lean on me, please do." Greg's voice was quiet and full of sincerity and concern, and Allen let himself believe it. Not that he doubted the words—he always believed Greg's words. But he also needed to let himself believe that Greg actually wanted to be here with him and really did support him and that, despite the fact that his husband had a different view, he wasn't going to resent Allen for standing up for his own beliefs about how this needed to go.

Greg pulled his hand away to turn into the parking lot at the police station, and Allen took the moment as Greg was finding a parking spot in the small lot to close his eyes and try to let his mind settle.

He'd recognized one of the three other cars already in the lot as belonging to David Johnston—the father of one of the teens—and suddenly everything seemed more real.

He didn't even realize he was shaking until Greg reached over and put his hand on Allen's. "You can do this, darling. I'll be there for you. Are you ready?"

No, he wasn't. But he had to be. This was how it needed to go. He nodded. "Yeah. I'm ready."

The two teenagers stood together with their parents near a desk just off to the right as Allen walked ahead of Greg into the building. Right away, Allen could see they looked remorseful—their shoulders hunched and their hands shoved in their pockets. And although everyone else seemed to turn to him as soon as he walked through the door, both boys continued to stare at their feet, unmoving. Allen forced himself not to lower his own gaze when the boys' parents looked at him, and instead, he gave a tight smile.

Sheriff Mike, whom Greg and Allen had known for decades, met them near the front door, his expression serious but welcoming.

"Thank you both for coming. I realize it wasn't an easy decision," Mike said, and Allen nodded slightly. He felt Greg's hand slip into his, and the familiar touch was comforting. Mike cleared his throat and spoke quietly. "Both boys have written letters for you, but I think those are for you to read later. Jan has them, and she'll give them to you when you leave. And Allen, I know you said you didn't want to press charges, but they were both arraigned this morning, both pleaded guilty to vandalism and destruction of public property. Judge Hawthorn took your statement into consideration, Allen, and gave them *a whole lot* of community service hours. Their parents had to pay sizable fines as well."

Allen had known or assumed most of that already from earlier communications with the sheriff, but he nodded as Mike explained, trying to keep himself focused and calm. Greg squeezed his hand gently, a silent reminder of his support, and Mike gave Allen and Greg a small nod.

"Ready, Allen?" Mike asked.

"Yeah." Allen's voice sounded hoarse to his own ears, but he forced a smile and let Mike lead them the rest of the way into the bullpen, over toward where the boys stood with their parents.

Allen recognized all of them—David and Sue Johnston with their son, Owen, and Pete and Heather Tanner with their son, Christopher. Next to them was Cheryl, one of the deputy sheriffs, who gave Allen a kind smile and nod as they approached. The two boys still didn't look up.

David stepped forward first, offering his hand. Allen tried to steady himself as he reached out and shook David's hand, but he could feel that he was still trembling.

"Mr. Westin, I know my son will have his own apology to make," David started, "but I'd like to say, on behalf of my wife and I, that we are deeply, deeply sorry for Owen's actions. We raised him to be a respectful young man, and he failed you and the whole community."

Pete nodded in agreement and put his arm around his wife's shoulders. "Christopher too. We're appalled and disappointed that this happened, and—" Pete cut himself off, his face turning red with anger as his eyes shifted to his son.

Allen pursed his lips, holding his breath for a second while he gathered his courage. The boys both seemed to shrink more, both frowning, both looking as uncomfortable as Allen felt. There were no hints even of the hate and bravado they'd both had on Sunday afternoon. And neither of them looked the least bit threatening.

"Sometimes . . ." Allen paused as both boys looked up at him. Owen seemed as though he was close to tears, and Christopher's expression held an anxiety that Allen was all too familiar with. Allen shook his head gently and gave the boys a smile, which seemed to come easier than he'd expected. "Sometimes," he started again, "people make mistakes. Sometimes they're just little mistakes that don't mean much, and sometimes they're big mistakes that have . . . massive repercussions or are . . . harmful."

Greg's hand squeezed his again, and Allen returned the gesture, then he blinked and let himself look down for a moment.

"Your actions were harmful, both in terms of property damage and—and to me, personally," Allen continued, keeping his eyes down still. "I don't know if either of you understand just how much. And I hope you never have to experience my side of this."

He finally looked back up, and both boys were watching him still. In fact, he could feel everyone's eyes on him. He let out a shuddering breath and then smiled at them again.

"I don't know what led to your decision that day, and I don't need to know. But I hope"—his breath hitched as Christopher sniffled and then reached up to wipe a tear from his cheek—"both of you take the time to think about your actions and how they affect others. And I hope both of you realize that anger and hatred shouldn't have a place in how you interact with others and the world."

From next to him, he sensed Greg nodding, and the boys' parents were also nodding.

Allen took a deep breath to steady himself. His chest felt tight as he looked from Christopher to Owen, and he tipped his head to them as he blinked back his own emotions, which were strong and intense and even a little unbalancing.

"I forgive you," he said to Christopher, and he stepped away from Greg and offered the boy his hand. Christopher hesitated for a second, biting at his lower lip, but then he reached out and shook Allen's hand.

"Th-thank you, sir," the boy said.

Allen nodded and turned to Owen. "I forgive you," he repeated, and again, he offered Owen his hand. Owen's tears fell freely now, and he sniffled, swiped at his cheeks, then wiped his hand on his pants before shaking Allen's hand.

"Thank you, Mr. Westin," Owen said. He couldn't quite look at Allen, and he shoved his hands back into his pockets and stubbed his shoe into the floor. "I—I was the one who filmed it, and it was my idea, and I just—it was a shitty thing to do and—"

"Owen!" his mom, Sue, interrupted, and Owen flinched.

"Sorry, Mom. It—it was a mean thing to do. And it was stupid of us. I don't really know why we did it, and I—I'm sorry, sir. I'm really, really sorry."

Christopher nodded. "Me too, Mr. Westin. I'm sorry. I-I mean, we both knew it was wrong, and we shouldn't have done it. And—and . . ." The boy was visibly shaking now, and Allen had to look away.

He shifted just slightly so he was standing a little closer to Greg, needing to feel his husband's warmth, and Greg took his hand again. Allen lifted his eyes once more to the boys and their parents, and he managed another tight smile.

"I accept your apology. Thank you. Both of you," Allen said, not surprised when he heard several of the other adults inhale sharply. The boys, for their part, both held his gaze, and he could see the regret and remorse in their eyes. "I accept your apology, and I forgive you both. And I . . . expect that you will both come to volunteer at the library as part of your community service hours."

He glanced at Sheriff Mike, who nodded, and then back at the boys.

"Thank you, sir," they both said in unison.

Allen bit his lip, struggling this time to hold back all the things he was feeling. He nodded again and turned to Greg. "Let's go," he said quietly. Then he looked up at Mike and Cheryl and managed another "thank you" before tilting his head to the boys' parents.

Without another word, Greg then led him back out toward the entrance. Allen was barely aware when they paused at the front desk for the receptionist, Jan, to hand Greg a couple of envelopes—the boys' letters they'd written him, he supposed. A short moment later, they were at the SUV. As he had earlier at the library, Greg stepped ahead of Allen and opened up the door.

Before he got in, Allen paused and closed his eyes. Greg's hand came to rest on his upper back, rubbing gently.

"Are you okay, darling?" Greg asked, his voice quiet.

Allen didn't answer right away because he wasn't sure what the answer was. He'd said what he'd needed to say, and he'd even surprised himself with feeling in control most of the time. But now, the tightness in his chest seemed to become more uncomfortable, and he leaned into Greg, who shifted to wrap his arms fully around Allen.

With a deep, shuddering breath, Allen rested his head against Greg's shoulder. "I-I don't really know yet. But, um, take me home. Please?"

"Of course."

Allen's strength was gone, and he let Greg help him into the SUV. Then he leaned his head back against the headrest, closed his eyes, and didn't hold back as his tears finally fell.

Chapter Nine

Greg

"PAUL, HI! NICE TO finally talk. Sorry I had to reschedule Monday. This week has been—well, let's just say I'm glad it's finally Friday, and I'm looking forward to the weekend." Greg shifted his cell phone to his left hand as he slipped into his office chair and scooted it up to his desk, pushing aside piles of invoices and other documents.

"No worries about rescheduling. It's been a beast of a week here too. Hang on just one second." Greg heard some rustling on the other end, and then Paul, his friend and long-time client, cleared his throat and continued. "And you know what, this actually works out better for me. Meghan's out of town today, so there's no chance she'll overhear."

His curiosity sufficiently piqued, Greg leaned back in his chair and adjusted the phone slightly. "I'm intrigued. What exactly are you looking for? You'd mentioned wanting a custom print made?"

"Well, not exactly. So, I'm not sure if this is something you even do or might be able to fit in, because it *is* time-sensitive, but I've got a vision about something, and it's more than just a custom print."

"Tell me more," Greg said, pulling a notepad out of the mess on his desk. He scrounged around for another moment to find a pencil and then listened carefully, his enthusiasm building, as Paul explained his idea.

They talked for nearly an hour, and by the time Greg hung up, he was buzzing with excitement. He scanned the several pages of notes he'd taken as his mind raced with all the possibilities.

Custom shoot . . . Jack Mountain area and summit . . . For Meghan's birthday in late October . . . Photo collage book plus extra-large print . . .

His energy spiked, and Greg buried himself in research for the next few hours. He studied the mountain, roughly mapped the nearly fifty-mile path to circumnavigate it and nearby Crater Mountain, and read stories online from the few who had climbed to the summit. As Paul had mentioned, there seemed to be a complete absence of high-quality, professional photos from the summit.

It seemed like the trip of a lifetime, and he vaguely wondered why he hadn't ever considered it until now.

But then he frowned and stared at his computer screen, the tab still showing one hiker's detailed topographical map. The hike would take a week. Maybe more. And it was probably nearly twenty thousand feet of elevation gain to summit both peaks and complete the circumnavigation path. Plus there were several stretches that were designated as class-four climbs.

That was no small feat, especially considering that he'd have to be carrying a week's worth of supplies, all of his camping gear, and his camera and equipment.

His younger self wouldn't have hesitated to go on a fully funded trip like this. But now, at fifty-six, even with as fit as he still was, it would be a challenge.

And that wasn't even considering the timeline.

Paul wanted the gift for his wife, Meghan, for her sixtieth birthday. Paul and Meghan had been avid hikers themselves, but Meghan had fallen ill shortly before their planned summit of Jack Mountain, and they hadn't been able to go. That had been over a decade ago, but Paul had said Meghan still mentioned the mountain and their planned hike all the time, describing it with a yearning that Greg fully understood.

Meghan's birthday was in late October, and the mountain wasn't really accessible after the end of September anyway due to the potential for snow and unsafe weather conditions. He'd also need several weeks at least to edit the photos and prepare the photobook and the print.

He'd be very well compensated; the number Paul had suggested had been more than generous.

But there were a lot of factors to consider.

Greg loved a good challenge—and this was a huge one on many fronts. The desire to take photos of that landscape and to explore somewhere he hadn't yet been was already burning deep in his belly—a familiar excitement and longing. But he *was* getting older. It would be difficult—physically difficult to do, that is, and it was not without risks. In fact, he realized, it might be the last time he'd have the opportunity to do something like this before his body forced him to slow down.

But his hesitation wasn't just about the physicality of it. No, it was more than just that. It was also that he'd have to be gone from home for more than a week. And soon. He'd have maybe a week or two to prepare, and then he'd be gone for probably at least a week and a half. And Allen would be alone.

That thought stopped him, and he ran a hand through his hair and blew out a short breath. He had his answer. He couldn't do it. A sinking feeling grew in the pit of his stomach.

"You look like you just got some bad news. Is everything okay?" Allen's quiet voice asked from just behind him.

Greg looked up as Allen's hand settled on his shoulder, and he gave his husband a small smile, then swiveled in his chair to face Allen and let his arms wrap low around Allen's waist.

"No, no bad news. Just . . . thinking."

Allen's hands rubbed lightly down his back, and Greg leaned forward to rest his head on Allen's stomach.

"Jack Mountain, eh?"

Greg laughed and shook his head, then released Allen and turned to shut off his computer. "It's nothing, darling. Paul had an idea, but I'm going to have to tell him I can't do it."

"Oh?"

Greg's hand paused on his mouse, and he stared at the image on the screen in front of him—a picture of the mountain taken just with someone's cell phone camera from miles away. The longing and pull in his chest grew again, and he could almost feel the fresh mountain air around him, the rough trail under his hiking boots, the freedom and wonder and excitement. God, he wanted to be there. He closed his eyes.

"Yeah. I can't do it," he said simply, and he'd tried to take the emotion out of his voice, because he knew exactly what that would do to Allen, but even he heard his own disappointment. Quickly, hoping to redirect the conversation, he opened his eyes again, clicked on the Windows icon in the corner of his screen, and shut down his computer. Then he pasted a small smile on his face and turned back around to Allen. "So, I've got pot roast cooking in the slow cooker. It's"—he glanced at his watch—"probably pretty close to done. How was work today?"

Allen's expression was tight, but maybe not in the way Greg had expected. Instead, he looked concerned, maybe. Greg wasn't quite sure.

"Is everything okay, darling?" he asked, reaching out to take Allen's hand.

With a short nod, Allen stepped closer to Greg, and his free hand came up to cup Greg's cheek. Greg expected some sort of discussion—Allen obviously knew there was more to his short answer that he couldn't do the job for Paul. But rather than a discussion or a question, Allen's expression seemed to darken slightly, and he leaned down and captured Greg's lips in a rough kiss. The intensity of it surprised Greg, and a heat coursed through him as Allen's tongue ran insistently along his lower lip, requesting entrance. With a groan, he released Allen's hand to set both of his hands on his husband's waist, then he stood slowly, their lips not losing contact. As soon as he was upright, Allen's hands were around the back of his neck, keeping him close, and Greg pulled Allen flush against him, their hips meeting with an ache of deep longing.

God, they hadn't made love in over two weeks.

The realization sent a rush of heat straight to Greg's groin, and he groaned into their kiss and let one of his hands run along Allen's back. Allen must have come into the garage straight from work, because he still wore his button-up tucked into his slacks, and the unavailability of bare skin for Greg to touch made him groan again.

Allen pulled back from their kiss, breathing hard, and with a huff of laughter, he slid his hands down Greg's chest. "Impatient, dear?"

Greg just grunted a nonresponse as he tugged Allen's shirt out of his slacks and lowered his mouth to Allen's neck. His husband's skin was slightly salty but still fresh, and Greg sucked gently, letting his tongue tease in small circles. At the same time, his hand finally found what he'd been searching for, inching under Allen's shirt.

Allen moaned and tilted his head back as Greg's fingers grazed along the warm, smooth skin of Allen's lower back.

He let his kisses trail down and then back up, and when he kissed a spot right under Allen's ear, Allen sucked in a sharp breath. The sound as Allen moaned again, this time a little softer, sent more heat straight to Greg's groin.

"Oh, my love . . ." Greg trailed off, his whispered words warm against Allen's skin. His hands rubbed up Allen's back and then down again, and when he reached Allen's backside, he paused, shifted, and found his husband's lips again. Allen met him kiss for kiss, their mouths moving in a pattern that was familiar and yet arousing. Allen's hands had made their way down to the hem of Greg's shirt, and when Greg felt Allen's fingers tease at the waistband of his shorts, giving a little tug at the button, he pulled back from their kisses, breathing heavily. Allen pressed on, seeming undeterred by Greg's need for air, and their lips crushed together again as he made quick work of Greg's shorts, unbuttoning and unzipping them, then pushing them down off Greg's hips.

It was intense, and a new rush of desire had Greg's arousal straining in his briefs. He quickly brought his hands around to Allen's chest and began unbuttoning his shirt, fumbling as Allen assaulted his mouth with deeper and needier kisses.

"Ah, god, do—do you . . ."

"Do I what?" Allen murmured. Then his hand slipped under the waistband of Greg's briefs, and all of Greg's thoughts fizzled away into nothing as Allen's fingers wrapped around the base of his shaft.

"Uh . . . oh, god. I don't know," Greg admitted, and he pushed open Allen's dress shirt and lowered his head to Allen's shoulder as his erection swelled in Allen's hand.

Lips grazed his cheek then, and Greg let his hands slide up his husband's chest, reveling in the familiar roughness of the thin layer of coarse hair covering Allen's upper body. He flattened his hands and ran his palms firmly over Allen's nipples, which hardened under his touch. Greg groaned again.

"God, I love your body," Greg rasped. "I love every inch of you. I love you."

Allen's breath shuddered, hot against Greg's cheek, and Greg straightened up and lowered his mouth to Allen's again, immediately deepening the kiss as he brought both hands to frame his husband's face. After another slow, deliberate pump of Greg's erection, Allen released him, and Greg whimpered a protest, his hands sliding back around to Allen's lower back and then down farther to his backside. He pressed his hips against Allen at the same time as he pulled Allen closer.

"Ah, god," Allen huffed, breaking the kiss again and lowering his head to Greg's chest.

They rocked against each other once and then again, and Greg groaned. "Do you want to go upstairs—that's what I was going to ask earlier," he said, his voice low and husky. He gripped Allen's backside again, holding them together, and Allen let out a long, low moan.

"Upstairs is good. I'm sorry, I should have—" Allen stopped abruptly as Greg tensed and then loosened his grip on Allen's waist and backed up a step so he could see his husband.

Allen's cheeks were flush, and his chest rose and fell rapidly with each breath. His dress shirt was halfway off—sort of pushed back off his shoulders, but not enough that it had fallen to the floor. His eyes were partly closed, and his lips slightly red and swollen from their kisses.

God, it was sexy. If he hadn't heard the hitch in Allen's voice with his unnecessary apology, Greg might not be able to resist just picking right back up where they'd left off. His fingers flexed gently into Allen's sides, wanting to continue their exploration, but he shook his head and frowned as he hesitated, unsure what exactly to say.

The week had been such an emotional roller coaster, and now, this intense buildup and rush of intimacy. Of course it was emotional. Of course they were both maybe just moving a little too fast, both of them needing the comfort they always found when they were intimate. At least, he was sure that was what *he* needed.

He shook his head. "I'm sorry, darling. What were you going to say?"

Allen's lips twitched up into a soft smile, and he leaned in and pressed a kiss to Greg's lips. It was light and undemanding—nothing like the kisses they'd just been sharing. And when Allen pulled back, he smiled again.

"I know why you're worried, but I think this apology is . . . um, okay?" He laughed lightly. "I was just going to say that I'm sorry I should have showered first before getting you all worked up. I should probably still shower. I just . . . I got lost with you there and didn't want to stop."

The feeling was quite mutual, and Greg nodded, sighed deeply, and wrapped both arms around Allen, pulling him into a warm embrace. Then, after another moment, he kissed Allen's cheek again.

"Let me take care of you," Greg said, knowing Allen would understand what he meant.

"That would make me happy," Allen agreed with another soft smile.

Greg gathered up his shorts, and together, the two made their way inside and upstairs. Beans was sleeping soundly in his bed, snoring away, and Greg chuckled.

"I took him out to Tiger Mountain just after I dropped you off this morning. He's been sleeping all day. I doubt he'll be bothering us tonight."

"Good," Allen said, his rough tone sending a rush of heat to Greg's belly. Allen tugged at Greg's hand. "Come on."

Once in the bathroom, Greg turned on the water in the shower and then lovingly and slowly finished undressing his husband. He touched and caressed and kissed every inch of Allen's chest before slipping off Allen's briefs, and he quickly undressed himself as Allen stepped ahead of him into the shower. By the time he joined Allen, Allen was leaning his back against one wall, breathing deeply as he lazily pumped his own shaft.

"Getting started without me?" Greg teased, closing the shower door behind him.

"You were taking too long," Allen said, his voice husky and low again. He let go of his shaft and closed the distance between them. Greg met him, their mouths coming together in a kiss that was everything—slow but urgent, sensual but needy. And despite its familiarity—over three decades of similar kisses—Greg still felt all his husband's love.

The warm water hit his back, and conscious of his husband's comfort, Greg broke the kiss and carefully turned them around so the water would be keeping Allen warm. Allen closed his eyes with a long breath, and Greg bent down, tracing a path of kisses down Allen's neck to his collarbone. He paused for a moment to soap up Allen's loofah and then slowly, lovingly washed him, his hand following along behind the path of the bath sponge. He took his time, knowing how much Allen loved this, and after Allen was thoroughly clean and the soap had all rinsed off, Greg washed Allen's hair just as gently.

It was something they'd done early on—one of the first deeply intimate acts they'd shared, actually—and Allen had admitted to Greg a long time ago that, for whatever reason, this act of love made him feel so treasured, so cherished, so precious.

Greg kissed Allen's forehead after he finished rinsing all the shampoo from Allen's hair. "I love you," he whispered, dipping his head down to place another kiss on Allen's cheek. "Let me finish up here?"

Allen gave a soft nod and then stepped aside, leaning back against the wall again. Greg saw his eyes lingering on Greg's semi-hard shaft, and he wasn't surprised at all when Allen reached down to start stroking himself again.

Greg groaned. "God, that's sexy," he rasped, and Allen just hummed a quiet response and closed his eyes.

Quickly, keeping his eyes on Allen, Greg washed himself, rinsed, and then shut off the water. He helped Allen out and toweled both of them dry. And by the time they were in their bed under the covers a few minutes later—Greg settled over Allen, kissing his neck again—all the stress of the week seemed to have melted away.

It was just the two of them, together. And it felt as it always had—so good, so right.

"God, I need you," Allen breathed against his cheek as Greg reached between them, finding Allen's hot, hard arousal. He closed his hand firmly around the base and stroked slowly, rocking his hips at the same time to alleviate some of the growing pressure in his own groin.

"What do you want tonight, darling?" Greg asked, not giving Allen a chance to answer before he lowered his lips to Allen's again. The kiss deepened quickly, Allen's hands coming up to the back of Greg's neck and holding him closely. When Greg finally tore his lips away, he didn't go far, breathing a path of kisses down toward Allen's collarbone as he continued pumping his husband's hard shaft. Allen's hands played up into Greg's hair, the little tease sending tendrils of warmth all the way down into his toes, and he heard a soft moan from Allen as he stopped to linger at a particularly sensitive spot right at the base of Allen's neck.

The moan was followed by a sharp intake of breath, and Greg continued his gentle touches until Allen reached down between them to wrap his fingers around Greg's swollen shaft. With a rough groan, Greg buried his head into Allen's shoulder as a rush of heat and desire pulsed through him, his erection throbbing. The arm he'd propped himself up on began to tremble, and he released Allen so he could support himself.

"Ahh, yeah, that's . . . that's good." He moaned again and rocked his hips with Allen's slow stroke of his shaft. "Tell me—tell me exactly what you want, darling," Greg breathed, and he pressed his lips to Allen's shoulder.

Normally, Allen would do just that—he'd always been assertive in bed, a contrast to his personality outside the bedroom. Tonight, however, Greg felt Allen hesitate. The hand stroking Greg's shaft faltered, and a short breath escaped Allen's lips.

"I just want . . . I just want you to love me," Allen said quietly.

His tone was unsure and shaky, and it tugged at Greg's heart. Greg lowered himself down to his elbows and then captured his husband's lips again in a tender kiss. "Always," he promised.

He pulled back, shifted off Allen to grab the lube and a small towel from the drawer in the nightstand on his side of the bed, and then settled on the bed, next to his husband this time, the comforter pushed back so he could see all of his husband's naked body. He set the bottle of lube on Allen's other side and then took a moment to trail his fingertips down Allen's chest and stomach. Allen's shaft twitched with need, and Greg's body responded, a flood of heat and want shooting through him. He inhaled sharply and repositioned himself to kneel between his husband's legs again.

Allen had opened his eyes, but only partway, and in the dim light of the bedroom, Greg wasn't entirely sure what he saw in his husband's expression. But he was intent on making Allen feel good. Good and loved and cared for and cherished.

He ran both his hands up Allen's thighs. "Turn over, darling?" he said softly.

Allen nodded, and Greg scooted back to give Allen room to roll over onto his stomach. Silently, Greg began loving his husband—caressing up Allen's back, kissing every spot his hands touched. He encouraged Allen to arch his back and get his knees slightly under him, bringing his hips off the bed. Then, Greg lowered his mouth to Allen's shoulder and trailed a path of warm, wet kisses all the way down, stopping only when he reached the top of Allen's crease.

There was a soft moan as Greg reached between Allen's legs to find his shaft, and he stroked gently as his mouth dipped lower. He kissed and licked, working his way downward with a deliberate slowness. When Greg reached the sensitive skin around the outside of Allen's hole, Allen moaned louder and writhed slightly, pressing his backside into Greg's mouth. With a grunt of his own, Greg released Allen's arousal and shifted so both of his hands were on Allen's backside, spreading his cheeks wider. Then he dipped back in again, kissing, sucking, licking. He knew just what his husband liked, and Allen's increasingly demanding moans of pleasure, the occasional grunt of "oh, god," and his much-too-fast breathing further directed Greg's efforts. Needing some relief, he shifted one hand to his own shaft, pumping urgently for several strokes as his tongue continued to explore. When he pushed lightly into Allen's hole, Allen groaned quietly and pressed back into him again.

"Ah, yeah. That's good. That's . . . ah, god." Allen trembled and let out a short breath, and Greg pulled back briefly before dipping in again. At the same time, he released himself and shifted his hand between Allen's legs until he found his husband's hard shaft, and he began pumping, matching the rhythm he'd had a moment ago with his hand on his own shaft.

Allen continued to make small sounds—needy whimpers and rough, breathless moans—and Greg probed a little deeper and stroked Allen's arousal a little faster. When he was sure Allen was just on the edge, Greg backed off slightly, pressed a light kiss to each of Allen's cheeks, and straightened up as he slowed his stroke. He was warm, his heart racing and his fingers buzzing, and when Allen whimpered in protest, Greg bent back down to plant wet, soothing kisses on Allen's back.

"I'm here, darling," he breathed, and he kissed Allen again as he released Allen's erection and sought out the bottle of lube. He squeezed some into his palm, lightly slicked his own shaft, and then circled his husband's hole briefly before easing one finger in. Another heady rush of heat and desire flooded Greg as Allen muffled a low moan into his pillow, and Greg continued, slowly thrusting first one finger and then two in and out of his husband's tight channel. He pressed his hips up against Allen's backside, his shaft sliding between Allen's legs, and when Allen reached down to stroke both of them together, Greg inhaled sharply.

God, he was close already, the familiar tightening low in his groin sending a jolt of heat and pleasure through him. He groaned, but shifted his hips backward to separate them. Allen let out a short breath and turned his head to look back at Greg, his eyes half-open.

Greg's free hand ran soothingly up Allen's back. "Sorry, darling. That's as much as I can take until I'm inside you," he said, his voice low and husky.

Then, he carefully curled his fingers to find the spot he knew would bring Allen even closer to the edge. Allen's body jerked slightly, and Allen screwed his eyes shut as he cried out Greg's name and arched back against Greg's hand again.

Greg loved the feeling—knowing that he was bringing his husband so much pleasure. Gently, he kissed Allen's back one more time, letting his lips linger there on his husband's warm skin for an extra moment. Then he slipped his fingers out of his husband's channel.

"Please, Greg." Allen's words were muffled into the pillow where his head rested, but the need in his tone was obvious.

Greg trailed a slow path of kisses up Allen's back to his cheek, taking his time. Then he caressed between Allen's legs again in one long, gentle stroke, and Allen gasped softly.

"I love you," Greg whispered, his voice somehow catching on the words. Allen turned his head slightly, and Greg met him in the lightest of kisses.

"I need you," Allen rasped when Greg pulled back.

Greg could only nod slowly, then kiss Allen one more time. He straightened up, found the lube, slicked his hard shaft again, and wiped the excess off on the towel before repositioning himself behind his lover, the tip of his erection right at Allen's entrance.

This part—the part where they finally joined together after all the foreplay and prep—was one of his favorite moments. And part of that was the knowledge that his husband trusted him so much, found safety and love in this intimate act. It filled his heart, and he closed his eyes and rubbed one hand down the back of Allen's thigh as he brought the other to the base of his shaft to guide himself.

With the sureness of experience, Greg started to inch his way in, and Allen met him eagerly, grunting and pushing back into him. Greg's hard length slipped in easily, almost immediately buried deep in the tight, hot warmth of Allen's channel. He groaned again as he settled his hands on his husband's hips and held Allen back against him.

It was as overwhelming as always, and for just a moment, his chest tightened. Then he leaned forward, letting his hands soothe slowly up Allen's back before dropping to the bed on either side of him.

"Kiss me," Allen said, his tone almost demanding, and he tilted his head back in invitation. Greg met him in a lopsided kiss before he started thrusting with a slow, deliberate rhythm, just as he knew Allen liked. "Ah, god, yeah, that's good. Good," Allen murmured, letting his head drop back down onto the pillow in front of him.

Greg kissed Allen's neck and rubbed his back, then slipped one hand around to find Allen's shaft. He stroked his husband in time with his own thrusts, and Allen's pants and moans and whimpers of pleasure became more and more insistent. Greg felt his own climax building right along with Allen's, and he shuddered as he struggled to hold out just the little bit longer that he knew Allen needed.

"Harder now. Oh, god," Allen huffed, and he pressed himself up onto his elbows and arched slightly, meeting Greg's thrusts with a slightly different angle. Both of them moaned, and Greg picked up the pace for just a few more strokes before Allen clenched around him, cried out his name, and collapsed again, burying his head into the pillow to muffle his moans.

Greg thrust one final time, and then he fell forward and grunted, throbbing hard with his own release. It was another familiar thing—the intense pleasure, relief, and love that rippled through him in waves. Yet every time they made love, it seemed to renew him, to remind him just how strong their connection was.

He panted as he lowered his head to Allen's back, reaching under his husband to run his hand along Allen's chest. He could feel Allen still trembling underneath him, his breaths uneven and stilted, and he wanted to move to Allen's side, gather him up in his arms, kiss him and make all the declarations of love and forever that he was feeling. But he also wanted to stay just where he was for another moment, still joined together with his husband in this intimate act that they'd only ever shared with each other.

So he settled for kissing Allen's back, letting his hand continue to caress lightly across Allen's chest and then down to his abdomen, and murmuring a quiet "I love you" as his spent arousal softened. Only when he heard a muffled sob from his husband did Greg finally move, allowing himself to slip out of Allen and then shifting over to Allen's side.

He swallowed hard as he heard it again—a low, shuddering breath that caught and hitched—and his stomach clenched.

"Allen, are you—"

"I'm okay. I'm fine. I'm just . . ." Allen trailed off as he shook his head. Then, without looking up, Allen scooted over, turned so he was facing Greg, and curled up into his spot, his head on Greg's shoulder and one hand resting against Greg's bare chest. There was a quiet sniffle, and Greg closed his eyes for a second. Then he reached up, touched Allen's cheek, and kissed his forehead gently, lovingly.

"How about I just hold you for a little while?"

Allen seemed to hesitate for a second, and Greg could almost hear the battle in his husband's mind, no doubt running through all the reasons why them lingering in bed—rather than getting straight up to get cleaned up, change the sheets, have dinner, get back to work or whatnot—would be a burden, disruptive, troublesome. Finally, though, Allen let out another short, shuddering breath and nodded into Greg's chest. "Please."

Greg kissed Allen's forehead again. "Of course, my love," he whispered, and he pulled the comforter up over them, settled down deeper into the bed, and held Allen to him tighter.

Chapter Ten

Allen

SUNLIGHT PEEKED THROUGH THE shutters as Allen blinked his eyes open Saturday morning. He should probably get up and start his day. But it was still too early, and he was still too exhausted. So he just closed his eyes again and hoped Greg wouldn't feel that he'd shifted slightly in the bed.

He hadn't really slept much at all the night before, even after a second shower and a wonderful, home-cooked dinner of pot roast and potatoes and quiet cuddling with Greg on the couch as they'd watched an old movie. When they'd finally crawled into bed well after eleven and Greg had wrapped him up in his arms and kissed him good night, Allen had felt good. Settled. Relaxed. It wasn't until he'd remembered that he'd needed to set his alarm clock—for 7:00 a.m., since he was heading into work on what was normally his day off—that uncertainty had started to cloud his thoughts again.

And that uncertainty had kept him up nearly all night, lying stiffly in bed, trying desperately not to move so he didn't wake his husband.

Today—Saturday—was the first day Christopher and Owen would be coming to the library to start working on their community service hours. Both boys had apparently wanted to get started right away, saying they needed to show their commitment to making things right and doing better. So, midafternoon yesterday, their parents had called the library and spoken with Annabeth, who had arranged everything. The boys would be in from nine to noon today, and although Annabeth had assured Allen it wasn't necessary for him to come in on his day off, he'd insisted on being there at that same time.

He hadn't even gotten a chance to tell Greg yet.

He'd planned to yesterday evening, but when he'd gotten home and gone out into the garage and seen Greg working, something had cracked inside him. He'd *needed* Greg like he hadn't in quite some time.

They had what he considered a healthy, active sex life, and they usually made love at least once or twice a week, even now, with both of them well into their fifties. And it was always fulfilling. Renewing. Comforting. He loved the way Greg made him feel—whole and loved, even when he was struggling emotionally, as he had been all week long. And last night had been no different, no less wonderful.

But he wished the feeling had carried over, that the unease he had about the upcoming day hadn't tarnished the intensity of the love and belonging he'd felt after he and Greg had made love and spent the entire, blissful evening together.

And he also wished he didn't feel so, so bone-tired.

He took a long, deep breath and opened his eyes again, blinking several times as his vision adjusted to the brightening light of the bedroom. And before he could even react to seeing Beans sitting just at the edge of the bed, the pup's muzzle resting on the comforter, Beans let out a low growl-whimper-bark and jumped up to put his paws on the bed.

Allen groaned, and behind him, Greg stirred, his arm tightening around Allen's midsection.

"Ugh, Beans. Go back to bed," Greg complained. But of course, that just made Beans bark again, louder and more insistently this time.

"I'll let him out," Allen said, but when he started to scoot away, Greg's arm held him.

"Let me, darling," Greg murmured, pressing a soft kiss to Allen's back. When Beans barked again, Greg groaned and started to push himself up. "Yeah, yeah, shush, you little stinker. I'm getting up," he grumbled.

Even though it was somewhat of a lighthearted grumble, Allen felt something shudder inside him. Some deep, dark pang of guilt and shame. *He* should be the one to do it. *He* should get up and go downstairs with the dog. After all, Greg was probably tired after having to take care of Allen all night last night and the whole last week, really.

Allen's chest tightened, and his stomach clenched. Greg probably was really tired, not just *from* taking care of him, but *of* taking care of him too. He'd been asking so much of his husband. And now, Greg was thinking he needed to be the one to take care of Beans as well?

Allen shook his head slightly. "No, I can . . . I mean, I'm already awake and—"

He stopped himself, screwing his eyes shut and sucking in a sharp breath. He shouldn't argue; arguing was wrong and would only cause more strife and stress, and he'd already caused enough of that, hadn't he?

God, he had. He'd caused so much trouble for Greg this whole week. It had been hard and trying, every day some new struggle, and it was all his fault. He was such a burden, and it was too much. *He* was too much, and he wasn't really even sure why Greg put up with him.

Greg would be so much better off if he weren't here.

If he just ended it all.

Ended himself.

Twisted images and thoughts bombarded him. Half-formed plans showing him how easy it would be. How easy it would be to do just that. To just—

"God, what's wrong with me, Greg?" The words slipped out without him really meaning to say them, and along with them came a rush of feelings—shame right at the forefront of the wave. He quickly turned over and buried his head into his husband's chest, needing the comfort he knew he'd find there. He felt Greg tense up briefly, but then Greg wrapped both arms around him and kissed his forehead.

"Nothing, darling. There's nothing—"

Beans barked again, cutting off whatever Greg had been about to say, and Greg let out what sounded like an exasperated sigh. "Beans, bed. Now," he said with a quiet but firm voice.

The dog whimpered but then must have listened, because Allen heard him trot away, and then there was a soft rustle as though Beans was lying down in his bed in the corner.

Allen shook his head slightly. "I'm sorry, I . . . I should take him out. He needs to go out," he mumbled.

"He'll be okay for another few minutes," Greg reassured, his tone gentle now. Greg's lips brushed Allen's cheek lightly, and his hand rubbed gently along Allen's back.

The touch didn't make Allen feel better, however, and he shook his head again. "I-I don't want to . . ." He trailed off, not quite sure where he'd been going with his thought. All he knew now was that all the feelings were overwhelming him, and he couldn't stop them.

Guilt. Shame. Self-loathing. And that much darker and more terrible something that had just had him contemplating how he could end his life.

A sudden pounding at his temples had all the air leaving his lungs.

And somehow, Greg seemed to know. He kissed Allen's cheek again and kept rubbing his back, and he started to whisper words of reassurance, his voice calm, soothing, loving. "My darling, Allen, you are so loved. I've loved you from the beginning, and I'll be here with you, always. I love you just as you are. You are loved, and you are enough." There was a pause, and Allen pressed himself up against his husband more as though that might help ease his pain.

"I don't know why it's so bad, Greg. Why is it so bad?" He didn't really expect an answer, since Greg surely didn't know why either, but the words came anyway, and he heard the desperation in his own voice—raw and deep.

"It's been a long week. And I know you didn't sleep well last night. That always exacerbates things. But Allen, please"—Greg's hand came up to touch Allen's cheek softly—"please talk to me. Is this . . . the usual stuff, or something more?"

He could hear the worry in Greg's voice, and it was warranted. Especially given the thoughts he'd just been having—the ones he'd been trying to stop. But Greg's concern just made them echo again. *He'd be so much better off if you weren't here. It would be so easy to just end it all . . .*

"It's more. It's worse. It's really bad," he managed, the words muffled against Greg's chest. "Please, Greg, I . . ." He could feel his heart's irregular rhythm in his chest, the strain each breath was taking, the pain now slicing through his head. Maybe he was having a heart attack. Maybe he'd just have a heart attack and die. Then he'd no longer be a burden, no longer be holding Greg back, no longer be the cause of any stress and pain and . . . "God, Greg, tell it to stop. Please."

"Allen?"

He couldn't speak, but he clung to his husband and fought the words as best he could, and when Greg started telling him again that he was loved, over and over, something inside him finally began to calm again. The thrumming of his heartbeat became steadier, and the weight on his chest lifted just a little. Each breath took less effort.

But it was some time, fifteen or twenty minutes maybe, when the suffocating dread had finally eased enough. Greg's voice faded into a soft kiss pressed into his hair, Allen let out a shuddering breath and reached up to wipe the tears from his cheeks.

"Thank you," he whispered, his voice hoarse and low.

Greg answered with another kiss. "We should go to see Dr. Schultz," Greg said quietly.

"Probably," Allen agreed, though part of him just really didn't want to. Dr. Schultz was wonderful, and she did always seem to help him. But he hated that he still needed help after so many years in and out of therapy.

"I know that's not what you really want to do, darling. But something is different now. I can . . . I can feel it. And I'm worried about you. And please, *please* don't take that the wrong way, because I know that's a part of it. I worry about you because I love you, and—" Greg's voice seemed to crack, and Allen felt his husband's breath shudder as his lips pressed to Allen's forehead.

He took two deep breaths and nodded. "I-I'll call her first thing on Monday," he said. It was probably the right thing to do. In fact, they probably should have already called her to schedule an appointment after everything that had happened the previous week.

Greg's hand rubbed up his arm gently. "Let me take Beans out, darling? And then we can make breakfast. Maybe we can go to Seattle today, maybe grab lunch at Ivar's, see that new exhibit at the art museum. Or—"

"Maybe." Allen's chest felt tight again as he closed his eyes. "Let me—let me get up with you, though. I . . . I think I probably shouldn't be alone right now." He somehow managed to keep himself from saying anything more, but he could feel Greg tense up, his hand stopping its soothing motion on Allen's arm. The air around him felt thick and too warm, even though he knew it was cool in the room, and Allen closed his eyes again as he pushed himself up to sit.

Shaky and weak. That was how he felt. Shaky and weak and unsettled.

But when Greg scooted up behind him, wrapped his arms around Allen's midsection, and placed a light kiss on Allen's bare shoulder, he let out some long, shuddering breath that somehow released a good amount of the tension that had built up. Then he collapsed back into Greg and allowed his husband's embrace to soothe him. And it did. It was soothing. Even more this time than earlier.

"I'm . . . okay now. We should take Beans out."

"Okay, darling."

Greg quietly scooted off the bed ahead of Allen and then helped Allen to his feet. And they both got dressed as Beans jumped around barking and whining and generally being impatient. When they finally made it downstairs, Beans had both front paws up on the back door and was whimpering as he scratched at the wood of the doorframe. Greg huffed some reprimand, and the dog lowered himself to the ground and sat until Greg made it over and opened the door.

Allen stopped at the kitchen table and watched, somehow managing a half-smile, as Beans tore out of the house and zoomed around the yard, racing all the way to the back fence before spinning around and racing back. After several laps, he stopped to sniff the ground and find a place to do his business.

Neither Allen nor Greg said anything for a few minutes, but Greg moved back over to where Allen stood, stepped behind him, and slid his arms low around Allen's waist, pulling Allen back against him. It felt good again, and he let the warmth of his husband's love wash over him.

He was loved. He wasn't a burden or too much or not enough. He was exactly as he should be. The words swirled around, repeating in his head as he leaned back more against Greg's solid chest.

"I love you," Greg murmured, his lips brushing just below Allen's ear. "Are you feeling a little better?"

The softness of Greg's voice, the gentleness of his touch, the warmth of his kiss all made everything just that much better in the moment, and Allen had the fleeting thought that it shouldn't be so difficult. Everything shouldn't be so difficult when he had this. He knew he had this—he knew Greg was here with him and for him, always.

So why had he wished earlier that he wasn't . . . alive anymore? It wasn't the first time he'd had these thoughts, not by far, but it *was* the first time the words had really coalesced and been so clear and coherent and strong. The first time he hadn't immediately dismissed the notion. The first time he'd actually wished it were true. And he didn't think he'd ever before gotten to *that* point—where his brain had started imagining *how* and *what* he might do, how easy it might be . . .

What was wrong with him?

He pushed the thoughts away and nodded. "Yes. Yes, you're . . . helping a lot right now. Just holding me."

Greg chuckled quietly. "I'll hold you all day if you need it."

"I have to work today," Allen finally admitted, and he turned around in Greg's arms and slid his hands up Greg's chest to rest on either side of his neck. He didn't miss the concern in his husband's expression. He closed his eyes and rested his head against Greg's shoulder. "Just from nine to noon. I should probably call out, but I can't. I promised to be there. Christopher and Owen are—"

"Allen, no. No. No, you can't be serious? Not after—not after what just—" Greg seemed unable to finish his sentence, and Allen's stomach churned.

Part of him wanted to be angry. But that reaction felt juvenile at best. He took a deep breath and tried to explain himself.

"It's only three hours, and—"

"No. No. I-I mean . . ." Greg faltered again, and Allen pushed back slightly to look up at his husband. Greg's face was pale, and he was shaking his head slowly, his eyes pleading with Allen. "I understand, Allen. I really understand why you want to be there. But I think you're not really letting yourself admit just how much what those boys did to you hurt." Greg pulled Allen back up against him and buried his head in Allen's hair. His warm breath felt soothing and yet stifling at the same time. And Allen's heart started pounding again.

"I-I know what they—"

"You're hurting, my love. You had a panic attack just less than an hour ago, and it was worse than I remember you having in a very, very long time. I'm . . ." Greg seemed to hesitate, and Allen felt tears pricking at the backs of his eyes. "I'm really, *really* not comfortable with this. Please . . . please reconsider."

Allen couldn't answer right away, and Beans chose that moment to scratch at the door to be let back in anyway. Needing to move, Allen pulled out of Greg's arms and silently headed over to open the door and let the dog back in. Then he turned back around and watched as Beans circled the kitchen, his nose in the air, sniffing as though he'd caught some very interesting scent. Greg hadn't moved from his spot, but Allen couldn't bring himself to meet his husband's eyes.

"I'm . . . going," Allen said finally, after Beans had taken off out of the room and clambered back up the stairs. Allen stared at the ground now, and his resolve felt about as shaky as his hands. Why was he being so stubborn? Greg was probably having the same thoughts.

Yet the words that came from across the room didn't indicate that. Nor did Greg's soft tone.

"Okay, okay," Greg said. Allen closed his eyes again as Greg moved closer. Two strong hands settled on his upper arms. "You'll let me walk with you? And pick you up?"

There was a plea to his husband's voice, and Allen swallowed hard as he nodded. "Of course."

"Okay." Lips pressed lightly to his forehead. "Can I make you toast and an omelet? We've got peppers and spinach and those fresh chives."

"That sounds good."

With a nod, Greg moved away from him, over toward the refrigerator to get started making breakfast. After a moment, when Allen had gathered himself enough, he followed, taking his spot next to Greg along the counter.

Chapter Eleven

Greg

GREG CHOPPED THE PEPPERS while Allen cracked the eggs, and in not too long, they were sitting down at the table, eating breakfast. But the conversation between them had been stilted, the air thick with tension and uncertainty. Greg just didn't know what to say. Or what to do.

It seemed like a very bad decision to him—for Allen to go into work today to supervise Christopher and Owen. A very bad decision. Particularly after the morning Allen had had—the shaking and trembling, the spiral, the panic.

He wanted to be supportive. He knew Allen needed that above all else. Only, Greg wasn't so sure being supportive was the best thing in this instance. His gut was telling him he needed to try a little harder to convince Allen to stay home . . . in the most supportive way possible.

He took the last bite of his omelet and glanced up across the table at his husband as he chewed. Allen had the newspaper open in front of him, but he wasn't moving—his eyes were unfocused and looking elsewhere, not at the newspaper, and his omelet sat almost untouched, one hand loosely holding his fork.

Greg frowned again and then lightly cleared his throat. "Joe's barbeque is tomorrow afternoon," he said, hoping to break the silence and the tension that had come with it.

From across the table, Allen lifted his eyes, looking up at Greg over the top of his reading glasses. His expression seemed dull, or resigned, maybe. Whatever it was, it wasn't an expression Greg liked or was used to seeing. Greg shook his head softly.

"We don't have to go, if you're not up to it. I just . . ." He trailed off, wholly unsure—again—of what to say or do.

As he watched, Allen's expression tightened even more. "We can go," Allen said simply, and although he looked about ready to say something more, he didn't. Instead, his eyes dropped to his plate, and he seemed to force his hand to move, the motion stiff and hesitant as he cut off a small bite of his omelet.

And it was painful again as Greg clearly heard the words Allen hadn't said but was obviously thinking. About how he didn't want Greg to change or cancel plans because of him. How he didn't want to be a burden. Or disruptive. Or . . .

Greg nodded a response, although he wasn't sure Allen saw it. Then he silently pushed back his chair, stood, and picked up his plate to move it to the dishwasher. He was aware that he needed to reassure Allen he wasn't upset, since he knew Allen would be reading much too much into everything, including Greg's silence. But at the same time, he couldn't do that because he actually *was* upset.

He closed the dishwasher and rested his hands on the counter, staring blankly out the window. His mind kept replaying earlier that morning in bed, when Allen had begged him to "make it stop." Allen had been shaking, his whole body trembling, and he'd felt cold and clammy. Greg had done the only thing he'd known to do—hold his husband, talk to him, reassure him. And eventually, Allen's shaking had stopped.

But this *was* different than he was used to. Scarier somehow than the panic and anxiety Allen had had in the past. There was something deeper happening, something that Allen hadn't quite told him.

"I can handle it, Greg," Allen said quietly, and Greg felt one of Allen's hands on his back. "I have to go. I said I would, and—"

"You don't have to," Greg interrupted, shaking his head. His hands gripped the counter tighter. "You don't have to go. Someone else can handle it today. Annabeth or—or your intern, Casey, right? He can handle it. You"—Greg turned around slowly and had to resist the urge to gather Allen up in his arms and just hold him—"should *not* be the one handling it today. Not today, Allen. Not after this morning. I can't . . . agree with you on this. I won't stop you, because it's your decision. But it's—but I think it's the wrong one."

His chest ached as he watched Allen recoil a step, his hand dropping down to his side. Allen's mouth had tightened into a frown, and his gray-blue eyes held Greg's gaze but were clouded with pain. Greg's stomach lurched, and he swallowed hard as he reached out and took Allen's hand.

"I know you feel an obligation, and I know you want to show those boys what true kindness and compassion are. I understand that, really I do. But you've been struggling all week, and even before that, and you said it yourself earlier—this is bad, worse than normal. Allen . . . please. Please, think about this."

Allen's eyes had dropped, and he now stared at their hands, his face taut. Greg moved a step closer, and he watched Allen's eyes close. The tension in the air between them was almost palpable. He shook his head gently.

"Allen—"

"I feel like I want to die." Allen's voice was low, and he didn't look up at Greg, even as he stepped closer, wrapped his arms around Greg's waist, and blew out a short breath. Greg's stomach clenched with a nauseating uncertainty, and he automatically returned the embrace, holding his husband tightly. With a shudder, Allen buried his head against Greg's shoulder. "I don't really want to, I mean. I . . . wouldn't ever do . . . that. I-I think. But the thoughts are there. And insistent. And—and that's what was so overwhelming earlier, in bed."

"And . . . now?"

The temperature in the room seemed to plummet as Allen's arms tightened around Greg's waist again.

"Now it's like . . . it's still there—that feeling. And I've acknowledged it and told it it's not welcome, but it didn't leave. It's still there." Allen paused, and the moment seemed to stretch on and on.

Greg closed his eyes and took two measured breaths. Over thirty years together. Over thirty years, and this might be the most scared he'd ever felt for his husband. His heart stuttered in his chest, and he pressed a light kiss into Allen's hair. He tried not to let himself think how he must have done something wrong this last week—not been supportive enough or not taken care of Allen enough or something. But deep down, he knew that wasn't the case.

"It's not forcing me to think it, not anymore," Allen continued, his voice still quiet, still shaky. "But it's still . . . there. And I—god, Greg, I have no intention of—of trying anything. I hope you don't—I hope you don't—"

Greg shook his head quickly, then he pulled back just enough while his hand reached up to cup Allen's cheek. The familiar roughness of Allen's neatly trimmed beard felt different somehow, and as Greg tilted Allen's chin up and searched his eyes, there was another uncomfortable tightness in his chest. "I love you, and—and I'll help you through this, and we'll get through this together, as we always, always have. Okay? Okay?"

There was a desperation in his tone, and he could hear it. He was sure Allen could hear it too. In fact, he *hoped* Allen heard it—heard it and believed him and trusted him.

But he felt it before he saw it and before Allen spoke—that chill again. The distance between them somehow grew, even though neither of them had moved. Allen swallowed, closed his eyes, and just nodded with a quiet "okay," mumbled through a tight jaw. That was all. And the uncertainty that hit Greg then was strong and intense and sent a fierce shiver through him.

At the same time, he felt Allen cling to him, leaning against him, and he slipped both arms low around his husband's waist to support him. He inhaled deeply, then blinked and closed his eyes again.

"Has it ever been this bad before?" he asked quietly. He thought maybe Allen had already told him earlier, but he wanted to hear Allen's thoughts again now—now that he was a little calmer and thinking a little more clearly.

"No."

"Have you ever—have you ever had these types of thoughts before?"

There was a pause, and Greg felt warmth seep through his shirt as Allen let out a long breath. "Yes."

"Allen . . ." He breathed his husband's name and pulled Allen up against him more, letting his hands smooth up and down Allen's back. "Allen, you never told me . . ."

"It wasn't really like this so much," Allen admitted, and he straightened up just slightly and lifted his eyes. Greg saw tears in them, and he shook his head weakly as Allen continued. "It was just a fleeting thought here or there. Really, Greg. I-I thought it was maybe something everyone thought about, from time to time . . . ?"

"No, no, I don't think so, darling," Greg answered softly, and Allen blinked several times with a weak nod.

"I didn't mean to worry you, but—" With a rough exhale, Allen scrunched his eyes closed, and his hands pressed into Greg's back as though needing him to be even closer, to hold him even tighter. "I-I'm scared, and I need you. But I also . . . I also need you to let me go to work today."

"Why?" Greg tried to deliver the question without any sort of accusation to his tone, but he wasn't sure if he succeeded. Allen tensed in his arms. "Please explain it to me," he added quickly. "I need to understand."

With a nod, Allen pulled away, and he didn't look at his husband as he dropped his arms to his sides and then tilted his head slightly toward the living room. "Can we go sit?"

Greg agreed immediately, and he followed Allen over to the couch. Allen sat down first, lowering himself stiffly into the middle couch cushion. After Greg took his spot next to Allen, one leg hiked up under him so he could face his husband, Allen scooted all the way over until he was once again in his husband's arms. Greg kissed the top of his head and then held him while Allen started talking—his words slow and punctuated by long pauses.

"I do know that what Christopher and Owen did is likely the reason things are this bad for me right now," Allen began. He swallowed hard and rested his head against Greg's chest, and Greg rubbed his hand up Allen's forearm to his elbow. "I understand how you see that and know that, like I do, and you're thinking . . . and you're thinking, *why the heck does Allen want to spend more time around them?* And you see how that's a bad idea, and I-I understand that too. Because maybe—maybe it is. But I—"

Allen stopped talking abruptly as he started shaking again, and his hand moved to the middle of Greg's chest. Greg could feel Allen pressing into him as he had earlier, as though he needed to feel Greg's closeness. He breathed another kiss against Allen's temple this time and stayed silent, waiting for Allen to continue.

"I know, Greg, I just know that I need to feel . . . wanted and needed. Whenever I've been most down, it's been reminders of things like that—that I'm loved and that I'm a part of something, like this community and my job and our relationship. Those things, those reminders are what have always given me strength and helped me the most. And I—and so what I think I really need is your support now, Greg. And—"

"You have it, darling," Greg cut in, and even though he tried to maintain an even tone, he heard the strain in his own voice. "You've always had my support, but—"

"But I don't. Not really. Not *this time*." Allen didn't move or pull away, and Greg was thankful. But his words were filled with an emotional distance, almost a numbness or detachment, and it made Greg's worry spike even more. "You don't want me going in today, and I understand that. But I need to, and I need—I really, really need for you to agree with me and support me. Greg, I need to be there. And yeah, maybe I'm—maybe I'm wrong. But I need—"

Allen stopped as he sucked in a sharp breath and then tensed, his whole body tightening in Greg's embrace.

"I need—"

Again, he started and stopped, and his hand, which had been pressing strongly into Greg's chest, fell away, down to Greg's thigh. Then, Allen's whole body began to shake with sobs, even as he buried his head into Greg's chest more and began mumbling nonsense words. Something about being sorry, and something else about probably being wrong anyway. Something about how he felt such a deep, utterly dark hopelessness sometimes, and how he was so sorry he needed all the constant reminders that he was loved. And then Greg heard him say how he knew he was loved, how he really did know, because Greg showed him all the time, but the negative thoughts and the despair could somehow sneak in, take over, snuff out all the good and all the love and replace it with an intense sadness. All the words were jumbled, stuttered, out of order. Wetness seeped through Greg's shirt, and his own tears stung at the corners of his eyes, but he barely noticed. He just held his husband tightly and started reciting his own truths.

"Shh, my darling. You are loved and wanted and needed. And you are worthy of that love, you are enough, just as you are. I love you and need you, and I always have and always will. Please, please, Allen . . ."

He knew Allen still hadn't really even given him a clear explanation about why he absolutely insisted on going to work. And he was sure Allen knew that too. But he'd heard enough of Allen's argument to know one thing—his husband absolutely *needed* him to be okay with it.

And that felt heavy. Heavy and difficult, and Greg wasn't entirely sure what to do. Because even though he really did want to be okay with it so he could support Allen—he really still . . . wasn't.

And he couldn't—wouldn't—lie about that. That would serve no purpose and would only make things worse. He knew that from experience.

Greg took a deep breath and continued rubbing Allen's back with long, slow, gentle strokes. When Allen's body stopped shaking, and his shuddering sobs quieted into more regular breathing, Greg lowered his cheek to rest on the top of Allen's head, and he closed his eyes. "Allen, I'm so sorry," he started, because he didn't know what else to say. "I'm so sorry I gave you reason to doubt that I supported you. I *do* support you. I always will. I just . . . I just can't . . ."

The short silence as Greg's voice trailed off was thick and yet sharp at the same time. A ragged exhale from Allen broke the quiet after a moment, however, and Allen sat up and pulled away, wiping at his cheeks with one hand.

A strong tug in Greg's chest sent him reaching for his husband again, but Allen shook his head once and stood, his eyes downcast and his hands balled up into fists at his sides.

"It's okay," Allen said, his voice unusually taut and hard. "But I need to go get ready now or I'll be late."

"Allen—"

"I'll walk myself. And I'll be home maybe around twelve thirty. Maybe we can still go to Seattle after." His words were clear, but his tone was filled with pain and hurt and doubt.

Greg shook his head, starting to push himself up to stand. "No, I'll walk with you still, I—"

"I can walk myself, Greg. I'm not a child," Allen stated, and he turned away from Greg and, without looking back, headed toward the stairs.

Greg's mouth hung partway open as he watched his husband stalk off, and he quickly closed it and sat back on the couch, his gaze still following Allen up the stairs. His heart ached in his chest, willing him to rush after Allen and apologize, but his legs wouldn't respond, and instead, he just sat there, staring as Allen disappeared down the upstairs hallway.

A moment later, he heard the bedroom door slam, and then, all was silent.

He closed his eyes and let out the breath he'd been holding.

A fight. How long had it been? Years maybe? They just didn't really fight. Little disagreements here and there, sure. All couples did that. But a real fight, with Allen getting angry and stalking off?

He actually wasn't sure if that had ever happened. Allen just didn't get angry like that; he didn't argue or raise his voice, didn't yell, didn't stomp off. In fact, Allen could barely stand when they'd disagree about simple things, like what to have for dinner. It just wasn't *him*.

And he certainly didn't slam doors.

A part of Greg still wanted to hop up and follow, apologize or . . . something. But another part of him felt too lost to do that. Lost and unsure. And Allen was right. He wasn't a child, and he could make his own decisions. They didn't always have to agree on everything, did they?

The simple question didn't really account for all of the factors in the equation, Greg knew. But he just didn't know what to do, what to say, how to react. So instead, he stood on shaky legs, turned in the opposite direction, and headed out into his office in the garage.

Chapter Twelve

Allen

ALLEN STOOD BACK A bit, watching as Annabeth pushed a book cart up to the first of several rows of bookshelves. The two boys, Christopher and Owen, trailed behind her, both of them quiet and looking rather uncomfortable.

Annabeth stopped and turned to face the boys, offering Allen a soft, understanding smile as her eyes met his for a brief moment. Then she blinked and shifted her attention back to Christopher and Owen.

"So, this is called shelf reading," she started, and Allen smiled inwardly as he saw both of the boys straighten up a bit and nod. "Basically, you're each going to work your way down your shelf, checking the call numbers to be sure every book is in the right place. If you find one that's not, you can reshelve it—put it where it belongs—if its proper place is close by, or if not, just set it aside on the cart for now, and when you're through with your shelf, then you can take care of them."

She continued her explanation, but Allen stopped listening as he turned and headed back toward the desk at the front of the library. It wasn't far, but by the time he got there, he felt winded, and he moved around behind the desk and sat heavily, closing his eyes for a moment. He couldn't seem to catch his breath. Not since earlier that morning.

He heard the echo of the door slamming behind him and felt the sting again, like shards of glass piercing his heart. And the cold—he felt the cold too, seeping into him and numbing his fingers.

He was broken. Completely broken. Something inside him wasn't working right. And it had caused him to go and overreact. Start a fight with his husband. A real, actual stomp-off-and-slam-the-door fight. All because he was stubborn and needed validation that Greg couldn't—or wouldn't—give. Just the thought of that—the reminder of their morning conversation—sent an unpleasant rush of nausea through him. And all those same feelings he'd been trying to tell Greg about that morning came back full force, as though trying to crush him. Smother him. Suffocate him.

That had to be why he couldn't really breathe right. Why his hands were numb and his chest ached. Why all he could really feel was this overwhelming sadness and this odd detachment from the world around him. All of it mixed with a deep, simmering fear of the dark thoughts still swirling around in his head.

Unwanted. Unloved. A burden. Shouldn't be here. Shouldn't. Be. Here.

There was a soft noise in front of him, and Allen looked up to see his coworker standing on the other side of the desk, her kind brown eyes watching him.

"That should keep them busy for a while," Annabeth said with a small smile. But then her smile morphed into a frown, and she shook her head and raised one eyebrow at him. "You, um, you don't look so great. Maybe, you know, you should head home. I can handle everything. Really. And Casey will be here in about an hour anyways."

A sick feeling in the pit of Allen's stomach had him shaking his head. "No, I'm fine. I need to be here. I need to work on that proposal to the city council for funding to expand the after-school program, and—"

"Um, excuse me, Ms. Jones." The voice from behind Annabeth was quiet and reluctant, and Allen recognized it immediately as Christopher's. The nausea turned into a sharp pain that seemed to stab him in the gut, but he ignored it. "I found a book without a call number, and, um, what—what do you want me to do with that?"

Annabeth hadn't turned away to acknowledge the boy and instead seemed to be watching Allen with even more concern. She opened her mouth, probably to ask him if he was alright, but he quickly nodded at her and forced a smile, even as his chest tightened more. "Go on and help them, and I'll just get started on this proposal," he managed, and he tore his eyes away from hers, gave Christopher another short nod, and shifted in his chair so he was facing his computer.

He was vaguely aware of Annabeth hesitating next to the desk for just a moment and then ushering Christopher away, presumably back to the bookshelves to take a look at the book he'd found. He knew she was worried about him. She'd been worried since he stepped foot in the library about a half hour ago, and she'd tried to talk to him several times. Before the boys had arrived, she'd even tried to convince him to go home.

A part of him wondered if Greg had called her and talked to her. Although he was pretty sure Greg wouldn't do something like that.

Mostly, though, he felt this growing sadness that was much too deep to just brush off. And it was sadness mixed with something else intense and raw. Something that had made his heart start racing and his whole body feel off. Like there was something sitting on his shoulders, trying to bury him. And he just wanted it to disappear. *He* just wanted to disappear.

With fingers that didn't quite feel like his own—because he couldn't shake the sensation that his mind was occupying this foreign space that was not really his—he switched on his computer and opened up the file he needed. Around him, the air felt thick and stale, and when Annabeth returned to check on him a moment later, he waved her off, barely hearing her as she asked whether he was okay.

But she didn't just leave. In fact, as Allen blinked and glanced up at her, she pursed her lips, shook her head gently, and then moved around behind the desk and took the seat next to him.

"This proposal is due next week," he said quietly, faking another smile as he adjusted his reading glasses and set his hands on the keyboard. He tried to read the words on the computer screen, but his eyes wouldn't really focus. And why did his chest hurt? "I-I should really try to get it finished, and—"

"Talk to me, Allen," Annabeth cut in, her voice low but insistent. "No one's here. The boys are working. You're insisting on being here, when you should be home. And I say this in the most loving way, because I'm your friend, but you look like shit."

Allen closed his eyes and blew out a short laugh, though his stomach seemed to knot up painfully at the same moment. "Gee, thanks a lot."

"Seriously, though. Please tell me what's going on," she said again, her voice gentle now.

But he shook his head. She wouldn't understand. She wanted to be supportive, sure, and he appreciated that. But she wouldn't understand, just like Greg hadn't. And she didn't need to be burdened by all of his uncertainties and pain and fear. Just like he shouldn't have burdened Greg with all of it either. He shouldn't have asked for so much, expected so much. He shouldn't have made Greg worry. He shouldn't have confessed as much as he had, since he knew it would just make Greg worry more. And then he shouldn't have gotten short with Greg, stomped off, slammed the door.

God, he was just making a bad situation even worse. Just like he always did. It was too much. *He* was too much. No wonder Greg hadn't come after him when he'd stalked off and hadn't insisted on walking him to work. No wonder Allen had left home earlier without so much as a kiss on the cheek or a goodbye.

The numbness in his fingers spread all the way into his hands.

He faked another smile and lifted his eyes to meet Annabeth's. "Really, it's nothing," he lied, although he regretted it immediately as guilt flared up inside him again. "There's nothing going on. It's just hard to be here and not remember last Sunday. That's all. I promise."

Annabeth was silent for a minute, and the guilt mixed with that deep sadness inside him. He swallowed hard.

"I'm sorry," he added, lowering his eyes to the computer screen again as he doubled down on his not-quite-truth. "I'm sorry. I'm fine though. I'll be fine. And the truth is, this *is* hard. It's harder than I thought it would be. But I need to stay here while they're here. I said I would, and so I will."

Her hand settled on his shoulder and then gave a gentle squeeze.

"Okay, Allen. But if you're not feeling well, let me know, okay? I can call Greg to come get you, and—"

He didn't hear whatever else she had to say, because at that moment, the pain in his head intensified, and he sucked in a sharp breath as his vision blurred. He screwed his eyes shut and reached up to rub the bridge of his nose underneath his reading glasses.

"Yeah, okay," he agreed, without really knowing all of what he was agreeing to. But it did the job, because Annabeth squeezed his shoulder again and then disappeared, maybe off to go get the rest of the library ready for their Saturday morning.

The pain slowly waned, fading from a sharp stabbing right behind his eyes to a dull throb across his whole forehead. And he waited with his eyes closed for a few more minutes, trying to steady himself using a grounding exercise Dr. Schultz had given him some years ago where he visualized drawing the sides of a square as he breathed in and out. It maybe sort of worked. Or at least, things didn't get worse.

With another deep breath, he finally opened his eyes again and looked out around the library. The bleariness in his vision had mostly cleared, but the numbness in his hands had not. Nor had that strange detachment he felt. Across the library, he saw the two boys, working quietly in the same row, carefully scanning each of the books on the shelf. As though they knew they were being watched, both boys seemed to sneak a glance in his direction, and Allen had to force himself not to look away. But his stomach dropped, and a cold chill settled over him. Christopher was the first to lower his eyes, shifting his gaze back to the book he had in his hands. Owen kept his eyes on Allen for a few extra seconds, his expression tight, and then the teen bit his lip and gave Allen a weak, hesitant smile before turning back to his work.

Allen let out the breath he'd been holding. He took off his glasses and set them on the desk, then stood to go speak with the boys, since that was something he'd wanted to do but hadn't been able to convince himself to earlier. He noticed Annabeth glance over at him from the other side of the library, where it looked like she was starting to reorganize some of the items on the display they had for local hiking trails and maps. She smiled kindly and looked like she was maybe about to say something.

But then the room around him began to spin. Or swirl. Or tilt. Dangerously. Sideways. And everything seemed to seep out of him—his strength, his breath, his warmth—out of him and downward, into the ground.

He tried to suck in air, but his knees gave out, and slowly, he began to fall. It seemed slow, at least, and he even had time, somehow, to register Annabeth's eyes widening in fear from the other side of the room.

Then everything went dark.

"Mr. Westin! Mr. Westin, please wake up."

"Move please, Owen. Christopher, call 9-1-1. Allen? Allen?"

He groaned, and pain shot through his back into his legs. His head hurt too. And his wrist.

More voices spoke to him, muffled though, and he felt Annabeth's hand on his forehead. He forced his eyes open and blinked to clear his vision.

"Oh god, good, you're not—"

"Ms. Jones, they want the address?"

Allen squinted and slowly brought one shaking hand up to his face, covering his eyes to block the bright light.

"Tell them it's the library. They'll know where to come. Allen, talk to me, please." There was a desperation in Annabeth's voice, and Allen felt her hand touch his forehead again.

"Wha—what happened?"

"You're gonna be okay. You fainted or something. How do you feel?"

He'd fainted? Groaning again, Allen set his hands down on either side of him and tried to push himself up, but his wrist flared with pain, and he just had no strength. That, and a strong hand pushed against his shoulder.

"Don't try to sit up, Mr. Westin." Allen recognized Owen's voice, though it sounded shaky. "You probably had a sudden drop in blood pressure, and you should lie still until the paramedics get here to check you out."

If he'd had any energy, he might have wanted to ask Owen how he knew that much. But he didn't. He felt more exhausted than he'd maybe ever felt in his life. And weak. Like he could barely lift his own head.

"They're on their way, Ms. Jones. Is he gonna be okay?" Christopher's voice sounded far away. And scared.

Allen closed his eyes and brought his hand up to cover his face again. God, he was still shaking. And it hurt. Everywhere hurt. And . . . and he'd never fainted before. Something like panic rose up inside him, and his chest tightened. *Was* he okay?

The quiet voices continued around him, and Annabeth's hand didn't leave his forehead. He heard bits and pieces of the conversation, and he tried to focus long enough to listen, but it was a massive jumble of words that he struggled to follow. And his head was pounding. And his chest hurt.

"Allen, we called the paramedics, and they'll be here soon, okay? And—shit, I've gotta call Greg. Dammit. Ah, boys, pretend you didn't hear me say that. Owen, can you go unlock the front door so they can get in? Here's the keys. Christopher, my cell phone is on my desk in the back office. Can you grab that for me please? Hang in there, Allen. Can you hear me?"

"Yeah," he answered, but his voice was raspy. He coughed to clear his throat, and his head hurt even more. "Sorry—sorry about this. Sorry, I'm . . ."

"Shh, no, Allen, you're fine. I'm calling Greg right now, okay?"

He gave a weak nod and let his hand fall back down to his side. The numbness in his fingers had turned into a tingling, buzzing sensation that was both uncomfortable and rattled him.

"Mr. Westin?" It was Owen again, and Allen forced his eyes open to find the teen kneeling next to him, his lips pursed with concern.

"Yes, Owen?" he managed, and he closed his eyes again, too weak to keep them open. God, what was wrong with him?

"Sir, I'd like to elevate your legs a bit. That could help bring your blood pressure back to normal. Is that okay with you, sir?"

Again, Allen wondered how Owen knew this, but now wasn't the time to ask, and so he just nodded with a feeble "yes." A moment later, he felt his legs lifted and his feet settled onto a chair.

"There you go, Mr. Westin."

"Thank you, Owen," he said.

Annabeth's hand moved to his shoulder. "Greg, hi . . . No, actually, he— . . . No, he's . . . Yeah." With effort, Allen opened his eyes again and turned his head toward Annabeth, who was setting her phone down on the floor next to him and shaking her head slightly. Her eyes met his, and she seemed relieved somehow, offering him a gentle smile as she squeezed his shoulder. "Greg is on his way."

He didn't get a chance to respond because the paramedics arrived right then, and there was a flurry of activity around him. A young woman maybe in her early twenties knelt down next to him and began asking Annabeth and the boys questions, and someone took his blood pressure and listened to his heart. He closed his eyes just to block out all the activity around him, and he focused instead on his breathing. In and out. In and out.

Not more than a couple of minutes later, one of the paramedics lowered Allen's legs from the chair and then helped him to sit up slowly. He still felt weak, a bit dizzy. And the intense throbbing right behind his eyes had only gotten worse.

It wasn't until he opened his eyes a moment later that he noticed Greg standing a few feet away, his arms crossed over his chest and his face taut with worry.

Pain and hurt and sadness hit him, and he clenched his jaw and blinked his eyes closed. How long had Greg been there? Why wasn't he sitting there next to Allen, helping to support him, telling him he loved him? Had he finally realized—

"Mr. Westin?"

Allen heard his name from the woman on his left, and he tilted his head slightly in her direction. "Yes, sorry, I . . . What did you say?"

She seemed to give him a reassuring smile. "I need to ask you a series of questions to determine whether we should take you to the hospital or whether you should just go home and rest and then follow up with your physician. Do you understand?"

Allen swallowed and gave a weak nod. Then he lowered his eyes to his hands and did his best to answer all of her questions honestly. When she was finished, she told him to sit tight and relax for a few more minutes, and then she stood while her colleague took Allen's blood pressure again.

The general commotion in the room seemed to have quieted down, and Allen lifted his eyes to take in the scene. But he immediately saw Greg, still watching him, still standing just a few feet away, and his heart ached. He swallowed as he held his husband's gaze for a moment before his jaw started to tremble.

"Greg . . ." He could barely form the word for some reason, but the instant it left his lips, his husband was at his side, sitting next to him on the floor. Greg's hand took his, and Allen closed his eyes again as a comforting warmth replaced the chill that had been with him all morning.

Soft lips grazed his cheek. "I'm sorry, darling. They told me to stay back until they were finished, and I . . . I'm sorry. I'm here now. I'm here."

Allen just gave a weak nod and leaned against his husband's shoulder as the other young man on his right began to remove the blood pressure cuff from his arm.

"What was it?" he heard Greg ask.

The sound of the Velcro unfastening on the blood pressure cuff grated on Allen's ears, and he almost flinched.

"One hundred over seventy."

"Is that okay? It's lower than normal for him."

"It's within an acceptable range, yeah," the paramedic said. His hand settled lightly on Allen's shoulder. "Mr. Westin, can you hear me, sir?"

Allen cleared his throat and nodded but kept his eyes closed. "Yes."

"Alright, sir, so we don't need to take you to the hospital, but we do recommend you see your physician as soon as you can for a follow-up." Allen nodded again, and the man continued. "From what we gather, the fainting episode was likely a combination of situational and postural syncope. The emotional stress you've been under can cause fluctuations in your blood pressure, and then when you stood up, that may have also caused another drop. Given the lack of history of any other medical issues, we don't see a need to take you to the ER. But like I said, you should follow up with your physician as soon as possible to rule out any other causes. Does that make sense, sir?"

Before Allen could answer, Greg squeezed his hand and then listed off a set of rapid-fire questions to the paramedic, speaking too quickly for Allen to follow. So instead, he just let out a long, slow breath and continued to lean up against his husband as the paramedic addressed each of Greg's concerns.

"That's right, yes. Rest and stay hydrated. And he said he's not on any medications. Right, Allen? So that's not something to worry about."

Allen finally opened his eyes, blinking at the light that seemed much too bright. He tilted his head slightly to look up at the paramedic, who still knelt next to him, on the opposite side as Greg. The man was watching him with a kind smile, and Allen nodded. "No medications, yeah."

Greg's thumb ran along the back of his knuckles, and Allen looked down to where their hands were clasped together on his thigh.

The paramedic cleared his throat. "Okay, let's see if we can get you up on your feet, eh?"

It was slow. Greg lifted him from one side, and the paramedic lifted him from the other. And he tried to tuck away his embarrassment at the fact that they were actually lifting him because he was physically incapable of standing on his own. But he managed to get his feet underneath himself, and though he felt lightheaded and dizzy, his legs seemed to hold him up. Sort of. He found himself leaning heavily on Greg as Greg's arm wrapped around his waist.

"I've got you. You okay, darling?"

He answered the best he could, a low mumble of something in the affirmative, though he wasn't sure that was the most accurate response.

"Owen, get that chair for him," the paramedic said.

"Yessir."

"Sit here, darling. There we go. Breathe slowly. In and out. Are you okay, Allen? Is he okay? Are you sure?" Greg's voice sounded . . . terrified. Without opening his eyes, Allen reached up to place his hand over Greg's, which now sat on his shoulder.

"Yes, he just needs to take everything slowly and rest."

The conversation continued around him for another few minutes, but he let all the words pass by, too exhausted to try to pay much attention. Eventually, Annabeth came over to check on him again, and then the paramedics left. He heard Greg's voice a few feet away, low and whispering but firm, upset. And then Annabeth responded, her tone also sounding tense.

He blinked his eyes halfway open to see his husband looking angry, arguing in hushed tones and motioning to his left. When Allen followed the direction of Greg's gesture, he saw Owen and Christopher standing there looking guilty as hell, both with their hands stuffed in their pockets and their shoulders hunched.

Owen glanced in his direction, and when their eyes met, Allen saw regret and some sort of apology in the boy's expression. Allen gave him a small smile and lifted his hand slightly. "C'mere, kiddo," Allen said, his voice still hoarse.

The conversation between Greg and Annabeth stopped, and Owen's eyes darted to Greg for a moment. His frown tightened, but he looked back at Allen and then approached cautiously and knelt down next to the chair where Allen sat.

"Thank you for your help there," Allen said, trying to infuse all the kindness into his voice that he possibly could. But god, he was also exhausted. He closed his eyes for a long blink and took another careful, deep breath. "How . . . did you know to have me raise my legs up? And about my blood pressure . . ." He trailed off, not quite able to finish his thought. But when he looked back at the teen, Owen's frown had turned into a cautious grin.

"I'm part of the Health Sciences CTE program at school," Owen started, and he bit his lip and lowered his eyes for a brief moment. "I'll start training to become certified as an EMT when I turn seventeen next year. I learned about how to handle patients with syncope a couple weeks ago on a ride along."

Something about that made Allen smile, and he closed his eyes again and nodded. "Well, I definitely appreciate your quick thinking there. And—and Christopher . . ."

"Yessir," Christopher said from just in front of him.

"Thank you for making that 9-1-1 call. Are you okay, kiddo?"

"Me, sir?"

Allen nodded and opened his eyes to see Christopher standing awkwardly, his eyes darting over to where Allen knew Greg was standing. Allen smiled weakly and let out a long breath.

"Yes, you. Are you okay?" Allen repeated. The boy looked like he had no idea how to respond, so Allen just smiled again. "I'll be okay. But it looks like the two of you . . ." A heaviness sat on his shoulders again, and Allen let his eyes close. "The two of you will need to finish . . . the shelf reading and then . . . probably help Ms. Jones set up for the chess club meeting. Follow her instructions, okay? And I'll see both of you next weekend. You'll be back next Saturday, right?"

Allen was sure he heard a huff of something from Greg, but when he glanced at his husband, Greg's eyes were soft and sad.

"Yessir," both boys said in unison.

"Good."

"Okay, back to work now, boys?" he heard Annabeth say, and then she and the two boys moved away, probably off across the library to get back to work.

As his eyes lingered on Greg's, there was a moment then where Allen had a flashback to a memory from so long ago. Thirty something years ago now. Thirty-three? Thirty-four? His brain didn't want to do the math. And as cliché as it sounded, he somehow remembered the day as though it were only yesterday.

He smiled up at his husband and, with effort, lifted his hand in invitation. Greg closed the distance between them immediately, kneeling next to Allen's chair, and Allen reached up and set his hand on Greg's upper arm.

"Remember the very first day we met?" Allen said quietly, and he saw the second Greg's expression changed, a flicker of love and joy interrupting the constant swarm of worry and concern.

"Of course. I'll never forget. Seattle Public Library. January 5, 1990. I came in, fresh from hiking Wright Mountain, which was really stupid of me since the snow made it just—just ridiculously unsafe."

Allen nodded with another smile, and he let his hand find Greg's. "You were still wearing that puffy blue jacket you used to have, and your hiking boots. And you came right up to the information desk and said, 'I need to find a book.' And I said something about—"

"You said, 'Well, if you were looking for books up in the mountains, it's no wonder you didn't find them. But I bet we've got exactly what you need right here.'"

Allen let out a short huff of a laugh, which felt good. But then his smile faded slowly, and he looked down. "I love you, Greg." He felt his husband squeeze his hand, and he returned the gesture. "And I love books and libraries. Especially this one. My job and my work are very important to me. But . . . you were right. I shouldn't have argued with you this morning. And I shouldn't have come in today. I'm really sorry that—"

Greg leaned in and stopped Allen's apology with a light kiss to his forehead, and he closed his eyes and tried not to get more emotional than he already was. He could feel all of it again—the guilt and shame and self-doubt, now loaded with a heavy dose of embarrassment, all those feelings starting to fill his chest again.

"Actually," Greg said quietly, "I think I was the one who was wrong, darling. But let's not talk about that now, okay? Let me take you home, so you can rest?"

Home and rest sounded like the only things he might be capable of right then, and so Allen nodded. A moment later, Greg's arm was around him again as they made their way slowly toward the front entrance.

Just before they reached the door, Christopher came jogging up and moved ahead of them to push the door open, his expression strained. "Here, I-I'll hold it here for you," the boy said.

Allen smiled weakly and started to thank him, but he stopped when Greg's arm tightened around his waist.

And it was Greg who spoke first. "Thank you very much, Christopher."

The boy's eyes dropped to the ground, and he nodded and held the door as Greg and Allen shuffled through.

Chapter Thirteen

Greg

GREG CLOSED THE SLIDER behind him and reached up to shield his eyes from the early afternoon sunlight. Clouds were moving in from the east, edging up over the top of the mountains and beginning to obscure their view of Mount Si. But the sun was just overhead, and he could still feel its warmth.

Maybe it would rain later.

It was such a mundane thing to think about—the weather. Mundane and normal and easy. And for some weird fleeting second, Greg found himself angry at the clouds and the sun and the heat. Angry at how they could just *be* when the world around him was spinning out of control.

Allen sat just at the other edge of the patio, resting back against the cushions of their outdoor sectional with his eyes closed. He looked almost relaxed, almost like it was a normal Saturday afternoon. But Greg could see Allen's chest rising and falling just a little too fast, his jaw held shut with just a little too much tension. His mostly uneaten lunch sat on the patio table in front of him, and his hands were clasped awkwardly in his lap. Definitely not the picture of relaxation.

And Beans was still in protective mode, curled up right at Allen's feet.

Greg swallowed hard, attempted a smile, and stepped out across the patio to join his husband.

"So, Tina and Joe should have been the last visitors, I think," Greg said quietly as he lowered himself onto the couch next to Allen.

"That was a lot of people." Allen shifted until he was leaning up against Greg, his arm coming to rest across Greg's midsection and his head on Greg's shoulder.

"Everyone was worried about you, darling." When Allen didn't say anything, Greg turned his head to press a gentle kiss into Allen's hair. "Everyone was worried because they care. Because you're an important part of this community. Because *you matter* to them."

Allen still didn't respond, but that was okay, Greg knew. He'd heard the words, and Greg would repeat them again and again and again if he had to. He rubbed his hand slowly up and down Allen's arm and kissed the top of Allen's head again as his husband settled up against him more with a long sigh that shuddered at the end.

They sat there together for several minutes, the shade provided by their oversized patio umbrella inching closer to the back of the couch as the sun shifted in the sky. Finally, Greg coughed quietly to clear his throat and squeezed Allen's shoulder lightly.

"How are you feeling? Can I get you something else to eat or drink? Or do you want to go lie down again?" He could predict what each of Allen's answers would be, and he knew he probably shouldn't have asked so many questions all at once. Just the first question would probably be difficult enough for Allen to answer. With a gentle shake of his head, he closed his eyes and rested his cheek on the top of Allen's head. "Sorry, darling, one thing at a time, huh?"

"Y-yeah, um . . ."

"Take your time, my love. How are you feeling?"

There was a quiet huff, like Allen wanted to laugh but couldn't quite do it. The hand resting on Greg's stomach pressed down into him just a little, and he felt as Allen tensed.

"Exhausted. And . . . detached. And like any effort is too much. Still foggy, like after a migraine. And . . ."

"And what, darling?"

"Scared," Allen breathed, the word slightly muffled into Greg's shirt.

Something sharp seemed to rattle through Greg's chest at the obvious fear in Allen's words, and he nodded into his husband and kissed the top of his head again. "I'm here with you. What is it you're scared of?"

But Allen couldn't seem to answer, and that was okay too. Greg just held him, sure to let Allen know exactly how much he was loved with the little touches and caresses he knew his husband needed.

When Allen spoke again, his voice had an odd sort of monotone to it. "I should probably just go back upstairs and rest. And then you can get back to your work. I've been keeping you from working lately, and I-I'm sorry. I . . . I mean . . ."

Greg waited patiently, giving Allen a chance to continue. But his heart ached again, and for a moment, he was reminded of the panic—his own panic. Twice in one week now. Twice in one week, getting a call from someone at the library, telling him to hurry and get there because Allen was not okay.

From his left pocket, he felt Allen's cell phone buzz, and he frowned. "Hang on, darling," he said, and he shifted slightly and pulled the phone out of his pocket. There were eight new notifications, all from their group chat with the neighbors. Greg let out a short breath and scrolled through them briefly. It was more of the same—wishing Allen to get well soon. Rest and lots of fluids. And another invitation to the barbeque at Joe's tomorrow. And a picture of Marcia's twins smiling, with the caption of "Sending baby smiles and giggles just for you, Allen!"

Greg smiled weakly and turned the phone so Allen could see the screen. "Those two little babies adore you."

Allen reached out to take the phone with a shaky hand, and when he tilted his head just slightly and a hint of a smile formed on his lips, Greg felt the tiniest bit of hope.

"Will they be there? Tomorrow, at the barbeque?"

"I think so," Greg said. He took the phone back from Allen gently and scrolled up a bit to the conversation from a day or two ago. "Ah, yep. Marcia is bringing the twins, and she's making that Jell-O fruit salad you like—with the mandarin oranges and pears."

"Ahh, yum. Good, I . . . I hope I'll have an appetite by then. I'm sorry, I—"

"Shh. Shh, darling." Greg shoved the phone back into his pocket and then reached up and cupped his husband's cheek. He brushed his thumb along Allen's cheekbone as he gently encouraged Allen to look up at him, then he lowered his mouth to capture Allen's lips in a soft kiss. He lingered there for a moment, letting his lips caress his husband's, and when Allen pulled back, Greg still held them close, resting his forehead against Allen's and slipping his hand down lower around to the back of Allen's neck.

"I know I need to eat, but I . . . feel nauseous. And tired. Maybe . . . maybe I'll just go upstairs again and take a nap or—or something," Allen said. "But I—" He sighed and pressed a light kiss to Greg's lips, and it was needy and had some desperation to it this time. "But I don't want to be alone. And Beans doesn't really count. So, um, I'll just stay with you. Whatever you were going to do today. I'll just . . ."

Allen's words trailed off as though he had no more energy to speak, and he took a short but deep breath. The moment felt heavy, and Greg knew why. He wrapped both arms around his husband and held him tightly, letting his hand stroke Allen's back.

"My only plan today was to spend my time with you," Greg whispered, and he brushed his lips against Allen's cheek. "Even before everything, that was my only plan."

"Somehow, I doubt that," Allen said, but there was a hint of playfulness to his tone, and Greg smiled.

"You're my only plan, my love. I might have considered going out this afternoon—"

"You'd mentioned Seattle."

"Yeah. But only with you. Only to spend time with you," Greg murmured, and he pulled back a little to find Allen's eyes. God, he looked exhausted. Greg brought his hand up again and settled it on Allen's neck as he bit his lip.

"You know how cheesy that sounds, don't you, dear?" Allen's smile flickered very briefly, and Greg's heart stuttered.

"I do. But I mean every word." He leaned in again for another kiss, and then he pushed himself to his feet. "They said you need to rest as much as possible today, and you said you want a nap . . ." Greg took a breath and offered Allen his hand. "How about I'll grab my laptop so I can edit those photos for that client in Mukilteo, and I'll lie in bed with you while you rest. Okay?"

Allen's hand tightened in his, and Greg stepped just a little closer to offer as much support as his husband needed. With a nod, Allen stood slowly, letting Greg help him. Beans jumped up and just out of the way but still stuck to Allen's side as they made their way into the house and up the stairs.

Greg stared at the photo open on his laptop, trying to focus. The final image for his client needed to be sent out to be printed no later than tomorrow, which normally wouldn't be a problem. The edits he needed to finish were straightforward—just applying a preset filter and making some final touch-ups. But he couldn't seem to settle down and get working.

True, he wasn't used to working while sitting in bed. And Allen's soft snoring next to him was distracting, though not intrusive.

He glanced down at his husband, whose hand rested lightly on Greg's thigh. Allen had been sleeping now for at least a couple of hours, though it had taken him some time to fall asleep. And every once in a while, he shifted with a quiet moan or other indistinct sound as though he were uncomfortable or even in pain.

It hurt Greg's heart.

Especially because he knew how much of that pain he'd caused.

They hadn't gotten to talk much yet. They'd had visitors and had to make phone calls—both to Allen's physician and to Dr. Schultz since their decision to wait until Monday didn't really seem like the best option anymore. And then they'd tried to have lunch, although Allen really hadn't been able to eat. Greg hadn't even gotten a chance to apologize to Allen for his behavior that morning or to tell Allen how proud he was and how he'd finally seen *exactly* what Allen's kindness had done with the two boys at the library.

And that hurt his heart even more.

He pursed his lips and glanced back at his computer screen. The scene—the photo he was supposed to be editing—was of a waterfall. A small one that he'd found months ago when he'd gone off the main trail somewhere deep in the Mount Rainier wilderness. He'd followed a stream to where it had ended in a quiet pool fed by the small waterfall. It had been secluded and idyllic and serene—a huge contrast to many of the busy trails in the national park. And he'd taken his time, set up his tripod, sat and waited to capture the exact moment as sunlight filtered in through the trees, creating a prism of rainbow colors that danced around in the mist surrounding the ripples of water at the bottom of the falls.

He remembered wishing Allen had been there with him.

And as he stared at the photo now, he wondered just how many of the amazing photos he'd taken over his career had been taken when he was out alone and Allen was home. Just how much time had he made them miss together?

Too much time, he decided. Much too much time.

Yes, he'd gotten amazing photographs, and yes, Allen had supported him and his career, never complaining about him being gone, never asking him to stay home, never expecting anything different of him.

So maybe he shouldn't be feeling guilty about it all. Allen knew him and loved him for who he was, and that included his need to be *out*. Out in the forest. Out on the trail. Out seeing the world, exploring, discovering, photographing.

But going forward . . .

Greg reached down and set his hand on top of Allen's. His husband's skin was warm, but the slight wrinkles on the back of his hand gave Greg a sense of fragility, thinness, like tissue paper. Easily ripped apart. Allen didn't wake, which was good—he still needed the rest. But he seemed to let out a long sigh, and Greg smiled sadly to himself as his thumb rubbed along Allen's knuckles.

Going forward, he wanted things to be different. He wanted more time together with his husband. No more long work trips—like the one Paul had offered him. No more disappearing for days at a time to go off backpacking in the Olympic Wilderness or traversing the local-ish stretch of the PCT. He could get his dose of the forest and the mountains and trails on day hikes or on trips Allen could also make. He could stay close by, be the husband Allen needed him to be, show Allen exactly what he meant every time he said "I love you."

There was already a pang in his gut as he glanced back at the photograph on the computer screen in front of him. He bit his lip and tabbed to another open window on the laptop. The towering peak of Jack Mountain stood off in the distance of the photo from some hiker's blog. It was a beast. Not harder than some other mountains he'd climbed, but harder than anything he'd done in a long time.

And a part of him yearned for it still. Even with his new resolve. Even with the knowledge that he wasn't going to go. He still felt the pull as he studied the photograph for another few seconds. But then, Allen shifted slightly next to him and mumbled something in his sleep, and Greg closed his eyes with a small, sad smile.

He wasn't really sad, though. He'd done so much, seen so much. And some of that didn't have to end. It just had to be modified to fit this new phase of his life.

He clicked the x in the corner of the screen, and Jack Mountain disappeared from view. The small waterfall with the rainbow glimmering in the mist popped back up in its place, and Greg smiled again. He could take Allen there. It was a couple of hours to drive there and then maybe two or three miles of easy hiking. No big hills or elevation gain. He could take Allen there and show it to him. And maybe they'd be lucky enough to have the sun peek through the trees, as it had on that day months ago, and he could show Allen this same view—the one Allen hadn't gotten to see before.

And that would be infinitely better than any solo hike up Jack Mountain. Because he'd be with his husband.

"I love that photo." Allen's hand pressed into his thigh a little, and Greg smiled softly as he glanced down. Allen's eyes were half-open, and he seemed to be studying the image on Greg's computer. "It's peaceful. Beautiful. And the colors are just right. Deep and rich and vibrant. I'm sure there's a word for it that I don't know. This is the one . . . you need to get off to the printer by when? Tomorrow?"

Greg lifted Allen's hand to his lips and brushed a gentle kiss on his knuckles. "Yeah. I just need to finish a few adjustments, but"—with his free hand, he closed the laptop and then set it aside—"I can do that all later."

He watched as Allen gave a small nod, shut his eyes, and then let out a long, shuddering breath. "How long have I been sleeping?"

"A couple hours, about. How are you feeling?"

"Um, I—oof!" Allen's response was cut off as a wiggly brown ball of coarse fur clambered up onto the bed, climbed right over Allen, and settled in between the two of them, stretching out until he could stick his nose right into Allen's face. Beans's little pink tongue started licking Allen's cheek as the pup wriggled up the bed even more, his tail thumping eagerly. "Beans!" Allen exclaimed, and Greg opened his mouth, ready to scold the dog and send the little furball back to his own bed. But then Allen laughed—the sound deep and hearty—and Greg closed his mouth again as he watched Allen pet Beans, still chuckling, still smiling.

It warmed his aching heart.

"You know that silly dog hasn't left your side all afternoon, darling," Greg said quietly as Beans calmed down a bit and rested his head on Allen's shoulder. Allen opened his eyes again to meet Greg's. "He's been lying right next to the bed there the whole time."

"Poor thing. Relegated to sleeping on the floor. He'd have been much more comfortable up here on the bed," Allen teased. There was a tiny twinkle in his eyes, and Greg let out a huff of laughter.

"Ah, yes, the poor, poor neglected dog."

"Big, bad Greg won't even let you up on the bed, will he? But I said yes, so now it's okay, huh?" Allen had turned his attention back to the dog and was scratching the terrier behind his ear. Beans closed his eyes like he was in heaven.

Greg shook his head with another small smile. He let the silence settle between them for just a moment as Beans rolled over onto his back, clearly taking advantage of the freedom he'd been given to be on the bed. Allen dutifully scratched the pup's belly, and Beans began panting, his tongue lolling out the side of his mouth.

After another couple of minutes, Greg cleared his throat quietly. "You're feeling a little better?"

Allen's hand paused on Beans's belly, and he gave a short nod. "The exhaustion is gone. It was intense earlier. I'm not sure about . . . about everything else, though. I mean, I'm not sure how I'm feeling about . . . how we . . ."

". . . left things this morning?" Greg finished for him, shifting on the bed to lie on his side facing Allen. Beans was still between them, but Greg reached over the dog and cupped his husband's cheek. He wanted a kiss—to reassure both of them, honestly. But Beans was too in the way for that, so he settled for stroking his husband's cheek with his thumb.

"I don't like when we argue, and I don't like how it made me feel this morning. I was already hurting, but I got more upset and angry." Allen had closed his eyes, maybe unable to look at Greg. But he leaned into Greg's touch slightly and then inhaled a shuddering breath. And he didn't seem to want to skirt talking about the hard truths in that moment. "You were right that I shouldn't have gone in today. No matter how things turned out. I was stubborn about it, trying to ignore how I've been drowning. It's all been too much lately, Greg. It's all been too much. And I need to be surrounding myself with . . . people and situations where I feel loved *and* safe. Not—not pushing myself because I think I have to fix everything for everyone else right away. I need to listen to those I trust—you and Annabeth, both—because I'm obviously a terrible judge of—of what's good for me right now. Especially with . . ."

He finally trailed off, his last words having lost all the conviction and sureness of his earlier ones. Beans wriggled a little between them, and Allen opened his eyes, but looked down at the dog, not at Greg.

Greg wasn't sure whether he should say anything then. Did Allen want to continue, or had he said all he wanted to say? And the same uncertainty Greg had been fighting with all day—a feeling of being lost, ill-equipped to handle this situation—chose that moment to flare again. He let his hand drift slowly down Allen's neck and shoulder, stopping on the bare skin of his upper arm, just above his elbow. He squeezed gently.

"I was scared this morning, Allen," he admitted after another moment of silence. "I don't want to see you hurting, and when you told me that you'd been having dark thoughts—feeling like—like you—" He couldn't quite say the words, and he shook his head a little, then swallowed tightly. "That scared me. A lot. And I want to be supportive. I really, really do. I saw how much it was doing for those boys—you being there today and showing them your kindness and your vulnerability. I *saw* what you were trying to convince me of this morning. You were not wrong about that, and I'll admit I was. But . . ." Greg's throat constricted, and he pursed his lips together as he scrunched his eyes shut.

"But I shouldn't have gone today."

Greg shook his head, blinking his eyes back open. Allen was watching him now, and in the dim light of the bedroom, with the shutters closed, his eyes looked dark gray rather than blue. And they were filled with this deep hurt and sadness. Greg saw Allen's lower jaw tremble slightly.

"I shouldn't have gone, and I-I'm sorry I put you through all that," Allen added, his voice now shaking. "I'm sorry, I feel like I've been trying to tell myself I'll be okay, and that everything's okay, because I need it to be. But I've been drowning. Or suffocating. I don't know. I'm unsure and scared, and then the words in my head, telling me"—he paused and took a deep breath—"that I don't deserve to live. That everyone would be better off if I weren't here. That—that—that—"

This time, his pause was accompanied by a shorter breath and some uncomfortable sound in the back of his throat. Greg swallowed hard, gently pushed Beans out of the way, and gathered Allen up in his arms, pressing a kiss against his forehead. "It's not true, darling. You know that, right?"

"Yeah."

"Good, because, I—" Greg's words caught, and he shook his head and kissed Allen's forehead again, holding his husband tightly. "Because I don't even want to think about living a life without you in it. You're the best thing that ever happened to me, Allen Westin. You're my reason for everything. You're the most important thing in my life. And I love you and value you and cherish every single moment we've been together. All these years, I wouldn't trade a single moment, even the hard ones. And I . . . I don't want to lose you."

Allen was nodding into Greg's chest. "I don't want that either," he said, his voice low and muffled. He tilted his head back and finally looked Greg in the eye. Greg could see his regret and pain, the battle he was still fighting against himself. "You remember when I first told you about my parents?"

Greg nodded silently and rubbed his hand up and down Allen's back. He remembered that conversation clearly. It had been early on—maybe too early, looking back on it now. Allen had been having a particularly rough day, although Greg couldn't remember now why that had been. They'd had a date planned—something simple, like dinner and a movie—but when Greg had arrived at Allen's to pick him up, he'd found Allen curled up in his bed, the apartment dark and cold. He remembered the moment he'd realized Allen hadn't been out of bed all day, and he remembered the moment he'd decided to crawl into bed with his then-boyfriend for the first time just so he could hold Allen because he hadn't a clue what else to do. And he remembered Allen opening up to him then, not about everything—because, god, there was a lot—but about how he'd battled with depression and anxiety most of his life, how his parents had treated him like a burden, taught him to feel ashamed of himself, said he was an inconvenience. Counted down the days until he'd turned eighteen so he would no longer be their responsibility.

He'd since learned how much worse than that it had actually been.

And now, as he lay there, holding his husband and lover and best friend, Greg wondered why he hadn't realized sooner that Allen had probably been having suicidal ideations for a long, long time. It fit. And it was scary as hell to him, especially if it was getting worse.

"I was so scared to tell you all that," Allen continued. "I was so worried, you seeing me like that, finding out how much . . . work I'd be . . . I was so scared you were going to leave. But it—but I figured it was better to have it end sooner, if you were going to leave. You didn't, though. You—you did the thing I never thought anyone would ever do for me."

"Which was . . . ?"

"You stayed." Allen let out a huff of warm air as he buried his head into Greg's chest, and Greg instinctively tightened his arms around his husband. "You stayed, and instead of being mad or telling me to get over it or trying to get me up and make me go out when I was feeling so low, you cooked us dinner at home. And you went and rented us a movie to watch at home. And you were just there with me. You even—gosh, you even brought those donuts the next morning, do you remember? That was what I needed. You to just be there for me. Then and now. Thank you for staying, Greg. And thank you for reminding me . . . *why* I need to keep fighting those words in my head. It's really hard sometimes. It's really, really hard. Especially this week."

Greg rested his cheek against the top of Allen's head as the quiet settled around them. It was a comfortable quiet, though, and Allen seemed to relax slowly, the tension that had gathered in his shoulders fading. It was several minutes later when a familiar whine broke the silence, followed by a series of barely contained whimper-barks. Allen let out a sharp breath that might have been a laugh, and Greg lifted his head off his pillow to see Beans's muzzle resting just on the edge of the bed. The rhythmic thump of his tail wagging accompanied another low whine that turned into a bark.

"He wants to cuddle again, dear," Allen said, pressing his hand into Greg's chest. Greg looked down at Allen to see amusement in his husband's gentle eyes. "You can't deny him that, can you?"

Greg laughed and rolled his eyes, then shook his head. "Get on up here, you silly dog," he said, patting the bed. The dog leapt up, not wasting any time, and after several minutes of cuddly pets and belly rubs, Beans settled down at the foot of the bed, curled up into a ball.

And Allen snuggled up in his spot again in Greg's arms. Greg planted another kiss in Allen's hair.

"Let me love you again tonight, Allen," he said softly. "Let me cook you dinner and hold you while we watch a movie. Let me take care of you. Whatever you want. Whatever you need." He didn't necessarily mean making love, that would be up to Allen, and he was sure Allen knew that. He touched Allen's cheek and gently tilted his husband's head back, and then Greg placed the lightest of kisses on Allen's lips. "Can I do that for you? Because I love you."

Allen nodded and settled his head back on Greg's shoulder. "I love you too."

Chapter Fourteen

Allen

THE WARM LATE-SUMMER SUN drifted high in the sky, just past its zenith as Marcia leaned over and carefully lifted baby Jackson from Allen's arms. The sleeping infant made some gurgling sound, which brought a small smile to Allen's lips, but didn't wake.

Marcia cradled the baby against her shoulder. "You're a miracle worker with him, Allen," she said quietly, and then she kissed the top of Jackson's head. "The only one who can get him to sleep like that. Thank you. I'll be back in a bit."

Allen nodded, and Marcia headed off towards Joe's house, where Jackson's sister, Danica, was already sleeping. Around him, there was general chatter and laughter, burgers and beer, fruit salad and coleslaw and cookies. The barbeque was an end-of-summer tradition for the neighborhood. Joe had been hosting it every year for at least a decade, maybe more. And nearly everyone from their little corner of the neighborhood was here.

Tina and her husband, Darren, sat at a table positioned under an umbrella, eating while chatting with Shane and Lily and
Jocelyn. Tina and Darren's three children were off on the lawn,
running through a sprinkler with Beans and Joe's dog, a Labrador
retriever mix named Poppy. Phyllis and Herbert, an older couple
in their mid-seventies, sat on a small patio sofa, watching the kids
and dogs play as they chatted with another older couple who had
just moved in two houses down from Greg and Allen. Then Brent,
who owned the hardware shop on the main strip in town, had just
joined Joe and Greg at the barbeque, where they both stood, beers
in hand, discussing something quite animatedly.

It was a wonderful group of people. And even though he wasn't
part of the conversation at that moment, tucked away on the quiet
side of the patio where he'd been cuddling baby Jackson to sleep,
Allen felt content knowing he was a part of the community.

He watched his husband take a sip of beer while nodding at
something Joe had said, and then Greg eagerly jumped back in,
speaking with certainty and sureness, his hand movements enthusiastic and an eagerness in his eyes. Allen was too far away to
hear the words, but he could almost imagine what Greg might be
talking about.

Some hike. Some photoshoot. Some amazing landscape,
maybe. Something wild and untamed.

When Greg nodded again and then pointed off toward the
mountains, his smile growing, Allen was even more sure. He
smiled softly, glad to see Greg so happy. It made him happy. Or at
least happier. A little lighter. A little more like himself.

Allen took a long, deep breath and closed his eyes, leaning back
against the cushions of the chair he sat in. Even though he felt
much more stable than he had the day before, even after another
relaxing night with Greg taking care of him, cooking for him,
holding him as he slept, Allen still felt everything. Pain and sorrow,

despair and desperation, shame, self-loathing, guilt. And he was exhausted, mentally and physically.

But being here helped. Seeing Marcia's twins, with their chubby, smiling faces, was always uplifting, especially when he got to help baby Jackson settle into his nap. Watching Tina and Darren's kids play with the dogs, seeing Greg so excited and happy, sharing food and listening to the chatter around him. All of these things let Allen forget just long enough for the tightness in his chest to ease slightly and for his mind to stop imagining scenarios in which he wasn't around.

Marcia plopped down in the chair next to his and offered Allen a bottle of water. "Hopefully they're both down for the afternoon," she said as Allen took the water with a nod of thanks. "Dani's been sleeping like a peach, no trouble at all going down for naps lately, but Jackson . . . he's been fighting it every time. Thank you again, Allen, really. He just adores you."

"They're both precious. I'm glad to help," Allen replied, giving Marcia another small smile.

She was watching him thoughtfully, her green eyes curious, and she looked like maybe she wanted to ask him something but wasn't sure whether she should. Allen had seen that look enough times to know what it was about. He blinked and looked down at the water bottle in his hands.

"We'd talked about adoption," he said quietly, and he glanced back up at Greg, who was still chatting with Joe and Brent. His smile faltered, and when he looked at Marcia again, her eyebrows had scrunched together slightly in confusion. "Greg actually *really* wanted children. I was the one who wasn't so sure, which is probably not what you were thinking, eh?"

"I would have guessed the opposite," Marcia admitted with an embarrassed smile as she tucked a loose strand of her dark hair behind her ear. "You're so good with children. And you seem so at ease with them. A natural."

Allen almost laughed, and he shook his head. "Maybe now. But babies scared me when I was your age." He paused and took a sip of water, then sighed. "I . . . I wasn't ready then, and I didn't know if or when I would be. I think I wasn't *really* ready until after we were finally able to get married. But by then, we were both well into our forties, and . . . and I think the time had passed for Greg."

He didn't talk about it much. It had been a hugely difficult decision for him and Greg to not pursue adoption. But it had been the right one, he thought. He'd never been confident that he'd make a good father anyway. After all, he hadn't had anything close to the right role model. And he was content just as they were. Or rather, he didn't feel like anything was missing in their lives.

Marcia had lowered her eyes, and she tapped the side of her water bottle with her finger, looking lost in thought.

"What about you? The twins. It's hard, but worth it? And Elijah will be back in what, another three weeks?" Allen watched as Marcia's lips turned up into a smile, and when she lifted her eyes again, there was a sparkle that hadn't been there before.

"Sixteen days."

"I bet you're counting down the minutes. I bet he is too," Allen murmured softly.

"He is. I can't believe they're five months old now and haven't met their dad. It's been a rough year."

"Has it been a full year now? Oh, that's right, that's right . . . He left right at the end of September last year. But the expedition? It was successful?"

Allen sat forward a bit and listened as Marcia grinned and then launched into an entirely-too-detailed explanation of her husband Elijah's research work. He could only understand part of it—like Elijah, Marcia was also a climate scientist, although she'd taken a year-long sabbatical when Elijah had left and the twins were born. But Allen did his best to follow along as Marcia explained how Elijah and the other scientists and graduate students in his research group had been working to collect and analyze samples that would give them information about the rapid changes occurring at the Earth's polar regions. He managed what might have been a few intelligent questions, and he just loved watching as Marcia lit up even more, nodded, and answered, her passion for her and her husband's research obvious in every word.

"So what that means is—" There was a quiet ding, and Marcia glanced down at the smartwatch on her wrist and frowned. "Ah, sorry, one of the babies must be awake. I'm sure it's Jackson," she said with an exasperated sigh. She hit a button on the watch, then wearily pushed herself to her feet. "Thanks for listening to me ramble on. I don't get to do that often enough anymore."

"Anytime," Allen said with a smile, and then Marcia disappeared back inside, leaving Allen alone again. Alone to his thoughts. Maybe a dangerous place to be.

He heard Greg's laugh from across the patio, and he looked up to see Greg patting Brent on the shoulder and shaking his head. This time, he could hear some of Greg's words.

"No, no, no. You've got no idea! If the hardest hike you've ever been on is that *easy* jaunt up to Snow Lake, wait until I tell you about this proposal I got . . ."

Allen's smile grew again as he shook his head. Only Greg would call Snow Lake an *easy jaunt*. Sure, Greg had hiked much, much more difficult trails, but for the average weekend warrior, that seven-plus-mile hike was definitely not easy on the knees.

He was just about to push himself up out of the chair and maybe go grab some more of Marcia's fruit salad when Greg glanced over at him, catching his eye. His husband's smile softened, and he quickly looked back at Brent and Joe, shook his head, and then motioned briefly toward Allen and said something to the two other men that Allen couldn't hear. A moment later, Greg was on his way over, his expression still soft as their eyes met again.

"Snow Lake is just an *easy jaunt*, eh?" Allen said as Greg took the seat in the chair next to his.

Greg just laughed lightly. "Ah, well, you know me, darling." He paused and seemed to study Allen carefully for a moment before clearing his throat. "Can I get you something else to eat or drink? Another bottle of water? Some more fruit salad?"

Allen instinctively closed his hand tighter around the bottle of water Marcia had given him, feeling its weight, and he shook his head. "No, no, I . . ."

"You were eyeing the fruit salad, darling. I saw you." Greg's voice carried a teasing tone, and Allen couldn't help but smile just a little wider.

"Maybe I was," he admitted, and when he glanced up at Greg again, his husband was nodding and pushing himself to stand.

"I'll be right back," Greg promised, but he didn't leave until after he'd placed a gentle kiss on the top of Allen's head.

The afternoon went on, and almost everyone stayed for a second round of food from the grill—hot dogs and barbequed chicken this time—as the afternoon turned to evening. Allen mostly watched, except when he was cuddling one of the babies, which he did several more times. When the sunlight finally began to dim, the neighbors started to head out, and soon, only Greg, Allen, and Joe remained. The three of them sat in the same cushioned chairs off to the side of the patio, watching Beans and Poppy as both dogs seemed to get a second wind, some extra burst of energy sending them zipping around the yard again.

"So, Greg, what was that about Jack Mountain earlier? You started to say something about a trip?" Joe asked, and then he took another sip of beer, shifting his gaze to Greg.

Allen tilted his head, trying to remember what trips Greg might have coming up, but he was drawing a blank. Greg seemed confused for a second as well, and then he shook his head and cleared his throat.

"Ah, well, no. There's no trip or anything," Greg corrected, leaning forward a bit to rest his elbows on his knees. He seemed to stare off toward Mount Si in the distance, but then he blinked and sat back up. "A long-time client of mine wanted to contract me to get photos from the summit of Jack Mountain for a birthday gift for his wife. But it's not in the cards for me this year, I'm afraid. Too short notice, really."

There was a hint of reluctance in Greg's voice that was unmistakable, at least to Allen. He swallowed tightly but forced his smile not to falter, even when Greg's eyes darted to his for the briefest of moments. And it was then that Allen remembered two nights ago, when he'd come home from work and found Greg researching Jack Mountain on his computer in the garage office.

He pursed his lips as he watched Greg's jaw tighten. When their eyes met again, the concern in Greg's expression was clearly etched across his face.

"Ah, damn. Too bad," Joe said, leaning back casually in his chair. "A client-funded trip like that? Would have been incredible."

It would have been. Allen gripped the bottle in his hand a little tighter, and it made a quiet crackling noise as the plastic bent inward slightly.

It would have been the trip of a lifetime.

With stark clarity, Allen suddenly remembered the look he'd seen on Greg's face Friday night, his eyes drawn to the photo of the mountain on his computer screen. Greg's expression had been filled with longing. Excitement. Awe. But had quickly made a sharp change to resignation.

"I can't do it," he'd said.

Because of me.

Allen tried to fight the thought, to ignore the drop in his stomach—that uncomfortable swoop that also made taking a breath difficult. He forced his gaze out to the lawn, where Beans had just been tackled by Poppy. The smaller dog jumped back to his feet, barked playfully, and zipped off again.

"Hey, Joe, thanks again for hosting. We should probably get back," Greg said abruptly, and Allen found himself nodding, pulling himself out of the daze. Sort of. He watched as Joe and Greg stood up and shook hands. They said a few more words. Joe came over and shook Allen's hand too, telling him something. *Take it easy*, probably.

But Allen felt miles away.

"Come on, darling, let's get home," Greg said after Joe stepped away.

Allen just nodded and then took Greg's hand and allowed his husband to help him to his feet. He stood slowly, as he'd been making sure to do since the incident at the library the morning prior, and Greg's arm immediately slipped around his waist to provide him just a little more support.

"Don't think anything of it, darling." Greg brushed a kiss on Allen's cheek. "We'll talk when we get home. It's nothing. I promise."

It didn't feel like nothing. But then again, Allen had been feeling everything at tenfold intensity lately. Every word and every thought. Everything amplified. Maxed out. So whatever he *was* feeling, he couldn't really trust it anyway.

"I'm fine. I'm fine," he said, as much to try to reassure himself as Greg, and he let Greg support him as they started toward the side gate that connected their yard with Joe's.

He was vaguely aware of Beans racing next to them, Joe calling out another goodbye, and Greg's arm tightening around him when they were in the privacy of their own yard again. But he felt off. Not like the day before—not weak and out of breath. Just . . . off. So when Greg led him up the steps of the back porch, in through the back door, and straight out to the garage, Beans shadowing them the whole time, Allen just followed wordlessly.

"I should have explained more to you on Friday night. But I want you to hear the whole thing now, so you're not worrying when you don't need to," Greg said as he directed Allen to sit at his desk.

"Greg, I said it's fine. I don't—" He closed his eyes as he cut himself off and his husband knelt down in front of him. Greg's hands came to rest on his knees, squeezing gently.

There was a pause, a few extra seconds of silence, and then Greg began speaking again, his voice sure and calm. "The last week has been one of the most trying I think we've ever faced together, Allen. Between what those boys did last Sunday and then what happened yesterday, it's been . . . more than difficult." He felt Greg's hands press into his knees just slightly, and he opened his eyes to see Greg standing up and reaching out toward his computer mouse. "Paul and I spoke on Friday, early afternoon," Greg continued as he clicked to open up a file folder. "He wanted to contract me for a custom photoshoot of Jack Mountain and the surrounding wilderness as a gift for his wife, just like I told Joe."

On the computer screen, several images popped up, along with a text document showing a list of bullet points. Greg had mapped a route with potential camping sites, estimated the time and distance and elevation changes, started noting all the equipment and supplies he'd need to carry with him.

Gently, Greg pushed a notepad in front of Allen on the desk. "This was the timeline. This was the problem," Greg said, pointing to the paper. Allen frowned as he saw the sketch of a rough timeline, with the words "Must be off the mountain by late September" double underlined.

"I-I don't . . . You don't have anything else going on," Allen argued. "I mean, there's the art festival in Edmonds that you might have to miss. But I can get Joe to help me, and we can still man your booth. It's short notice, but I can cover for you. I've done that before, and . . ."

Allen trailed off as Greg shook his head. "It's too soon, Allen. I'd have to leave in only a couple weeks. And I'd be gone for at least a week, a week and a half. And most of the time with no cell phone reception. I—"

"You can't miss this chance because of me," Allen cut in, his heart starting to pound in his chest. "Just because I—because I'm struggling with anxiety and—and whatever else is going on. Greg, I've *always* struggled, you know that. And I . . . *will* probably always struggle. You can't let that stop you from doing something like this. It's an incredible opportunity, and this is your career. It's your career and your passion, and—"

"Yes, that's true," Greg said gently as he turned back to Allen, knelt down, and set his hands on Allen's thighs. The seriousness in Greg's expression caused an uncomfortable tightness in Allen's chest, but he managed to hold Greg's gaze. Greg shook his head slightly. "And I won't even try to deny that I want to go. It's an amazing opportunity that I'll probably never be given again. It's my career and my passion. But Allen, it's also your *life*. Which of those things do you honestly think is the most important to me?"

Chapter Fifteen

Greg

THE SHUTTER CLICKED ONE more time, then Greg stepped away from the camera, letting his hand drop to his side. His eyes followed the rocky tree-lined ridge in the distance, out beyond the fork in the river. Straggling wisps of morning fog drifted low along the base of the mountain, though the sky above was bright blue. It was the perfect shot and exactly what he'd been hoping for.

He let himself linger there for another moment, committing the scene to memory. He'd have his photographs, of course, but a photograph couldn't replicate the sounds of birds chirping in the trees and the quiet babbling of the Middle Fork Snoqualmie River just to his left. Nor could it replicate the feeling of the fresh Wednesday morning air or the smell of the forest or the real, true grandeur of the mountains in front of him.

Somehow, it took the edge off all the tension and stress from the last week and a half. Grounded him. Refilled his soul.

With a final gaze out at the mountain, Greg turned back to his camera, sitting on a tripod right at the river's edge, and began to dismantle his setup. Carefully but quickly, he packed everything back up, then shouldered his backpack and started back toward the trailhead, picking his way slowly along the riverbank. The morning sun was well on its way up in the sky, and a glance at his watch told him he had just enough time to get home, put his equipment away, and make breakfast before walking Allen to work.

Allen had called out Monday and Tuesday after they'd talked more. The decision was made a little bit easier when Allen's therapist, Dr. Schultz, had called to tell them she had an opening for Monday morning and she wanted to see Allen right away. Then Allen had also gotten in to see his physician Tuesday afternoon.

Nothing of note had been found during Allen's checkup with his physician, which had been a huge relief to both of them. But the session with Dr. Schultz had been rough. Allen had asked for Greg to be there, which he'd sometimes done over the years. And Greg had of course obliged.

But it had been difficult to hear Allen talk openly about everything that had happened—rehashing all of the events of the last two weeks, admitting to all of the dark thoughts he'd been having. Greg had sat there with him and held his hand and listened. There'd been talk of scheduling an appointment with a psychiatrist to discuss medication, which Allen had quietly refused, as he always did, but the doctor had also reminded Allen of all the coping mechanisms and strategies he had at his disposal and walked both of them through some additional relaxation exercises that Greg and Allen could do together.

And they'd talked more about how Greg could support Allen when things got challenging and how Allen felt when he had to lean on Greg for that support.

It had been a lot. And since then, Allen had been more quiet than normal. Not unhappy or upset or anything. Just more quiet. Thoughtful. And he hadn't brought up Jack Mountain again, which both bothered Greg and didn't.

Greg frowned as he approached his SUV and pulled his key fob out of his pocket to open up the back hatch. They should talk some more, he knew. If anything, that was the most important thing that had come out of their session with Dr. Schultz on Monday. That, and the reminder that Allen's pain was still all there. Even when he seemed fine and happy and joyful, the trauma of his childhood was *still* there with him, buried below his comfortable smile and kind eyes.

That reminder only made Greg love Allen even more. Allen, who, despite *everything* he'd been through and experienced growing up, was the kindest, gentlest person Greg knew. Kind, selfless, loving, caring. Also brilliant and generous and thoughtful.

Greg sat on the back of the SUV and changed out of his hiking boots, trying to ignore the tickle of fear in his chest. That morning, he'd been reluctant to leave. They'd talked about it—that Greg would take a short outing to Snoqualmie if the weather was right to try to get some new photos of the mountains wrapped in the morning fog. They'd talked about it and agreed to it, and Greg had insisted that they tell Joe next door. And he'd only been gone for about an hour and a half now. But it was the first time since Saturday morning that he'd been away from Allen at all, and it was slightly terrifying to him.

He pulled his cell phone out of his pocket as he shoved his hiking boots into the hatch space in the back of his SUV. No reception still. He'd known that. He was more than familiar with this area and the spotty reception his phone got. But that didn't help his worry at all.

As quickly as he could, he closed the hatch and then took his spot behind the steering wheel, carefully setting his backpack in the passenger seat. Minutes later, he was on the road and headed back toward home, trying not to obsessively check his cell for notifications.

The drive from the trailhead wasn't long—only about a half hour—and by the time he pulled up into the driveway at home, it was about eight fifteen. He parked, grabbed his backpack, and headed inside.

Beans greeted him in the doorway, which Greg took as a good sign since the dog had been sticking to Allen like glue since Saturday. Greg knelt down for a moment to scratch Beans just behind his ear, right where he knew the dog would like it most, and when he stood up, Allen was starting down the stairs, dressed for work in his usual slacks and button-up. Beans rushed back to the base of the stairs and sat, his tail wagging as he watched Allen descend.

"How'd it go?" Allen asked. He had one hand on the railing and was taking each step carefully. "Did the fog stick around long enough for you to get the shot you wanted?"

Greg nodded. "Sure did. It was perfect. The lighting too—exactly as I'd wanted. I think this one will be pretty popular."

"Good." Allen's smile was tight, and Greg tried not to feel worried about that as he met Allen at the bottom of the stairs.

"You're okay? You're still feeling okay?" He reached out to take Allen's hand and then pulled his husband into a soft embrace. Allen nodded against him.

"Yeah. I'm okay. But . . . but I'm still tired, like I just can't shake it off, no matter how much sleep I get. But I feel better than I did over the weekend."

Greg appreciated the honesty, and he tried to push his worry away. He turned his head slightly to press a light kiss against his husband's cheek. "Good, good. Did you eat already? Can I make you something?" He stepped away, but let his hand caress down Allen's arm until their fingers intertwined.

There wasn't an immediate response to his questions, and when he squeezed Allen's hand lightly, all he got was a small smile and a weak shake of Allen's head.

"No to both?" he asked, frowning. He waited, but Allen didn't respond again. "You need to eat, darling."

"I know, and I—I just, um . . ."

"Some toast, at least. Here, I'll make you some toast. We have that sourdough I bought yesterday from Valerie. Okay?"

"Okay, yeah. That sounds great, actually," Allen admitted, giving Greg another smile. It looked forced though, and it really did nothing to placate Greg. In fact, if anything, he felt even more concerned now.

Still, he nodded and led them both into the kitchen. Beans didn't follow, and Greg thought he heard the dog trotting back up the stairs.

"You just take a seat here, and I'll handle everything, okay?"

"Greg . . ."

Allen stopped right at the threshold to the kitchen, and when Greg stopped with him, turning slightly so he could see his husband, Allen swallowed tightly and lowered his eyes. Their hands were still joined, but Greg could almost feel Allen pulling away from him.

"You're . . . not going to try and talk me out of going to work today, right? Even if I . . . even if I can't really eat much?" The serious question was tempered a bit when a small half-smile grew on Allen's lips and he said in a light tone, "Please say no."

Greg chuckled quietly as he shook his head. "No. I won't try to stop you today. But I think we should talk before we have to leave because I *am* worried."

Allen's gray-blue eyes softened, and he nodded. "I know. I'm sorry—or, I mean—" He screwed his eyes shut for a second and blew out a short breath. "I mean, I understand that you're worried, and I've already thought about it a lot this morning because I—because it was more difficult than I thought it was going to be when you were gone and I was alone. I actually, um . . ."

Greg felt some deep shiver run through him at Allen's words, and he stepped in front of his husband again and wrapped Allen up in his arms, pulling Allen up against him and kissing the top of his head. Allen seemed to melt into him, returning the embrace.

It felt like this had been their life for the last three days. Incomplete sentences that trailed off into a silence filled by long hugs.

He let his hand rub a familiar path up and down Allen's back, and he closed his eyes. "Sorry I was gone. I'd have stayed if I'd known," he said, suddenly feeling almost breathless.

"I know," Allen said quietly. "And I didn't think it was going to be so hard. But I . . . I knew you wouldn't be too long, and I could call Joe if I needed to. And Beans was here. The little stinker crawled up on the bed and *under the covers* this time. Give him an inch and he'll take a mile."

Greg gently backed up a step and then lifted a hand to cup Allen's cheek. There was an attempt at a small smile on Allen's lips, but his eyes were almost stormy. Greg bent down to kiss him, softly, lightly, and when they parted, he shook his head slightly. "He is a stinker."

"I'll try to eat some toast, if you still want to make it for me," Allen said, and he reached up to kiss Greg again. It was another soft kiss, but Allen deepened it just a little and let it linger just a little more.

A few minutes later, they both sat at the table to eat—Allen's slice of sourdough toasted but plain and Greg's toasted and topped with an avocado spread, turkey bacon, and chopped tomatoes.

Allen scooted his chair close to Greg's, and they worked on the weekly crossword puzzle in the newspaper for a bit. There were occasional laughs at some of the odder clues, and for a few minutes, Greg's head and heart seemed able to forget all the strife and uncertainty and just *be* with his husband.

When they'd both finished eating, Greg picked up their plates and moved them to the sink. "I'll take care of everything later. You're supposed to be at work by nine? We should leave, eh?" he said, setting the dishes down and turning back around to face Allen.

"Um, yeah, I . . . That's what I wanted to talk about actually. Are you . . ." Allen paused for a second, closed his eyes, and took a deep breath. "Are you, um, busy right now? This morning?"

Greg sat back against the counter a bit and shook his head, though Allen wasn't watching him. "I'm not busy, darling. I'm whatever you need."

That elicited a small laugh, and Allen finally opened his eyes again and looked back up at Greg. "Whatever I need, huh?"

"Yup," Greg replied. "Husband, chef, escort—to walk you to work, I mean." He pushed away from the counter and made his way back to the table just as Allen started to stand up, chuckling and shaking his head.

"Well, then, my husband and master executive chef, will you *escort* me to work? And . . ." Allen pursed his lips and frowned, but then seemed to find his resolve. "And then will you stay with me for a bit? Annabeth isn't going to be in until ten thirty, just before the preschool group is supposed to arrive, and I, um, don't want to be there alone. And it sort of . . . really hurts to even admit that, but I'm trying to be more honest with myself too, and that's . . . that's the real truth," Allen finished, his voice low and shaking with the last few words.

"I understand," Greg said softly. He pressed his lips to Allen's forehead in another light kiss. "I'll stay there with you as long as you need me to. Just let me wash up and change. Give me five minutes?"

After Allen nodded, Greg kissed him one more time and then headed quickly up the stairs to get changed and wash his hands. A few minutes later, he and Allen walked side by side down the street toward town, their hands clasped tightly together. The morning air was still a little crisp, even though the sun shone brightly in the sky, not a cloud in sight, and Greg was happy to have opted for a long-sleeve tech shirt rather than something with short sleeves.

As they rounded the corner, Allen finally broke the silence with a sharp laugh. "Ha! Proverb! How clever!"

Greg just lifted his eyebrows. "Proverb?"

"Number five across. 'Dog wearing lead.' The answer is proverb," Allen declared, a hint of amusement still in his voice.

"I'm . . . not following."

"I know."

"Care to explain it to me, darling?"

Allen tilted his head sideways as though considering but then shook his head. "Hmm, nah. You'll figure it out."

"Allen!"

Allen laughed again, this time deeper and heartier than before, and when Greg glanced at him, his heart lifted a little at the twinkle in Allen's eyes. "You'll figure it out, dear. It's not too difficult, even for an old geezer like you," Allen teased.

"An old geezer like me, huh?"

"Mm-hmm. Ancient."

The fullness in Greg's chest almost brought tears to his eyes, the gentle banter so much more . . . normal for them. Greg let go of Allen's hand and slipped his arm around his husband's waist instead, and their walking slowed just a bit to accommodate the embrace. He tried to think on the crossword puzzle clue, but he was too distracted by Allen's warmth next to him, and for a moment, it was all he could think of.

Allen was all he could think of.

His smile brightening up Greg's day. His touch making Greg's skin feel afire. His laugh and his eyes and . . . *him*. All of him.

They stopped at the base of the steps to the library, and Allen moved away enough to fish his keys out of his pocket. "Ah, you know what you can help me with this morning?"

"Hmm?" Greg followed Allen up the steps, reaching out to place his hand at the small of Allen's back.

"Unless Annabeth took care of it yesterday, and I'm guessing she probably didn't, we'd planned to set up the new rug in the children's reading room before the preschoolers came in today. And we'll need to stack up the chairs and move them to the storage room. The kids do much better sitting on the floor. Hence the new rug."

"I can take care of that."

Allen stuck the key in the lock on the door and then glanced at Greg with a soft smile. "Thank you, dear. I need at least a good half hour to work on that proposal for the city council, since I've gotta get it sent off by this afternoon. And if you can take care of the children's room for me, I should be able to get the proposal done with no problem. And that'll be a huge weight off my shoulders."

Allen grinned again, a little more broadly this time, and as he pulled the door open, he leaned over, stretched up, and pressed his lips to Greg's. It was a short kiss, but that warmth was there again, a slow burn radiating outward from Greg's chest. He whimpered a protest as Allen pulled back, and when he opened his eyes, he saw Allen watching him with an amused half-smile.

"And if you help me, I just *might* explain that crossword puzzle clue to you," Allen teased, and then he winked and headed inside the library, leaving Greg holding the door and staring after him.

When his brain finally caught up with Allen's tease, Greg let out a loud laugh and shook his head. "Hey, wait a minute now!" he called out, pushing the door open a little more and following Allen inside. "I didn't realize we were negotiating here!"

Chapter Sixteen

Allen

ALLEN STARED AT THE printed proposal on the desk, absently tapping the eraser of his pencil on the top of the page as he read through it one more time. The library had already closed for the day, and his 5:30 p.m. deadline was fast approaching. The proposal was probably about as good as it was going to get, he knew. He'd already spoken with two of the city council members who were in support of the expanded after-school program he and Annabeth had developed, but the other members of the city council were toss-ups. He hoped he'd done a good enough job explaining the benefits of the program to the community and how the added cost would be worth it.

Just as he'd flipped back to the first page of the five-page report, there was a light knock at the office door, and Annabeth peeked in. Her eyes were soft but showed a hint of concern.

"Hey, Allen. How's it going?"

"Not bad, actually," he said with a smile and nod. He was happy to be able to tell her that. He *had* been feeling surprisingly okay most of the day. Much more like himself. The exhaustion he'd been fighting that morning had even lifted shortly after lunchtime, when Greg had come back and brought takeout from Allen's favorite sandwich shop in town. "I was just about to email this proposal out. Did you want to take a look before I do?"

"No, no, I'm sure it's fine," she said, and he gave her a short nod before turning back to the computer.

"Great. So I'll get it sent off, and then I'll shoot Greg a text. Do you . . ." He hesitated for only a second, the part of his mind that hated feeling like he was a burden warring with the other part that just *knew* he shouldn't—couldn't—be at the library alone right now, regardless of how well the day had gone. He let out a sharp breath and then looked back up at Annabeth, who still stood there in the doorway, watching him with a kind expression. "Uh, that is, do you mind waiting until Greg can get here? It should only take him a few minutes."

"I don't mind at all."

"Thanks. I'll hurry here. Let me just text him first, then I'll send that email, and . . . yeah."

Annabeth chuckled quietly. "No rush, Allen. Really."

He gave her another nod, and she seemed to pause for a moment, studying him with her soft smile. Maybe she wanted to talk, to ask him something or other, but instead, she just said, "You look like you're feeling a bit better today. And I'm really happy about that."

He'd known Annabeth for over a decade now. The two of them had worked together at the library since shortly before he and Greg had gotten married, and he'd consider them to be pretty close. She certainly knew he struggled with his mental health, although she didn't really know any of the specifics. Despite that, he did know she was someone he could absolutely trust, and so, he should probably tell her a little more . . . of something.

He swallowed tightly and lowered his eyes to the proposal again, twirling his pencil around in his fingers. "I am, yeah. I saw my therapist on Monday, and that really helped. Plus, Greg . . ." Allen shook his head as thoughts of his husband distracted him momentarily. He smiled. "Greg's just been wonderful. He's—"

"Isn't he *always* wonderful?" Annabeth cut in teasingly, and when Allen looked up, she was grinning at him, her arms crossed over her chest.

He couldn't suppress a smile, and he leaned back in his chair and shrugged. "Well, I dunno. I mean, he leaves his dirty socks lying around in the living room. And he hogs the covers at night. *And* he puts the toilet paper roll on in the wrong direction. I'm really not sure why I still put up with him."

That got a chuckle from his coworker, and Allen found himself smiling yet again. Even still, he sobered up quickly when he remembered how their conversation had started. He cleared his throat.

"He *is* wonderful, and he's been reminding me . . ." Allen shook his head again, and his smile tightened a little. "You, too, really. You and Greg and everyone in this community—you've all been reminding me of—of why . . . I'm . . . here."

She'd read between the lines, he knew. Annabeth was a smart woman. Smart and caring and kind. And she *did* know him well, even if he'd never really opened up to her about everything.

He risked looking back up at her, and he saw the slow evolution of emotions in her eyes as she processed his words. Her smile faded to a frown, and then she pursed her lips and nodded.

"You're such an important part of this community, Allen," she said gently. "I know you know that, but just in case you need to hear it again, I'll tell you. You make this community better by just being here. You . . . make *me* a better person. And you bring joy and hope and happiness to all the kids who come in here every day." She inhaled sharply and held his gaze. "You're loved and important. And I'm so happy to know you. I'm so happy you're here, Allen. Please . . . please don't ever forget that. Okay?"

There were tears in the corners of his eyes now, and Allen blinked them back, willing himself not to cry. He nodded. "O-okay," he managed, but his voice trembled a bit.

With another gentle smile, Annabeth tipped her head toward the main room. "I'll just go finish tidying up until Greg gets here."

"Greg, yeah. I'll—I'll go ahead and text him right now. Shouldn't be long. Thank you," he said. And then, because he was feeling quite overwhelmed, he repeated it again. "Thank you, Annabeth."

She nodded and then turned and left.

Allen swiped at his eyes, brushing away the tears that hadn't really fallen. Then he pulled his cell phone out of his pocket and opened up his messaging app to text his husband.

"Glad the mushrooms were on sale, and the daikon too. Were you thinking ground turkey or pork?" Allen stopped next to Greg at the meat counter of the grocery store, scanning the selections.

"Pork, I think. It's more authentic Japanese, and I think that's what I want tonight." Greg leaned over slightly and shook his head. "Though with these prices, maybe we'll just need to go vegetarian soon."

Allen laughed, and Greg straightened up and slipped his arm around Allen's shoulders as Jillian, the butcher, came out through a set of double doors and stepped up behind the counter.

"Hiya, Greg, Allen. What can I help you with?" Jillian said as she started putting on some plastic gloves.

Allen was quiet as Greg greeted Jillian, asked how her two children were doing, and then requested half a pound of ground pork. And as Greg was prone to do, he stuck around for another minute or two, chatting with Jillian about something or other. Allen tried to focus, but he found himself having a hard time listening and following the conversation. Eventually, another customer stepped up behind them, and Greg politely said goodbye. Allen and Greg then continued on a familiar route around the small grocery store, picking up a few more things on the way—some milk and a few spices and a container of Greg's favorite local brand of salsa. By the time they'd checked out and headed back to their car with their couple of bags of groceries, it was nearly six thirty, and the beautiful sunny skies from earlier had darkened as clouds threatened to bring an early evening storm.

Together, they loaded the groceries into the back of the SUV, and Allen climbed into his seat as Greg put the shopping cart away. A minute later, they were on their way home, and just as they turned out of the parking lot, the rain started up. It was immediately a heavy downpour, huge droplets pounding the windshield and gusts of wind pushing their small SUV around on the road.

Greg talked casually as he drove, completely unperturbed by the weather. And Allen did his best to keep up. But just as it had been with Jillian at the grocery store, he was only catching about half of what Greg was saying. He was just too tired—the exhaustion that had been plaguing him for the last few days beginning to creep back in. Their short trip to the supermarket seemed to have used up all of whatever energy Allen had left.

He hoped he could still manage to help Greg make dinner. He also hoped he had an appetite by the time dinner was ready.

"So, I already have a buyer for one of those photos I took when we were in Friday Harbor," Greg said as they pulled into their driveway a few minutes later.

"Oh?" Allen unbuckled his seat belt, but didn't move, not super keen on rushing out into the pouring rain. Greg seemed to feel the same. He shut off the engine but just sat there, staring off at the house.

"Yeah. I sent the unedited proofs to Mickey Stone—you remember her?" When Allen shook his head, Greg continued. "She stopped in at the Salmon Days Festival last year, and she's been emailing me every couple of months since, asking for new proofs. She was looking for something very specific, but she didn't really know exactly what."

"And one of the Friday Harbor photos was it, huh?"

"Yep. The one with the pelicans just taking off from the water."

"Ah, yeah. I liked that one too," Allen said, smiling as he closed his eyes and leaned his head back against the headrest. "It was peaceful. And the sunset—those vivid colors, and the reflection in the water. And then the birds too."

A sense of calm washed over him, just thinking about that view and the trip, and he remembered then that they'd mentioned maybe taking a vacation up there—just going to visit, not for something work related for Greg.

"What are you thinking, darling? Your smile, it's . . . You look happy." Greg's hand covered his, and Allen turned his hand over so they could intertwine their fingers.

The touch felt warm and welcoming, and the same sense of calm and contentment that he'd been feeling bloomed even more in his chest. He looked down at where their hands were now joined, sitting on his thigh, and he nodded. "I was just remembering that trip to Friday Harbor. We should go again. For, um, vacation this time, though."

"We should," Greg agreed, and then he lifted Allen's hand and brought it to his lips for a gentle kiss. "You get the time off from work, and I'll make it happen. And I'll even leave my camera at home, just like you said."

Allen laughed lightly and shook his head. "You don't have to do that. But a vacation sounds wonderful. Really, really . . . wonderful."

Greg pressed his lips to Allen's knuckles again and then lowered their hands back to Allen's thigh. With a sigh, Greg leaned forward and looked out the front windshield. "It's not letting up. Guess we'll just have to deal with it. Ready?"

While Greg headed around to the back of the SUV to grab the bags of groceries, Allen made the short trip to the front door. By the time Allen reached the front porch and stepped up under the overhang, he was dripping wet. He might have been laughing if he wasn't also so tired. He reached into his pocket and pulled out his keys just as Greg jogged up behind him, and for the first time that day, his hand started to shake just a little.

"Whew, it's really coming down," Greg said, and then, after a pause, during which Allen was unsuccessful at getting the key in the lock, Greg added, "You okay there, darling?"

Allen nodded but dropped his hand from the door. "Just tired, and . . . can you help?"

"Of course," Greg replied without hesitation. After setting the grocery bags down on the porch, Greg gently reached up and took the keys from Allen, then opened up the door and pushed it inward. Beans barked and jumped around in the entryway, though he calmed after a light command from Greg to back off.

And then Greg's arm was around Allen's waist, giving him the support he hadn't even known he'd needed.

"Thanks, dear. I-I don't know what's . . . I'm not feeling bad. Just tired. Suddenly really, really tired." It was the truth, at least, and Allen let Greg help him inside and over to the couch to sit.

"Here we go, here we go," Greg said quietly as he lowered them down onto the couch, settling into the seat next to Allen. "Just rest here for a few minutes, darling. Is there anything I can get you? Water, maybe?"

His chest felt tight and heavy, and he closed his eyes and shook his head as he leaned back into the couch cushions. "No, no, I'll be fine in a minute, I'm sure," he reassured Greg, even though he wasn't sure at all. He had no idea where this exhaustion had come from or what to do about it.

Soft lips pressed gently against his temple. "Okay. Let me get you a blanket, though. It's almost cold in here, and with the rain . . ."

He didn't protest, and Greg left and returned a moment later, then carefully laid a lightweight blanket over Allen and kissed him again, on the forehead this time.

"I'm going to get the groceries and start dinner. You can join me when you're feeling better? Is that okay, darling? Or if you want, I can put the groceries away and come back to sit with you."

The words ran together, and Allen screwed his eyes shut tighter as he tried to follow. "Um . . ." He hated the brain fog, the fuzziness, the whatever else it was that made it so he couldn't really answer Greg's questions. So instead, he nodded. "You can, um . . . Yeah, that's fine." Somehow, he knew his answer was wrong. But Greg just brushed another kiss on his forehead.

"I'll be right back," he murmured, and Allen nodded.

He heard the sounds of Greg moving around the house—first opening the front door to get the bags of groceries he'd left outside, then heading into the kitchen. Vaguely, Allen thought that he should get up and help. Or at least get up and go change out of his work clothes, which were still wet from the rain. But before he could make any decision, the couch shifted, and he felt Greg's warmth next to him, a solid arm around his shoulders and soft lips grazing his cheek.

"The food's put away. I'll cook in a bit, after I know you're comfortable."

"I'm sorry, I—" Allen stopped himself, let out a long breath, and leaned into Greg as Greg's arm tightened around his shoulders. The embrace was immediately comforting. It didn't chase away his exhaustion, but it made him feel all of his husband's love. And his words came a little easier. "Can you help me upstairs? I should change and probably rest. I'm tired."

"Of course," Greg said quietly and without hesitation. Another kiss brushed against his temple, and then Greg shifted away, stood, and helped Allen to his feet.

He let Greg help him, although with how tired he felt, he realized he probably didn't have much choice. But they made it upstairs, and Greg led him to sit on the bed.

"Let me grab you some dry clothes," Greg murmured with a light kiss to Allen's forehead. He left and returned a moment later, kneeling in front of Allen with his hands resting on Allen's thighs. "May I undress you, darling?"

Allen could only nod, though something inside of him reacted to Greg's words with a familiar desire. Greg's hands slid gently up his thighs and then his stomach and chest, and Allen closed his eyes and let himself feel loved as Greg's fingers carefully worked down the buttons of his shirt. The tips of Greg's fingers brushed against his exposed skin as each button came undone, burning a trail down his chest. And then Greg's lips were on his, kissing him lightly, tenderly. The bed shifted, and a warm hand smoothed across his abdomen to settle at his opposite hip. He turned slightly to meet Greg at a better angle, and their lips moved together in tandem for another moment. The kiss didn't become deeper or more intense. But Greg's hands moved up to his chest again, splaying out and then gently pushing his shirt off his shoulders. The touch felt intimate, like there was an entire three decades of love packed into the simple gesture.

With another light kiss, Greg pulled back, and Allen opened his eyes to watch as Greg continued undressing him. Deft fingers, strong and steady, slipped off Allen's shoes and socks, then unfastened his belt and the button at the top of his slacks.

"Lift your hips?" Greg's voice was low and so gentle, and Allen nodded before closing his eyes again and then pushing himself up off the bed just enough so Greg could slip off his slacks.

He wasn't so tired that he didn't react when Greg's hands caressed up his calves a moment later, and he let a soft moan escape him. The touch continued, light and undemanding, first up to his knees and then along the outsides of his thighs, stopping right at the hem of his boxer briefs. Allen sighed contentedly as Greg's hands then drifted inward, his thumbs rubbing in slow circles. There was a shift—one hand pressing more strongly than the other for just a moment—and Allen inhaled deeply when he felt Greg's lips place a warm, open-mouthed kiss just on the inside of his right knee. He reached out to set his hand over one of Greg's as Greg began working his way up along Allen's inner thigh with the same slow, lingering kisses.

"Is this okay?" Greg asked quietly as his lips stopped just below the bottom hem of Allen's briefs and his free hand rubbed gently along Allen's thigh again. "I can stop or keep going."

"Hmm." His noncommittal answer didn't really help Greg, he knew, but he didn't know how to respond otherwise. He was tired, but both his body and his mind craved his husband's love and closeness. So maybe that was his answer. "Will you just cuddle with me in bed for a bit? I-I think I might be too tired for anything else, but I . . . want you to stay here with me," he said, and when he opened his eyes, he saw Greg nod softly as he rested his cheek against Allen's thigh.

"We can do that. Anything you want, darling." Greg pushed himself up off his spot on the floor, then he leaned in and kissed Allen's forehead. "Here's your dry clothes," he said, picking up the T-shirt and shorts he'd set next to Allen a few minutes before. "I'll go change too, and I'll be right back. And then we can lie here together for a bit, and we can talk about . . ." Greg paused, but only briefly. "Ah, our trip back to Friday Harbor! We can talk about that. How does that sound?"

Greg's eyes sparkled with love and enthusiasm, though Allen also saw a hint of concern in them as well, which was understandable. The thought of their maybe-vacation made him smile, however, and he closed his eyes for a long second and nodded.

"That would be perfect."

After another light kiss to Allen's forehead, Greg picked up Allen's wet clothes from the floor and bed, then moved away toward the clothes hamper and dresser. Allen watched him for a moment, and when Greg pulled his own T-shirt off, Allen stared unabashedly, admiring his husband's strong, lean body. He felt the familiar stirring of arousal, and a big part of him wanted to tell Greg not to bother putting on a dry shirt, or pants for that matter.

Maybe that would be for later, though. Maybe tonight, after cuddling and talking and dinner and maybe a movie and a shower together.

Greg glanced over at him and caught his eye just as he pulled a clean T-shirt out of the dresser. Greg's eyebrows lifted in question, and Allen laughed quietly and shook his head.

"Later, I think?"

Greg grinned and nodded. "Whatever you want, darling."

A couple of minutes after that, Allen snuggled up next to his husband, in the spot that was just made for him, and he closed his eyes as he let his breathing deepen. Greg smelled good. And felt good. And . . . and Allen felt good in Greg's arms. Warm and comfortable and loved.

A wave of gratitude hit him, and he pushed himself up just enough to press his lips to Greg's for a brief kiss. When they parted, he settled back in his spot, with his head resting in the crook of Greg's shoulder, his arm draped over Greg's midsection, and one leg hitched up over Greg's. Greg brushed a kiss against the top of his head.

"Comfortable?"

"Mm-hmm," Allen answered sleepily. He didn't *want* to fall asleep, but he felt himself drifting in that direction. "Maybe too comfortable. I'm going to fall asleep like this. We should talk. Keep me awake."

A warm hand settled on Allen's forearm and then caressed upward to his elbow gently.

"I can definitely talk. But if you need to sleep—"

"No. No, I want to talk," Allen cut in, and he tilted his head back until he could see Greg's eyes. "Tell me about . . ."

He trailed off as his stomach dropped quite suddenly, the uncomfortable feeling slamming against him and nearly knocking the breath out of him. He knew what he *should* say. He *should* say "our trip to Friday Harbor." Because that was something he was looking forward to and something easy and nonconfrontational. And Greg would start talking quietly while rubbing his forearm softly, and it would be comfortable and warm, and he'd fall asleep within minutes.

But "our trip to Friday Harbor" were not the words on the tip of his tongue. No, what had suddenly popped into his head was much less relaxing to think about. He'd been doing such a good job of ignoring it the last few days, and he almost wanted to curse now as the two words settled in his mind.

Jack Mountain.

He watched Greg tilt his head slightly and give Allen a kind smile. Then Greg kissed his forehead again. "What is it you both want and don't want to talk about?" Greg asked, his voice as gentle as his kiss. And Allen almost laughed at Greg's intuitiveness. Greg squeezed him lightly. "And I'll remind you of what Dr. Schultz said, and that's that getting things out in the open earlier is always the best thing to do, even if you think it might be difficult to talk about. And I'll also remind you that I love you. Always. And if something is bothering you, I want to know about it so I can fix it. Or at least so I can support you in the best way possible."

It was true. Greg was right, as usual. They should talk. He shouldn't hold everything in, even if it was difficult. And though Greg was very good at interpreting Allen's moods and guessing what Allen might be thinking about, he couldn't *expect* Greg to know and understand if Allen didn't tell him.

Allen settled his head back on Greg's shoulder. "You know me too well," he said quietly. "I wanted to say, um, that we should talk about going to Friday Harbor. But then I . . . then I remembered . . ." He trailed off as something tightened uncomfortably in his chest, and he was unable to say it.

Jack Mountain. That trip—that adventure—that Allen just *knew* Greg really, really wanted to go on. *Would* be going on, in fact, if not for Allen's anxiety and depression and struggles all forcing Greg to stay home. Forcing him to miss out on what would surely be an amazing, life-changing experience.

And that last fact—the fact that Allen and his mental health issues were the cause of Greg missing this incredible opportunity—it sort of compounded everything, setting off this huge spiral of negative thoughts. He closed his eyes and clung to his husband as all the words he'd been so good at keeping locked away all day now zipped around in his head.

Needy. Disruptive. Burden. Shouldn't be here.

"Please . . . please just talk to me about Friday Harbor?" Allen mumbled, pressing his cheek harder against Greg's shoulder. "I think that's what I actually need right now."

There was a short pause, and Allen tried to ignore the fact that he could feel Greg tense up slightly.

But then Greg answered with a quiet "okay, of course," and he started once again to gently rub his hand up and down Allen's forearm as he began speaking, his voice low and soft and kind.

The warm, comfortable spot became warm and comfortable again, and Allen let out a long, slow breath and listened to his husband's budding plans for their maybe-vacation. He could ignore that other voice for now.

Though if he hoped to be successful in convincing Greg to go on that work trip, to not give up such an important thing that had to matter to him a whole lot, he knew the conversation would have to happen soon. Very soon.

Chapter Seventeen

Greg

THE HEAVY RAIN TURNED into light rain overnight, and by morning, the sky was cloudless once again. Greg was up just before sunrise, though he didn't wake Allen, and he made himself a cup of coffee and sat out on the patio, watching as the sun inched its way up into the sky. Beans tootled around the yard, alternately sniffing things, rolling around in the wet grass, and then joining Greg up on the patio before heading off again.

Just after the sun had reached clearly up over the top of the mountains to the east, Greg heard the slider door open and then close behind him. He glanced back over his shoulder and gave his husband a soft smile. Allen's smile in return was tight and uncertain, and Greg's stomach immediately knotted up.

"What is it?" He set his coffee down and started to stand, but Allen shook his head and motioned that Greg should stay put.

"I, um . . ." Allen dropped his eyes to the ground, closed the rest of the distance between them with a few slow steps, and then settled into the seat next to Greg. "I was actually thinking of . . . calling off work today," he said, his voice low and rough.

"Okay, okay." Greg wrapped his arm around Allen's shoulders and pulled Allen closer to him as he closed his eyes. "Are you feeling alright?"

Allen didn't answer out loud, but he shook his head and then buried his face in Greg's chest. The knots in Greg's stomach tightened. He'd seen and felt the moment something had started bothering Allen last night when they'd crawled into bed together before dinner. In fact, he'd almost argued with Allen then because he'd known they shouldn't put things off. They needed to talk more. Greg needed to know how Allen was feeling and what things were bothering him so he could best support him.

But he also knew it was really, really hard sometimes for Allen to do that, especially if the thing that was on Allen's mind had *any* potential to upset Greg. Or if Allen *perceived* that there was potential to upset Greg.

So last night, he hadn't pushed. Now, he was wondering if maybe that hadn't been the right choice.

"It's still early, but do you want me to call Annabeth for you?" he offered quietly, and when Allen didn't answer again, Greg rested his cheek against the top of Allen's head. "Did you have anything that you need to go in for today, or will she be able to handle things without you?"

Allen's voice was shaky, but he responded this time. "We have the homeschool group, but Casey will be there around that time, and—and . . . I think Annabeth should be fine."

"Okay," Greg said. He kissed the top of Allen's head, and then, without shifting them too much, he pulled his phone out of his pocket, unlocked it, and hit a few buttons to bring up Annabeth's phone number. The conversation was short, and Annabeth was just as understanding and kind as he expected.

After he hung up and slid his phone back into the pocket of his pajama pants, he heard quiet sniffles from Allen, and his heart ached again. Whatever was bothering him must really be hurting.

"I love you," Greg whispered as he turned slightly so he could wrap both arms around his husband.

"I love you too. I'm sorry for being so . . . so . . . me." Allen's lower jaw trembled, and he shook his head and ducked his chin down.

Dammit. Greg's heart clenched. The sadness and uncertainty radiated off Allen, again, and it hurt to see how much his kind, compassionate husband was struggling. Still. Again. Always.

Allen had reminded him the other day that he'd always struggled, that this wasn't all new to him. He'd even reminded Greg that he would probably always struggle. They'd talked at length about that with Dr. Schultz too. But even though Greg knew this, it didn't make things easier when he saw his husband not doing well.

Greg brought a hand up to cup Allen's cheek and repeated the words he'd said so many times before. "I love you, and I love caring for you. And I love having you here with me. I only worry because I love you." He pressed a gentle kiss to Allen's forehead. "And I also worry because I know that you wouldn't be calling out from work unless it's something really bad. So I hope we can talk about it—whatever it is that's bothering you—if it's something you're ready to talk about."

There was something else—some other nuance he'd meant to say—but his words hadn't quite come out right. He'd meant to ask, in a sense, whether there was something specific that was bothering Allen—and whether Allen himself knew what it was. *Not* whether it was something he was ready to talk about.

Greg could already almost see Allen thinking too hard on it, and he knew Allen well enough now. He knew what Allen would find if he thought on the words too hard. Greg let his thumb brush along Allen's cheekbone as he watched his husband's gray-blue eyes refocus on him. Then he leaned down and kissed Allen's lips softly.

"Darling, I didn't mean anything other than—"

"Can we go inside? Please. Sorry—sorry to interrupt you. I shouldn't have done that. I just . . . I'm just cold, and I want to go inside. Please."

"Of course, darling."

He didn't argue—Allen's reaction was just more evidence that they did need to talk and that Allen *had* made the right decision to stay home from work today. Instead, he stood and helped Allen up and whistled to the dog, who came bounding over to join them. Then he took Allen's hand and led him inside, pausing briefly at the door to towel Beans dry before guiding Allen the rest of the way to the living room and over to the couch.

After he got Allen settled, he knelt down in front of him and set his hands on Allen's knees. Allen blinked his eyes open, and Greg pursed his lips to avoid showing all of his concern. He took a deep breath and glanced up at the clock on the wall. 7:15 a.m.

"Are you better? I mean, is this better? Warmer, at least?" When Allen nodded, Greg pushed himself up onto his feet and then took a spot on the couch next to Allen. As he'd done when he'd sat outside with Greg, Allen nearly melted right into his arms, and Greg hugged him tightly.

"I have two deliveries later today. One at ten in Carnation and then one at noon all the way up in Everett. So we have time to talk before I have to leave, and . . . Actually, are you able to come with me? If not, I'll just reschedule."

A tickle of Greg's own anxiety started to nag at him as Allen didn't answer right away. He remembered their argument last Saturday. How Allen had gotten angry, stalked off, refused to let Greg walk him to work. And then getting the phone call from Annabeth that Allen had fainted and that they had an ambulance on the way.

Why did everything seem so . . . tenuous right now? So fragile? So ready to break? Even when he *knew* his love for his husband was as strong as ever.

And why was he worried he'd push Allen away more if he asked for answers? If he insisted on not leaving Allen alone?

And why did that all scare the hell out of him?

"I feel like I want to die."

Right. That was why. His stomach twisted painfully as he recalled Allen's words, and he tightened his arms around his husband again.

"Allen, talk to me. Please, please talk to me."

He felt more than heard Allen suck in a sharp breath, and then Allen nodded. "Don't reschedule your work stuff. I'll ride along with you. And . . ."

Greg waited patiently, though he felt very much the opposite of patient at the moment, his mind buzzing with too many what-ifs and uncertainties. Allen was taking slow, unsteady breaths, his hand pressing into Greg's side as though to anchor himself.

"And I want you to go on that work trip for Paul," Allen said finally. And once he'd admitted that, everything else seemed to spill out as Allen continued clinging to him. "I don't want you to stay home. I don't want you to stop working because of me. I don't want to be the reason you—you don't go places. You live for that stuff—those hikes and those trips and finding exactly the right photo and . . . and I don't want to ruin that for you. I've already messed everything up enough. I'm sorry. I've already made your life—"

"—wonderful," Greg cut in, interrupting Allen's rambling. "Wonderful and incredible and the best life, full of love and passion and happiness. Allen . . ." He took a shaky breath and buried his head into Allen's hair. "Allen, no, no, my love. You have made my life worth living. Being with you, being your husband—that's the most important thing to me. I wouldn't—"

Allen shook his head emphatically. "No. No, you have to go on that trip. It's . . . your only chance. I'm—I'm—no. No."

Tears burned his eyes, but Greg held them back as he kissed Allen's hair. "Allen, I won't leave you for that long. I can't do it. I would always—*always*—rather stay with you, rather be with you."

"Then I'll come with you. It might take a little extra time, because I'm not as fit, but—"

"No, Allen. That won't work. It's too difficult a hike. Dangerous, even."

"Then—then you have to go alone, and I'll—I'll be fine here. I've got Beans. And Joe's just next door. And—and I've got my work at the—at the library, and . . ." Allen took a strangled breath as he trailed off, his head still buried in Greg's chest. "You have to go. You have to."

Greg was quiet as Allen stopped arguing and began mumbling "I'm sorry" over and over. Still shaking. And still cold.

"Why . . . do you really feel so strongly about this, Allen?" he asked after Allen seemed to calm just slightly. "Because I can't—I *won't* leave you right now. Not for the work trip, not for some hike or some photo. They are things I don't need. I need you, though, Allen. And I *want* to be here with you. And if you think—"

"I'm horrible for you," Allen cut in. "You deserve so much better. I'm ruining—I'm ruining everything. I'm so sorry. I'm not . . . I'm not worth . . . I don't know why . . ."

Allen continued, his words becoming more and more muddled both in clarity and meaning, and Greg just held him as tightly as he could, rocking them slightly back and forth as his mind raced and his heart ached. It was as though every bad and terrible thing Allen had ever thought about himself needed to come out then, and the only positive Greg could even try to see in that moment was that Allen was still clinging to him, even as he spiraled.

And god, what a spiral it was.

Greg pressed a kiss to Allen's forehead as his words finally slowed down, but his stilted breathing and trembling didn't fade. And Allen uttered just two more words before he began sobbing against Greg's chest.

"I'm s-sorry."

Greg pulled the SUV and trailer up along the curb outside a huge two-story home in a small, newish neighborhood in southwest Everett. Allen sat quietly in the passenger seat next to him, reading a book, or at least pretending to read a book.

"Here we are. I'll just be a few minutes. I'm supposed to help them hang the prints too, but it shouldn't be long. That okay, darling? And since we're up here, we can grab lunch at that little café you like down by the waterfront when I'm done. How does that sound?"

Allen nodded slightly but otherwise didn't answer. It was as it had been since that morning—since their "talk." Since Allen had practically begged Greg to go on that trip for Paul. If he wasn't starving—having skipped breakfast in favor of spending more time comforting Allen—he would just say they should head straight home. Allen was clearly not okay still. Maybe they should go back to see Dr. Schultz as soon as possible. Or maybe Allen just needed to sleep more, although he'd been doing an awful lot of that lately. Or maybe he just needed to be somewhere safe and quiet so his brain could steady itself and reset. Maybe they needed to continue right on up the coast to Anacortes, hop on the ferry, and go take their vacation now.

Greg didn't know what was best.

All he knew was that he somehow needed to convince Allen that his life was worth more than any of Greg's hobbies and passions, including his career and his camera.

He reached over and touched Allen's cheek, and Allen closed his eyes with a short sigh.

"I won't be long," Greg said softly.

Then he grabbed his cell phone from its holder, shoved it into his pocket, and hopped out of the SUV. He jogged up to the front door and spoke briefly with Mitchell and his wife, Suzanne. They brought him inside and showed him where they wanted the prints hung on the walls. Then he got to work.

And he was mostly focused. And cordial and friendly. Mitchell and Suzanne were both chatty and open, and continued to rave about how wonderful the prints looked, how talented a photographer Greg was, how they couldn't wait to buy another print at some point. It was distracting enough for a few minutes.

When he finished, he shook hands with both of them, thanked them again for their business and support, and then turned to head back down to where the SUV and trailer were parked. Allen was watching him from inside the vehicle still, and Greg gave him a small smile as he headed down the walkway. Allen sort of half-smiled back. But his eyes were tired and sad.

Allen's words from that morning echoed in his head as Greg turned toward the trailer to make sure everything was secure and closed up.

"I don't want to ruin that for you."

"I've already messed everything up enough."

"You deserve so much better."

God, none of that was true. Allen hadn't ruined anything. He hadn't messed up anything. And Greg didn't want or need anything more. He had all he'd ever wanted, all he'd ever needed in his husband. Why couldn't Allen see that?

He knew the answer. He knew the depth and extent of Allen's traumas, rooted in his childhood. The neglect and abuse. The berating. The insults. The list went on and on.

But it almost hurt—the fact that Allen sometimes still pushed Greg away. Especially when things got really bad. Like now.

And everything—*everything*—that had beaten Allen down in the last couple of weeks . . . it all seemed to have this compounding effect. Allen's tiredness after their trip to Friday Harbor for the farmers' market. Then what happened at the library with Christopher and Owen. Then all of that aftermath, all of Allen's feelings growing and escalating, ultimately causing him to faint at work.

Greg took a deep breath and leaned his back against the closed door of the trailer.

No wonder.

He hadn't *really* been wondering. It all followed some terrible, logical progression, even if that progression had spiraled out of his and Allen's control. But when he let himself really think about it and remember all of those little pieces of the puzzle fitting together everywhere, it *did* make sense.

Allen's guilt and shame and depression and lack of self-worth.

God, his poor husband. All he wanted to do, all he *ever* wanted to do, was to show Allen all of the love he deserved. And he deserved it all.

Somehow, Greg needed to figure out how to convince Allen of that.

In a sudden burst of inspiration, Greg's hand shot down to his pocket, and he pulled out his cell phone, hit a few buttons, and lifted it up to his ear.

"Annabeth, hi. It's Greg . . . No, Allen's fine, he's just, well . . .
He doesn't know I'm calling to ask, but would it be an issue with
you if he were to take a few extra sick days, maybe through the
weekend?"

Chapter Eighteen
Allen

ALLEN TOOK OFF HIS reading glasses and closed his book since he wasn't really reading anyway—just staring at jumbled letters on the page while his mind raced in some continuous round of self-deprecating thoughts that hadn't really stopped since his conversation with Greg that morning. He glanced out the windshield ahead of him, trying to focus on anything else. But his chest felt tight and his hands felt clammy and tingly, buzzing with unease.

He forced himself to take a few minutes to count things in his visual field. Six western hemlocks, one Japanese maple, three western redcedars. Two seagulls. One small yacht—heading north up the Puget Sound. Fourteen—no, fifteen pyramid fence post caps along the wood fence outside Greg's clients' home.

It was distracting enough, but too temporary. Just like everything he tried.

He took a deep breath, closed his eyes, and set his hands on his thighs. The material of his jeans felt coarse against his fingertips, and he focused on that for a minute while using another deep breathing exercise. It, too, was temporary, but at least the tightness in his chest faded somewhat. When he opened his eyes again, his thoughts felt a little less intrusive.

He glanced at his watch and frowned as he realized it was taking Greg much too long to close up the back of the trailer. He leaned forward a bit and looked out his window into the passenger's side mirror. But he couldn't see anything. Maybe he should get out and check. After all, they should be back on the road by now.

Not that Allen was in a hurry—in fact, maybe he'd prefer to not be home for a while yet, to still be out and about and away from the house so he wasn't just sitting there fixating on their unfinished conversation this morning or how downright lousy he was still feeling in his head.

And even here, even now, sitting in the SUV with all the distracting things around him, that task seemed impossible. His thoughts still tried to swerve, still tried to take that dark turn he'd been so desperately avoiding. He closed his eyes and leaned his head back, unable to stop it. The whole morning replayed—beginning with him waking up to an overwhelming anxiety and uncertainty, every negative emotion and thought practically screaming at him that he needed to find a way to convince Greg to go on that work trip for Paul, and ending with his abysmal attempt and complete failure to change Greg's mind.

What a mess that had been. Not that he'd expected to be successful, really. He was terrible at arguing his point, even when it was important, like this. But now, he wasn't quite sure what to do.

Certainly at some point, Greg would realize how much he was missing out on, and he would realize it was all Allen's fault, because it was. Then Greg would surely be angry and upset, and he had all the right to be. All the reason to be.

Because it was Allen's fault.

All of it.

All of it was—

Allen's thoughts stopped abruptly as the driver's side door opened, the sound jarring in the otherwise quiet vehicle. He opened his eyes and squinted at the bright sunlight, which seemed somehow to pull him back to the present and away from the rough downhill slide he'd been on. Then he turned his head as Greg peeked in.

Greg had his phone in one hand, and the other was grasping the door, holding it open just enough. Greg's brilliant smile and sparkling eyes tugged at some deep emotion in Allen, and his heart seemed to stutter.

"Darling, a question for you . . . Do you trust me?" Greg asked.

Allen blinked, the question so out of left field that he had to think on it for half a second. "Of course." He nodded. "Completely."

"Good. Okay. One more minute, then we'll be on our way," Greg answered with another grin. He closed the door, lifted the phone up to his ear, and started talking as he moved back toward the trailer again. Allen couldn't really make out anything more than a muffled "yep, that'll be perfect" before Greg disappeared out of his view.

Do you trust me?

It was a funny question to ask, and Allen had no idea what it could possibly mean. If they'd been younger, he might actually have hesitated, since that look in Greg's eye could have meant *Let's go jump out of an airplane!* or *Paragliding! It'll be a blast!* or *A class five climb! Come on, let's do it!*

But even though he was ninety . . . eight? percent certain Greg wouldn't throw something at him that he couldn't handle, he found himself glancing back in the side mirror again, his teeth worrying at his lower lip.

186 BECCA NEIL

Maybe he did just want to go back home. Maybe that was the safest thing. The easiest thing. The predictable thing.

He'd said yes, though, because he *did* trust Greg. Especially now. Today. With everything.

Allen closed his eyes and forced his breathing to slow—again. And he counted backward from ten as he breathed in and out in controlled, measured breaths. Just as he reached zero, the driver's side door opened again.

"Sorry to take so long, darling. Everything's packed up. You ready to go?" Greg's voice sounded slightly different—both eager and nervous, Allen thought.

He turned his head slowly until he could see Greg, who was now seated in the driver's seat, fastening his seat belt. "Um, yeah, but . . ."

Greg tilted his head a little, still smiling, and he reached out and started up the SUV. "But what was that all about?" Greg said, his eyebrows raised in earnest.

"Yeah."

"Just some planning I had to do. You still trust me?"

"I don't know why you're even asking me that," Allen said, and though he'd meant to keep his tone light, his voice sounded more serious than he'd intended. He let out a short breath. "I mean, I do trust you. Of course I do. I just don't . . . trust myself. Which is . . . I don't even know what it means in this context because I have no idea what . . . you're planning . . ."

Allen trailed off as he watched Greg's smile fade and his lips purse into a frown. Shaking his head slightly, Greg reached over and set his hand on Allen's thigh. "I didn't mean to worry you, darling. I just got a little excited. Maybe a little carried away, and ah, well, I hope you'll love it. I think it'll be wonderful."

Allen gave a small smile and nod and somehow refrained from asking what exactly *it* was. Some last-minute excursion, an outing somewhere that he *hopefully* had energy for. And because he really *did* trust Greg, he was sure Greg wouldn't plan something strenuous. Because he very much didn't have any energy. At all. "I-I don't know if I can . . ." He shook his head, hating how he seemed incapable of finishing his sentences.

But Greg just squeezed his thigh gently.

"We're going to grab some quick sandwiches from Minnie's—I called ahead, so they'll be ready when we get there—and then we're heading up the coast a bit. Trust me, darling. I've taken care of everything. And today, tonight, tomorrow, the whole weekend, my only plan is to *take care of you*. Whatever you need."

"Tomorrow? The weekend?" Allen asked, now thoroughly confused.

Greg nodded. "We do sort of have to hurry, though. The ferry leaves at two, and we don't want to miss it."

"The ferry?"

"Yep. For our Friday Harbor vacation, which starts now."

It was the definition of spontaneous, and yet, somehow Greg had managed to fully plan and execute "spontaneous" in the ten minutes or so that he'd been at the back of the trailer, "closing it up." He'd called Annabeth to ask whether it would be difficult for her if Allen took the rest of the week off. He'd called Joe to ask if Beans could have a bit of an extended playdate with Poppy for the rest of the week and over the weekend. He'd called to reserve the ferry ticket for them and their vehicle. He'd called a friend who owned several rental properties on the island to check their availability—and when luck was on his side and their favorite cabin happened to be available, he'd reserved it for tonight through Monday morning. Then he'd called their friend Darryl and asked if Darryl could grab a few things for them from King's Market—a short list of clothes, toiletries, and groceries, which they'd pick up on their way through town after getting off the ferry.

It was completely spontaneous. Completely last minute.

And because of that, it both terrified Allen and felt exactly right. For one, it completely saved him from all the stress of decision-making, all the worry over planning and making sure everything was taken care of.

Greg had handled all of it.

And now, all Allen had to do was relax and let Greg take care of him . . .

Greg didn't even have his camera with him, or his laptop. It would just be the two of them. From now through Monday morning. No obligations, no worries.

They could just be.

He could just be.

"We can do as little or as much as you want," Greg had said as he'd pulled the SUV out onto the highway after they'd stopped at Minnie's to grab their lunch. "We can stay at the cabin the whole time, or we can go walking through town. We can go hiking or kayaking, or we can watch stupid movies and eat popcorn. We can do whatever you want, or nothing at all. It's all for you. All whatever you need, darling."

As Allen stood next to Greg on the outside deck at the back of the ferry, leaning against his husband and watching the mainland get farther and farther away, he still wasn't really sure what that meant. He still didn't know what he wanted or exactly what he needed. He'd had a flicker of anxiety about missing work, but then Greg had held his hand and kissed his knuckles and reminded him that his mental health was more important.

And he *had* already had to call out three of the four days so far this week because he was obviously not well. His mind obviously needed some time to heal . . . or something. So maybe this *was* exactly what he needed. And when he'd pulled out his cell phone just before they'd gotten out of the SUV to head to the outside deck, he'd seen a text message from Annabeth telling him not to worry about a thing except relaxing and getting better.

That *was* what he needed—to relax and get better. Or at least, he hoped that would be enough, that a quiet, relaxing weekend with his husband would be enough.

Greg slipped his cell phone into his pocket and then pressed a gentle kiss to Allen's temple. "Darryl just texted me. He's delivering everything to the cabin for us, so we don't have to pick it up as we go through town, after all. We can just head straight there. And after we get settled in, I'll make you dinner—filet mignon and asparagus and risotto."

"Dinner sounds lovely. And Darryl—gosh, that's so kind of him . . . I . . ." Allen shook his head and then settled it on Greg's shoulder again. "I mean, that seems like a lot of trouble for him to go through just for us, and I . . ."

"He was happy to oblige, darling. In fact, when I called him earlier, he happened to already be in town and at the market. He was glad to help. Really." Greg's voice was some mixture of quiet and reassuring that just made the slightly uneven beating of Allen's heart steady out.

"I might . . . not want to go out tonight. Or tomorrow. I-I'm not sure yet."

"Perfectly understandable, and perfectly fine," Greg murmured as he slipped his arm around Allen's shoulders.

"But I understand if you wanted to—"

"—stay with you the whole time," Greg cut in, though his voice was softer now. "I want to do whatever you want to do. And if that means all we're doing all weekend long is cuddling in bed, sign me right up."

Allen huffed a short laugh. "Well, when you put it that way . . ."

"I have no plans and no expectations." Greg's hand rubbed up and down Allen's upper arm, and Allen felt as Greg turned and pressed another kiss to his skin, this time just next to his ear. In a low voice, Greg whispered, "All I want is to take care of you"—kiss—"for the rest of forever."

Hearing the sincerity in his husband's voice sent rushes of emotion through him—a warm shiver first, followed by a wave of something more intense. Some combination of love and relief and safety. Allen closed his eyes and let out a shuddering breath as Greg kissed his cheek one more time, then pulled Allen up against him a little tighter.

A few more passengers joined them and the rest of the crowd on the much-too-small outer deck, and the general chatter around them became a little louder. Allen could hear two little kids having some playful argument about what island was the one to the north and a young couple to their right talking about the best angle to take a selfie from. Another group was oohing and aahing over a flock of pelicans that had just taken flight to the south.

So many people just going about their lives.

He felt silly for a minute—almost embarrassed at how he couldn't get rid of the dark thoughts in his head. How he couldn't just be in the moment, enjoy all the small things around them. Like the giggling of the two little kids, the breeze of cool, salty air, the warmth of the sun shining overhead, the comfort of his husband's embrace.

He opened his eyes again and found the flock of half a dozen or so brown pelicans gliding through the air, just feet above the top of the water. And he gave himself permission to just watch them. He tilted his head a bit to rest against Greg's shoulder as the birds continued skimming the water. Then, together, as though some silent signal passed between them, they all descended the final distance to settle into the water, causing the surface to ripple. A couple of them flapped their wings, and one lunged down and forward, submerging its head underwater, then floated upright again and lifted its beak up in the air, maybe swallowing a fish it had caught.

After another few minutes, when the birds were no longer in view, Allen closed his eyes again and took a long, deep breath. "How much longer until we have to head back down to the SUV?"

"Ten, fifteen minutes maybe," Greg answered quietly.

"M'kay."

"Are you okay? Did you want to go back down now? I know it's, um, a little loud up here, and I don't mind, either way."

"No, I'm . . . This is comfortable here. It's nice. I'm good." He turned his head and tilted it back a little. Greg was watching him with a soft smile, his expression hopeful and full of love. He stretched up as Greg dipped down, and their lips met in a short, sweet kiss.

When they parted, Greg was still smiling, and he reached up and cupped Allen's cheek before leaning in to kiss his forehead. Then, they both went back to looking out across the water as the ferry continued on its route.

Chapter Nineteen
Greg

GREG PULLED THE SUV up to the cabin, put it in park, and then shut off the engine. Everything looked perfect, as it always did here. Peaceful, quiet. He hoped he'd made the right decision—that this trip would be exactly what Allen needed. Time away from everything that had been causing him anxiety. Time to rest and relax and let himself be cared for.

God, he hoped it would be enough.

He glanced sideways at Allen, who'd been sitting quietly in the passenger seat since they'd left the ferry terminal. He was staring out toward the water now, but as though he sensed Greg watching, he turned to Greg and seemed to force a small, unconvincing smile that didn't quite reach his eyes.

Greg's stomach twisted just a little as he reached out and took Allen's hand, then brought it to his lips and placed a soft kiss on Allen's ring finger, just above his wedding ring. It was okay. It would all be okay. They had time—several days of time to focus on nothing else.

And he didn't doubt for one minute that Allen's real smile—the one he'd fallen in love with thirty-three years ago—was still there. He'd seen little glimpses of it earlier on the ferry, and he'd seen it yesterday too, when they'd been cuddling in bed and talking about low-stress things . . . like this vacation.

So he knew it was still there. He'd just have to work hard to bring it back more reliably.

He gave Allen another gentle smile of his own, which he really hoped conveyed everything he wanted it to—all his love and all the promises he had in his heart. Then he released Allen's hand and pocketed his keys.

"Ready, darling?" Greg asked.

"Yeah."

Greg nodded and hopped out of the SUV. The air was fresh, with a strong pine scent, so familiar and so tempting to him, like the forest was calling his name. He closed his eyes and inhaled deeply, letting the comfort of the forest surround him and wash away the little bit of worry he didn't *really* need to have anyway. Then he jogged around to the passenger side to meet Allen, who had just opened his door.

Greg reached out his hand, which Allen took, and then helped his husband out of the SUV. He paused there for a moment, holding Allen's hand and studying Allen's beautiful, kind eyes. Then he couldn't resist. He brought his free hand up and ran the backs of his fingers along Allen's jawline, the familiar roughness of Allen's beard providing another measure of reassurance that everything really would be okay.

The corners of Allen's lips twitched upward in a small smile, and Greg leaned in to kiss him. It was a light kiss again, but he lingered there for a moment, their lips pressed together tenderly, as he let his other arm wrap around Allen's waist. Then he pulled back just enough to shift slightly, and he buried his head into the crook of Allen's neck, holding him tighter.

"I love you," he murmured, and he closed his eyes and settled there for several long seconds, not wanting to let go.

The buzz of his cell phone from his pocket, however, pulled him out of the comfortable place he'd found, and he groaned quietly and straightened up. Allen chuckled and backed up a step.

"Ahh, I'll just ignore it," Greg said. "It's probably just the group text or something."

But Allen shook his head. "It could be important. But we can go inside first. I'd love to make some tea and then probably just sit out on the deck for a bit. Come on." Allen slipped his hand into Greg's, and they walked together toward the small, one-story cabin.

The cabin sat at the end of a rocky outcropping and was nestled among towering pines, which cleared along the back of the home to reveal a full, expansive view of the San Juan Channel and neighboring Lopez Island. They'd stayed there multiple times in the past, typically when they had been on the island for multiday events, such as art festivals or gallery shows or the farmers' market. But it was nothing short of a miracle that the cabin had been unoccupied and available; according to the owner, Janice, her booking for the weekend had literally *just* canceled right before Greg had called.

And it had made his decision feel even more right.

Together, he and Allen made their way to the front porch, input the code to unlock the door, and let themselves in. Several minutes later, their tea made but his text messages not yet checked, he and Allen settled down on the outdoor couch on the back patio overlooking the channel.

Allen took a cautious sip of his tea—a fragrant blend of chamomile and lavender—as Greg set his tea on the small patio table in front of them and then pulled out his cell phone. He'd gotten several more text messages while they'd been preparing the tea, and he smiled when he quickly scanned them. He opened up the most recent one first.

"Ah, look, darling, Annabeth sent a photo for you," Greg said softly, and he shifted to show Allen his phone screen. His heart warmed as Allen's eyes lit up and he reached out to take the phone.

"Wow, three new kids today, and I . . . Wait, what is . . . ?" Allen set his tea on the table next to Greg's and then brought the phone just a little closer to his face. His eyebrows scrunched together as he slid his fingers on the screen to zoom in on the image. "They made . . . for me?"

Greg slipped his arm up and around Allen's shoulders. "They did. Annabeth's text said it was Kiera's idea? I'm not sure who that is."

"This little girl right here." Allen pointed to the screen, where a tiny girl held up a piece of pink construction paper decorated with several colorful drawings and the words *Get Well Soon Mr. Allen* written in large block letters. "Last week was her first time at the library. Her family moved here from Pittsburgh, and . . . and I helped her find books on kittens and dragons. She's such a sweetheart. Gosh, I . . . All of them made cards? F-for me?"

"Yeah," Greg whispered, and he kissed Allen's cheek. "That's what Annabeth's text said. They all stayed an extra hour."

"Wow."

Allen's hand seemed to be shaking as he stared at the phone more, taking the time to zoom in on each of the handmade messages the children held. Greg's heart both ached and felt so incredibly full as he watched tears gather in Allen's eyes, and when

Allen had finally finished reading the messages, he sniffled, wiped his cheeks, and handed the phone back to Greg.

"Thank you for showing me that," he said quietly.

"You are so loved, Allen," Greg said softly. He switched off the screen on his phone—all of the other texts *were* from their group chat, and he could show them to Allen later. And though he'd planned on gathering Allen up in his arms and kissing him, it was Allen who melted into him first, falling against Greg and burying his head in Greg's chest. His arms wrapped protectively around his husband, and he closed his eyes and rested his cheek against the top of Allen's head. "You are loved, and you are important to me and to so many others. And you are enough just as you are. Always, my love."

His heart clenched as he felt Allen shudder against him.

"I don't—I mean . . . I can't . . ." Allen shook his head, even as he kept it pressed into Greg's chest. "My brain doesn't listen. It tells me the opposite. And worse. All the time. And I'm trying—I'm trying so hard."

"Shh. Shh, I know, darling."

Allen's voice was muffled as he started talking again, but Greg could clearly hear every word. Every sad word. "I know this was the right thing to do—to come here. I need the time away. With you. Just me and you, and I-I really hope this is going to help me, and I'm going to try my best to get better, to let myself get better." He paused for a second and took another deep, shaky breath. "But even now, even after those wonderful messages from the children—god, Greg, those just make my heart feel so full—but there's *still* this voice in my head saying how terrible it is that I have little kids worried about me. How I've made them worry. How I'm not strong enough, because if I was, I would be at work right now. How I'm not worth everyone's care or—or love. Even your love. How—"

"Shh, no, no," Greg cut in, and Allen stopped, exhaled roughly, and shook his head.

"It's . . . a constant battle. Especially these last few weeks."

"I know. I know."

"And I'm . . . so tired of fighting sometimes. Sometimes I just . . ."

Greg's stomach flipped and twisted and did all sorts of painful things as Allen trailed off and didn't say whatever horrible truth had been about to come. He closed his eyes and rubbed one hand up and down Allen's back slowly, lovingly.

"You can rest now, darling. Just rest and let me take care of you. Let me love you." Greg pressed a kiss into Allen's hair, even as Allen nodded into him, still shaking. "But please also . . . don't ever stop fighting those words. They're untrue—all of them. It's not terrible that the kids are worried about you. They just care about you because you've had a positive impact on all their lives. They're learning empathy and compassion, and they're learning how important it is to let the people they care about know it. And you *are* incredibly strong and brave. And you *are* worthy of love—my love, the love of our friends and neighbors and the whole community. You are worthy, and you *are* loved, and you are enough." Greg felt himself start to shake then, and he breathed yet another kiss into Allen's hair. "Please don't ever give up. Don't ever stop fighting. But also know that you don't have to fight this alone. I'm here for you, Allen. Now and always. You are not alone. No matter what mountains we face, we'll climb them together. I love you, Allen Westin—and that will *always* be true."

They sat there together for some time, neither of them moving, even to drink more of their tea. And Allen stayed silent, except for the sound of a heavy breath every once in a while. Greg both wished and didn't wish he knew what was running through Allen's head right then. More of the same intrusive thoughts, probably.

Which was why Greg should suggest they do something—anything—to distract him from all of that.

Greg looked out beyond the small, rocky beach in front of them, out across the water, and he thought back to the first time he and Allen had stayed here at the cabin nearly fifteen years ago, before it had become an official rental property. The owner, Janice, was a friend of Greg's mother, who was now living down in California in a small retirement village along the central coast. Janice had bought the place in 2007, with the intention of living here full time, and Greg and Allen had come up to help her with some repairs. They'd stayed an extra few days, and Greg had, of course, taken the opportunity to explore hiking on the island for the first time and had gotten some amazing photographs at several different locations on the island, and Allen had come with him. The hikes hadn't been terribly strenuous, at least not compared with some of the hiking he and Allen had often done on the mainland at that time, and Allen had been more than capable of it then.

But as he thought back on it now, Greg realized the hiking and the photography were not his favorite memories from that trip. Like so many other times, his favorite memories were of much smaller moments.

Like the time they'd been sitting here on that first trip—sitting in this very spot—and they'd seen a group of three humpback whales swimming south through the channel.

And that time—also on the first trip—that Allen had found some old poetry book in the bookstore in town, and his face had just lit up with the biggest, most brilliant smile Greg had maybe ever seen as he'd skimmed the pages.

And again on that same trip when Greg had found out Allen had never eaten s'mores before, and so they'd gone shopping and then made s'mores over the firepit. It had been so fun and messy, and afterward, they'd danced to soft music under the stars . . .

"We should make s'mores tonight," Greg said, finally breaking the silence. "We'll have to run into town—or I can go alone—but . . . we should definitely make s'mores tonight, after dinner."

Allen let out a soft *hmm* and then straightened up a tiny bit and tilted his head back. His eyes glistened slightly, but his cheeks were dry. "Only if you'll dance with me afterward," he said quietly, and a small but obviously hard-fought smile grew on his lips.

Greg blinked back tears of his own and reached up to cup Allen's cheek. Then he leaned in for a soft, warm kiss, and when he pulled back, he rested his forehead against Allen's. "Anything you want, darling."

Chapter Twenty
Allen

"Mmm, I think I agree with you, dear," Allen said as he sat back in his lounge chair and took a second bite of his s'more. "The dark chocolate *is* better. And it melts slower, I think?"

"Yes, exactly," Greg said, nearly beaming as he sandwiched a perfectly toasted marshmallow between two graham crackers. "The dark chocolate isn't as sweet, so it balances the sweetness from the marshmallow and the graham cracker. Plus, the melting temperature is higher, so it's not quite as messy too. And that method of toasting the marshmallow—good idea, darling. It worked just right."

Greg stepped away from the firepit and took a seat in the chair next to Allen's, biting into his third s'more of the evening. Allen was only on his second, and he figured it would probably be his last since he was still full from the incredible dinner Greg had cooked earlier. He licked some chocolate off his fingers and watched his husband do the same. Then he took another bite and looked out over the top of the fire toward the water. It was fairly dark since the moon wasn't out yet, and he could just make out a few lights dotting the shore on the other side of the channel.

It felt peaceful, and for the first time that day, he was starting to feel relaxed. Actually, really relaxed. No more buzzing in his fingers or that hazy sort of exhaustion that had been hanging over him all week long. No more weirdness in his chest—that feeling he'd had all day like his heart was struggling to maintain a constant rhythm. And no more overwhelmingly intrusive thoughts—at least, not so bad that he had to keep distracting himself with other things.

A warm, gentle hand covered his, and Allen smiled and turned to look at his husband. Greg was studying their hands, his expression soft and thoughtful, and when he finally glanced up at Allen, his eyes were just as soft and so kind. His thumb rubbed over Allen's knuckles, and he looked like he wanted to ask a question, but he didn't say anything. Instead, his eyes flitted down to Allen's lips, and then he leaned over toward Allen in invitation.

They met halfway in a slow, chocolatey kiss that deepened briefly as Greg's tongue teased its way into Allen's mouth, tasting and exploring in the most undemanding way. Allen made some quiet sound that was somewhere between a whimper and a moan, and Greg's hand caressed lightly up his forearm and then continued higher to cup his cheek.

"Mmm, yeah," Greg murmured as he pulled back just slightly. He dipped back in for another kiss, their mouths slanting together in a way that somehow just surrounded Allen in a swath of warmth and love. Greg hummed into the kiss and then broke away. "That *is* good chocolate."

Allen smiled in agreement and then turned his head and pressed his lips against Greg's palm. When he opened his eyes again, Greg was watching him with some content, hopeful smile, his thumb stroking back and forth along Allen's cheek. It felt good. So good.

And it was a deep feeling that seemed to spread through him, all warmth and certainty and love.

As though Greg knew what Allen was thinking, his smile grew just a little more, and he kissed Allen's forehead. "I love you, darling."

Allen closed his eyes again. "I love you too," he said quietly, and he leaned into Greg's touch, letting himself feel all the comfort and love Greg was offering. He wanted to say a little more too; he felt he should say something more. Greg had been just wonderful all afternoon—taking care of everything, making sure Allen was comfortable and happy, and somehow doing it all without any expectations and in a way that didn't make Allen feel any guilt about any of it.

He just felt loved. He felt that same deep feeling of warmth and certainty and love, and it was so much better than everything he'd been feeling for the last couple of weeks that it was almost overwhelming.

"This is perfect," he said, his voice low and maybe a little rough with emotion. He straightened up and smiled softly at Greg again before he looked back out over the fire toward the water. Greg's hand slipped down to cover Allen's, just as it had earlier, and they both sat in silence for a few more minutes, finishing their s'mores.

Eventually, Greg stood, gathered up all the leftover food, and disappeared into the cabin for a moment. When he returned, he stopped behind Allen's chair, set his hands on Allen's shoulders, and began massaging gently. It was another thing that felt good and relaxing, and Allen closed his eyes again and took a long, slow breath as the light touch continued. Greg massaged his shoulders and neck, then moved to his upper back, rubbing with sure, soft strokes. It was a slow burn—a glow that spread gradually, reaching all the way down to his toes. And when Greg's warm lips brushed against his cheek just below his ear, Allen shuddered as some stronger need tugged at him.

"I still owe you a dance, don't I?" Greg whispered, and he pressed a kiss to Allen's earlobe and then moved lower with another kiss and then another, trailing a quiet path down to Allen's jawline.

"Mmm, yeah. Yeah, I think you do," Allen managed as another jolt of heat rushed through him. He tilted his head back slightly, and Greg hummed as though in approval and shifted to press a kiss to Allen's lips, his hands stilling on Allen's shoulders.

With a gentle squeeze, Greg straightened up again, then reached into his pocket and pulled out his phone as he stepped around the side of Allen's chair. A moment later, Greg's lips twitched up into a half-smile, and some soft, melodic song began to play. It took a few seconds for Allen to recognize the tune, but when the artist began to sing their cover of "How Long Will I Love You," Allen gasped softly.

"Ah, I . . . I love this song," he said quietly.

Greg smiled again as though he'd known just that and reached out with one hand. "Allen Westin, my love, may I have this dance?"

There were tears in his eyes already, but Allen nodded and took his husband's hand. Greg helped him stand and then led him over to the other side of the firepit. And when Greg turned to face him and their eyes met, a wave hit him. It was one he'd felt so many times before—one of love and trust and belonging—and yet this time, for whatever reason, it hit harder. Maybe it was the atmosphere—the quiet, romantic night with stars twinkling overhead and the soft breeze bringing cool air off the water. Or maybe it was the music. Or maybe it was just Greg—Greg and his love and everything it meant. It filled him, surrounded him, made him feel whole and *wanted*. And that was huge, especially now. Especially today.

Greg's arms wrapped gently around his waist and pulled him closer, and that feeling—that feeling of being whole and wanted and loved—suddenly seemed *more*, deeper, amplified. Allen closed his eyes, slid his hands up around to the back of Greg's neck, and lowered his head to rest on Greg's shoulder. And as the lyrics continued with their soft piano accompaniment, Greg began to sway them to the music, humming along quietly and occasionally pressing kisses to Allen's temple.

The song was too short, the final notes fading into silence after only a few minutes, but Greg kept them swaying softly, and he started humming some other tune, an older melody that Allen also didn't recognize right away. But that didn't matter. What really mattered was how comfortable it felt being in his husband's arms, knowing without a doubt—without his brain even trying to convince him otherwise—that he was loved.

Nothing meant more in that moment.

Greg's swaying finally slowed and stopped, and Greg straightened up just enough and brought one hand around to cup Allen's cheek and tilt his chin back. Allen did as he had earlier, leaning slightly into Greg's touch, and this time, when Greg said his whispered "I love you, darling," Allen saw a glint of tears in the corners of Greg's eyes.

They came together in another soft kiss, and he felt Greg smile into him. When he pulled back, he looked up at his husband and lifted his eyebrows. Greg was still smiling but was also shaking his head almost imperceptibly as his eyes seemed to study Allen's expression.

"What?" Allen asked quietly.

He swore he saw Greg's cheeks flush, even in the dim firelight, and Greg ducked his head for a second before looking back up and letting his hand slip down to Allen's upper arm.

"You. You're just . . . so beautiful," Greg said. "And I think maybe I don't tell you that enough."

A warm shiver coursed through Allen then, and he blinked and then closed his eyes briefly as the tears he'd been holding back finally escaped.

"Ah, my love. My sweet, beautiful husband." Greg's lips brushed against one cheek and then the other, kissing away his tears, and then Greg pulled Allen up against him and wrapped him up in another wonderful, warm embrace.

God, it felt good. He felt so good. So much better. At least in this moment. It was a moment he wished could last forever, for always, because here in this moment, he felt safe from everything that he'd been battling with for the last few weeks. There was no doubt and no uncertainty, and the voice in his head—his voice—telling him that he wasn't worthy of any love, of his husband's love, faded until it was nearly inaudible. Just whispers somewhere far off in the background.

He breathed in Greg's scent as he rested his head in the crook of Greg's neck, and the strong hands holding him began gentle strokes up and down his back again. And there was more of everything: more love, more comfort, more of that feeling of safety. He sighed deeply and then straightened up as Greg's hands shifted down to his lower back and then to his hips.

Tilting his head back slightly, Allen met his husband's gaze, now filled with something else too, and that heat he'd felt earlier flared back to life when Greg's eyes seemed to darken. Greg bent down, and Allen stretched up, and their lips met again, their mouths moving in tandem and their tongues dancing. Greg broke away first to trail an indistinct path of slow, open-mouthed kisses downward to Allen's jaw and then to that sensitive spot where his neck met his collarbone. A quiet moan rumbled through Allen's chest as Greg continued, his kisses sending more heat straight to Allen's groin.

"Mmm, darling, let me . . . put out the fire . . . and then . . ." Greg spoke softly between kisses, but then he seemed to get distracted as Allen moaned again and slid one hand down to Greg's chest, palm open and splayed.

"And then?"

"Mmm. And then . . ." Greg straightened and reached up to cover Allen's hand with his own. Then he lowered his mouth to place the gentlest of kisses on Allen's forehead. "Let me take care of you."

The familiar words—words Greg had been telling him for over thirty years now—rippled through him, and he closed his eyes again, nodded, and pressed his hand into his husband's chest. He could almost feel Greg's heart beating fast, just like his own, and, one more time, he leaned up against Greg and let his husband's solidness support him.

Something felt different this time, despite the familiarity of it all. And as he watched Greg move away a moment later to put out the fire, Allen tried to figure out what that was. But his mind wasn't quite in step and his body was too distracted, and he just felt so overwhelmingly comfortable in the moment—in the knowledge that Greg loved him fully, completely, unconditionally. So he gave up trying to find an answer.

When they stepped back inside the cabin a few minutes later, Greg led Allen straight into the bedroom. He then kissed Allen's cheek and excused himself for a moment to turn off all the lights and make sure everything was put away so they wouldn't have to be bothered afterward.

Allen moved to the bed but didn't sit. Instead, he stared across the dimly lit bedroom and out the large window on the opposite side. The view was similar to what they'd had out by the firepit—darkness over the water with the lights from the small town on Lopez Island just barely visible. The lights flickered slightly as he studied them, and Allen found the view almost mesmerizing. He hadn't even realized Greg had returned until two arms slipped around his waist and a warm body pressed up against his back.

"Mmm, ready for bed, darling?" Greg asked, his voice both rough and soft at the same time and his lips now grazing Allen's neck.

Desire sparked in Allen's chest, and he felt it as a brightening of everything around him, a need—urgent and yet languid. All these contradictory things that somehow still made perfect sense to him. He closed his eyes as one of Greg's hands teased under his T-shirt and ran along his stomach and then upward, just a little, just a hint.

"God," he breathed, and he leaned back into Greg, his heart stuttering in his chest. This was what it felt like to be loved. He knew this. He'd known this for so long.

"You feel so good. I love touching you," Greg murmured, his breath still hot against Allen's neck and his hand now running in long, slow strokes back and forth just above the waistband of Allen's jeans. "May I . . . keep going?" Greg's hand moved upward again, and Allen moaned with want and need and something else as the slow move sent waves of pleasure rippling through him.

"Yes. Please."

"Good. Just tell me what you want tonight, darling."

The words sent another familiar flutter through his chest, and Allen felt his body shudder with need. He breathed deeply again as Greg continued a gentle exploration with his hands and lips, maybe waiting for Allen to reply, or maybe just moving forward with what he already knew Allen would love.

And he did. He loved it. The soft touches. The lingering kisses. The light fingertips grazing through his chest hair and over his sensitive nipples. The sounds in the room—a mixture of his own moans and Greg's quiet affirmations.

I love you.

God, Allen, when you make that sound . . .

Ah, darling, you feel so good.

Slowly, Greg undressed both of them down to their briefs, taking his time. Allen had mostly kept his hands to himself as Greg had explored everywhere he knew Allen loved to be touched. But when they settled on the bed together a moment later, Greg resting over Allen with one knee wedged between his legs, Allen found himself reaching out, running his fingers up Greg's solid chest, letting his thumbs brush over Greg's nipples.

Greg groaned and lowered his head to Allen's shoulder with a shuddering breath. "God, that's good."

"Mmm, yeah," Allen agreed, and he continued, palms smoothing up and down Greg's chest, then his back, then his arms, all while Greg fluttered kisses along his collarbone and up his neck and along his jawline. Heat and need burned deeper in his belly as he felt Greg's arousal pressing against his thigh, throbbing every time Greg rocked against him or moaned or trembled.

Above him, Greg shifted to prop himself up on one elbow and then paused to look down at Allen. Through half-lidded eyes, Allen watched as Greg's expression softened, intense desire and need giving way to love and something else. Joy maybe? Allen blew out a short breath, and then Greg smiled so tenderly and lowered his mouth again, their lips meeting in a much slower, gentler kiss.

Allen's hands slid around to Greg's back and then lower, slipping underneath Greg's briefs to grip Greg's backside. Heat rushed through Allen as his erection stiffened and pulsed with need, and he squeezed firmly and lifted his hips up at the same time, craving more pressure, more friction. They both broke their kiss, breathing hard, and Allen let out a rough moan, the sound rumbling deep in the back of his throat.

"God, that's sexy," Greg rasped. "I want to hear it again."

Allen huffed a weak laugh; he'd *never* thought of himself or any of the sounds he made as sexy, even when they were younger. Still, it was something Greg hadn't ever hesitated to tell him—not then and not now. And though he was pretty sure he'd never *actually* feel sexy, his husband's words never failed to ignite an even deeper desire in him or to make him feel loved and wanted.

Greg's lips captured his suddenly, this kiss hungrier and needy, and at the same time, Greg's free hand slipped down between them, teasing under Allen's briefs with sureness and confidence. Allen's hard shaft ached with the need to be touched, and when Greg finally stroked firmly down his length and then grasped him around his base, Allen whimpered and broke the kiss with a gasp, screwing his eyes shut and pressing his head back into his pillow.

"Ahh, that was also sexy," Greg said, his voice deep and rough, "but . . . not quite the same." Greg's breath was hot against Allen's throat, and when he trailed a path of wet kisses downward, the touch seemed to leave Allen's skin burning, making Allen ache with an even greater need. It was all heat and pleasure and some intensity that Allen hadn't felt in a while. And it was incredible. Everything.

And this time, when Greg's tongue flicked across Allen's nipple and tendrils of heat and tingling shot all the way down to Allen's toes, he did moan in a way that was much closer to that first moan—deep, thready, and rough.

"God, yeah, that's it," Greg said as he moved lower with his hot mouth and kisses. Greg rocked against him again with a moan of his own and began stroking Allen's hard shaft, the rhythm slow and deliberate.

A hazy pleasure surrounded Allen, his breaths beginning to come in faster pants and his heart racing. Out of a deep need to hit some new higher edge, he gripped Greg's backside with both hands again, a little harder even, and pressed Greg down into him as he thrust up into Greg's hand. God, it was good, that tightness growing deep inside him, coiling up, demanding to be let out.

"Close, I'm—I'm close," Allen panted. "But god, I want..." He trailed off and pushed his hands a little lower, dragging Greg's briefs down.

He knew what he wanted tonight, and it was simple. He just wanted his husband's naked body pressed against his own. He wanted to feel Greg's weight over him, their shafts rubbing together, Greg's hand pleasuring them both. He wanted to come hard and then be held in his husband's arms, where he felt safe and loved and whole.

And maybe, just maybe, the feeling would carry over, last longer than a moment, help him to get back to something closer to normal. Something not so broken.

"...I want you naked, now," he finished, his voice husky and deep as he slid his hands around to push Greg's briefs even lower in front as well, freeing his straining erection.

Greg inhaled sharply as though in relief and closed his eyes for a second. Then he released Allen's shaft and shifted on the bed so he could slip his briefs all the way off. He tossed them to the ground with the rest of their clothes and then settled again so he was kneeling on the bed next to Allen, his eyes dark with desire as his gaze drifted up and down Allen's body.

"And now me too. Finish undressing me too," Allen said when Greg's eyes stopped on his.

Another of those warm shivers coursed through him as Greg groaned quietly, then nodded and reached out to set one hand on Allen's stomach, palm flat. And Allen closed his eyes and breathed deeply as Greg took his time again, his hands smoothing over Allen's stomach in long, soft strokes. The bed shifted, and Allen felt Greg's fingers hook under the waistband of his briefs, teasing them down just an inch. A warm softness brushed against his exposed hip, and Allen sucked in a breath and opened his eyes halfway to see Greg bent over him, inching his briefs down, fluttering kisses along every bit of newly exposed skin.

"God, yes," Allen moaned, and he brought one hand up and ran it along Greg's shoulder, up his neck, and into his hair.

Greg continued, slowly working Allen's briefs down until his aching erection was no longer confined within the restrictive cotton. And Allen's heart pounded in his chest when Greg paused to graze his lips lightly around the tip of Allen's shaft, just barely touching him.

It was exquisite, and he closed his eyes again and groaned as his erection twitched hard. "God, Greg . . ."

"Hmm?"

He felt the vibration of the soft hum against the base of his shaft just before Greg pressed another kiss there—warm, loving, and tender, and it stoked the aching desire burning deep in his chest. "God, please, Greg. I need you. Now."

That was all he had to say. Greg finished undressing him without any more detours or distractions, and a short moment later, Greg settled so he was straddling Allen's thighs, as though he knew exactly what Allen wanted and how he wanted it.

Greg bent down to press a kiss to Allen's lips, and when they parted, he straightened up, running both of his hands over Allen's chest and stomach, and asked, "Just like this, darling?" He continued lower with one hand until he positioned their rigid, hot shafts together and took both of them in his fist, his fingers wrapping around them and holding them together.

"Yes, yes, just like that." Allen hissed out a short breath and lifted both hands to rest on Greg's thighs as Greg started to stroke them both together. "Faster though. Just a little." His hands ran up to Greg's hips and then around to grip his backside.

Then everything started to blur together as Allen let himself go, let himself be pleasured by his husband. It was warm and hot and bright, every stroke bringing him closer and closer to that edge. He was vaguely aware of Greg's free hand coming to rest on his chest and then over along his side as Greg leaned in and covered Allen's lips with his. It was a messy kiss, but one filled with love too, and Allen let out another low, rough moan as he arched his back, needing to relieve the pressure and tightening. Needing his release. His hands moved to Greg's hips, and he flexed his fingers into Greg's skin as he felt everything start to converge.

Greg sat back up, his hand settling on Allen's hip, applying some type of counterpressure, and Allen moaned and arched again, then thrust up into Greg's hand.

"God, I—I can't—I'm so close. Ahh, Greg, are—are you too?"

Greg grunted, his rhythm faltering slightly, and his hand pressed into Allen's hip again. Then his breath was hot against Allen's cheek. "Yes, yes, my love. Come now," Greg murmured. "Come with me now."

The whispered words sent a final jolt of heat and tingling through him, and Allen cried out Greg's name with his release. His shaft stiffened and pulsed hard, and a wet, sticky warmth hit his stomach. At the same time, Greg's movement stilled on top of him as Greg muffled a groan into his shoulder.

He was spent and out of breath, his chest rising and falling rapidly as he tried to steady himself. But also, he was completely sated, his body buzzing and trembling and full and relaxed.

Greg seemed the same, breathing hard but unable to move, his hand still wrapped loosely around their shafts. Greg was the first to

speak, his lips brushing against Allen's neck. "Mmm, ahh, you . . ."
He paused and kissed Allen's skin, lingering lazily for a moment.
". . . you're so perfect. So beautiful. Mmm, I could just . . ." Slowly,
Greg released them, his hand caressing down Allen's thigh as he
shifted to settle on the bed, his weight still partially over Allen.
Kisses feathered on Allen's neck and then up to his jaw and his
lips and his cheeks. "I could just stay here with you forever," Greg
whispered. "Just like this. You and me. Forever."

Allen couldn't respond except to hum in agreement. God, he
just felt . . . so, so good. He closed his eyes and turned his head
slightly, and just as he'd wanted and hoped for, Greg's lips found
his again. The kiss was longer this time, deepening briefly before
Greg pulled back and rested his forehead against Allen's.

"Let me help you clean up, darling? We can take a quick shower
together, and then I'll hold you so you can rest?"

"That would be perfect," he said, and though the words were
confident, his voice still seemed to tremble. He finally opened his
eyes and looked up to see Greg's soft, kind expression, and he lifted
a hand to cup Greg's cheek. "I love you. Thank you for today, for
tonight. For always."

Greg blinked slowly as he gave a small nod and a half-smile so
full of love. "Thank you for being here with me," he said quietly.
Then he pressed another kiss to Allen's lips, and when they parted,
Allen swore he saw tears glistening in Greg's eyes.

Chapter Twenty-One
Greg

SOMETIME IN THE MIDDLE of the night, Greg had gotten up to open the window and let some fresh air in the room. He'd then crawled back into bed with his husband, and they'd cuddled more until they'd fallen back asleep.

It was early morning when he woke again, this time to the sounds of birds chirping in the forest outside and Allen's quiet snoring next to him. He lay there for a few minutes just listening, feeling so content in the normalcy and peacefulness of the moment. Then he shifted onto his side to face Allen. Allen slept calmly, as he had all night long, and even though Allen was facing the other direction, Greg could see the lack of tension in his husband's back and shoulders and the way his breathing was slow and steady and deep. And that knowledge brought him a small measure of hope.

He was desperate to know he'd made the right decision in bringing them here. By all accounts, the way the previous afternoon and evening had gone, he should be feeling a resounding *Yes!* And he was hopeful. He really was.

But even *with* that hope, he couldn't forget all the ups and downs of the past couple of weeks, including the lowest lows he and Allen had probably ever had together. He couldn't forget all of the anxiety, the panic, the depression. Their argument. Allen's confession that there were times he didn't want to be alive anymore.

All of that really tempered the hope wanting to burst out.

Still, as he let his eyes wander across his husband's back, down to where his backside disappeared under the comforter, a fullness bloomed in his chest. Yesterday really had felt amazing. The relaxing dinner, the night out under the stars, s'mores, dancing, making love . . . Allen had seemed to have sort of given himself permission to be taken care of, permission to be whatever he needed to be, and Greg had loved being there for him—there *with* him in every moment.

In fact, the whole day yesterday had only further solidified his decision about cutting back on work and solo travel and challenging hikes. Any lingering doubt he'd had about how much he *might* miss doing those things just . . . wasn't there anymore. Instead, he was feeling a renewed sense of commitment, an even deeper love for his husband, and he couldn't wait to find out what this new phase of their lives had in store for them.

He also couldn't wait to share all of this with Allen.

Greg scooted a few inches closer. He yearned to reach out and touch his husband—to trail his fingertips lightly over Allen's skin and make him shiver. Then kiss him. Everywhere. Do whatever would make Allen feel good. Hell, Greg wouldn't even mind just staying here in bed all day. Just touching and cuddling and talking. Just being together.

But he also didn't want to wake Allen up yet—he wanted Allen to get as much sleep as he needed. So instead, he moved to the opposite side of the bed, careful to not make the bed shift around too much, and crawled out from under the covers, watching Allen the whole time to be sure he didn't wake. Quietly, he sifted through the clothes Darryl had picked up for them, setting aside a simple gray T-shirt and a pair of black joggers for Allen and selecting similar clothes for himself. After he dressed, he grabbed his phone and headed out into the kitchen to make himself a cup of coffee.

Greg spent the next half hour or so checking and responding to text messages from Joe (Beans was completely worn out from playing with Poppy in the backyard for hours on end), Annabeth (the city council had already reviewed Allen's proposal at their meeting Thursday morning and had tentatively approved the additional funding Allen had requested), and a potential client (would Greg have his regular booth at Issaquah's Salmon Days Festival next month? and could he bring a medium-sized print of "Misty Mountain Sunset" from his Mount Rainier National Park collection?).

Just when he was about to get up and go check on Allen, he heard quiet footsteps padding down the hallway to his left. He glanced up as Allen emerged, barefoot and yawning, his hair still ruffled from sleep, and an immediate warmth bloomed in Greg's chest.

He cleared his throat and set his phone down. "Good morning, darling. Did you sleep well?" he asked, pushing his chair back and standing.

Allen didn't answer except with a small smile and a nod, but he closed the rest of the distance between them and settled right into Greg's embrace. Greg wrapped his arms around his husband and inhaled deeply, humming with content as he pressed a light kiss to Allen's cheek. He loved this—this moment, his husband, this moment with his husband. And it just made him feel all of his earlier convictions even more strongly.

"I'd love to make you breakfast, if you're up for it," Greg said quietly, resting his cheek against the top of Allen's head. "Something simple, maybe? A toasted bagel with cream cheese and strawberries?"

He could feel as Allen smiled against him and buried his head deeper into Greg's chest. "You know that's my favorite. But, I, um . . . Darryl got all of that?"

"He did."

"Because you asked him . . . because you knew it would make me happy." Allen tilted his head back, and there was another small, soft smile on his face that made Greg's heart stutter. God, it was everything. A real, true smile. Something honest and full of love and not dulled by pain and anxiety and uncertainty.

He bent down and kissed Allen slowly, tenderly, then pulled back. "I did, and I did," he admitted quietly, and then he pressed another kiss to Allen's cheek before he dropped his arms from around his husband. "Would you like coffee? Or maybe tea?"

"Yeah, um, tea, I think. That's probably best."

With a nod, Greg started over into the kitchen, and Allen followed. "We had that chamomile and lavender tea last night, but I think I saw a few other teas as well. Green tea, maybe, and then something with ginger and honey."

Together, they rummaged through the cupboard to find the stash of about five different types of teas. Allen chose that "something with ginger and honey" Greg had thought he'd seen, although it ended up being a blend of lemon balm and ginger. Then, as Allen settled at the table, Greg got started preparing the tea and their breakfast.

The conversation stayed light, and that hopeful feeling inside him continued to grow, buoying his spirit. Allen was grinning, joking with him, and laughing, and it all just seemed right and made so much more sense than everything else had the last few weeks.

So when he moved their prepared bagels and tea and coffee to the table and then sat down next to Allen a few minutes later, the question slipped out before he could think whether or not he should have asked it.

"Should we go out somewhere today?"

As soon as he saw Allen blink and lower his eyes to his bagel, Greg realized his mistake. His voice had been *too* eager, *too* expectant, like he was hoping or expecting Allen would say yes. Like that mattered for Greg's own happiness. And of course, that was the farthest thing from the truth. He immediately opened his mouth to backtrack, but stopped when Allen looked back up at him, smiling.

"Actually, yeah, I was thinking we could," he said. "Remember that trail along the southern coast, by American Camp? I can't recall the name of the trail, but we went there a few summers back with Ron and Faye?"

Greg nodded slowly. "South Beach, yeah."

"I think it's fairly flat and—and I should be able to handle it. It's got some really gorgeous views, especially on a day like today when it's clear and sunny." Allen blinked, and his smile faltered just enough that Greg shook his head slightly.

"It's an easy trail, yes, but darling, I shouldn't have implied—"

"It'll be good," Allen cut in, his fuller smile returning and a twinkle in his eyes. "Relaxing. And I think the fresh air will be good for me. We should go."

Greg hesitated. He wanted to agree emphatically, immediately start planning their day, jog out to the SUV to grab his hiking backpack so he could load it up with water and trail-appropriate snacks. He wanted to believe the twinkle in Allen's eyes, not the falter in his smile. And he wanted to see this as a positive thing—Allen's willingness to go out somewhere and do something. But something in the pit of Greg's stomach wouldn't let him do any of that. At least, not without talking all of it through with Allen first.

"It sounds perfect," he said carefully. He turned his chair slightly so he was facing Allen more, and then he reached over with one hand and cupped Allen's cheek as he studied his husband's eyes. So wonderfully kind. A soft gray-blue. The same eyes he'd fallen in love with so many years ago. He wanted to find all the answers there—all the answers and all the certainties. But he saw a hint of something else, and his smile tightened just a little. "I'd love to go hiking with you, always. But not at the expense of your health, or just because you think I need to or want to, or if you still need to rest."

Greg let his hand slide down from Allen's cheek to his neck, and he tugged gently, pulling them together so he could kiss Allen's forehead.

"I promise you," he continued, "I will be perfectly content staying here and taking care of you all day. I will be perfectly happy, always, to just be here with you."

"And I promise you, I wouldn't have suggested it if I weren't ready and sure," Allen countered, though his tone stayed light. A playful smile lit up his face as he picked up his bagel. "I mean, if you want to stay here that badly, I can always just go by myself."

A light huff of laughter escaped Greg, and he shook his head. He still wasn't quite convinced—it seemed too soon, and he'd been mistaken to even suggest they head out—but when he searched Allen's face for any sign of reluctance or anxiety or exhaustion, he really couldn't find it.

"I'd love to go, darling. When do you want to leave?"

Greg parked the SUV in the otherwise-empty parking lot at South Beach and glanced over at his husband. Allen had been unusually talkative most of the drive, which had been great, but the last couple of minutes, he'd quieted down, and now, as Greg smiled and reached over to take Allen's hand, his stomach twisted in a knot.

Allen was shaking.

Just barely. Just a little. But Greg could feel it.

He squeezed Allen's hand gently, and Allen turned to him, his smile strained and not bright—nothing like it had been earlier that morning or late last night.

A string of silent curses ran through Greg's mind, and he fought to keep his own expression neutral. He brought Allen's hand up and brushed a soft kiss on his knuckles. "You know, maybe we should—"

"My hiking boots—they're still in the back, right?" Allen interrupted, pulling his hand away and reaching for the door handle. "I don't want my tennis shoes to get dusty."

"Yeah, but—"

"Good! Let's get going. It's what, a couple miles, right? Easy-peasy."

Before Greg had a chance to react, Allen was out the door, shutting it behind him. The knot in Greg's stomach tightened again, and he closed his eyes for half a second before grabbing his cell phone, stuffing it in his pocket, and exiting the SUV. Allen was already standing at the back, staring at his hiking boots, one hand resting on Greg's hiking backpack.

Greg stopped next to him, and Allen looked up with a small smile, though his jaw was clenched. It felt wrong. Something was wrong. Allen was pushing himself for whatever reason, and they needed to *not* go now. They needed to talk.

"Allen," Greg said, his voice quiet. He bit his lower lip and shook his head again, then he took both of Allen's hands in his. "Darling, I think we should go back. We don't have to do this. You don't . . . seem okay anymore." It was hard to say, but it was the truth, Greg knew. Allen didn't seem okay.

"I'm fine, Greg. Sorry if I'm worrying you. I'm—I'm . . ." Allen trailed off and pulled his hands away, and then he sat heavily on the back of the SUV and lowered his eyes to the ground.

"It's okay to not be okay," Greg said softly, and he stepped forward and then sat next to Allen, setting his hand on top of his husband's.

But Allen shook his head. "I know. I know that. But, no, I *am* fine. Really. I was just—" He looked back up, a forced smile on his face, and then he twisted and reached back behind him. "Here's your hiking boots, and mine too. We should get going, huh?"

Greg didn't respond, but he took the dusty boots Allen handed him and then watched as Allen hiked up a leg and untied his tennis shoe to change footwear.

"You know, since it's pretty flat and shouldn't be *too* dusty, maybe we don't really need the boots at all?" Allen said. He kicked off one of his shoes and slipped on his boot. "But it's probably better if—if—if we . . . if we, you know, um . . ."

All the signs were there, staring him right in the face, and Greg had no idea what the hell to do about it. Allen was not okay again, well on his way to some sort of spiral, it seemed. Maybe.

But then, maybe he was just a little nervous about doing something active—which was a good enough reason in itself to *not* do the thing.

Greg swallowed thickly and started changing his shoes, trying to clear his thoughts. It would be fine, either way, he decided. They'd do this little walk, maybe not even go quite to the end of the trail, and then they could head back to the cabin, and he could make sure Allen really *was* okay. It was a short, easy trail, after all.

By the time Greg had his hiking boots mostly on, Allen had finished and was standing, staring out to the west, toward the deep blue waters of Haro Strait. It was clear enough that they could see all the way across the strait to the southern tip of Vancouver Island looking to the west and to the northeastern part of Olympic National Forest on the mainland looking to the south.

The weather really *was* perfect—sunny and maybe sixty degrees, with a crisp breeze coming off the water. They'd be cool enough in the long-sleeve shirts they'd changed into before leaving the cabin. And the trail was just an easy path up on a low ledge set back a bit from the water. It was fairly straight, no real elevation changes to speak of, and very low-key.

So why was Greg so nervous?

Allen turned away from the water to look at him, and when their eyes met, he was smiling again. "Hurry up, old man. Let's go," Allen teased.

And Greg finally let himself smile too, because it felt good and he wanted to believe in the levity Allen was trying to infuse in the moment.

"That's Mr. Old Geezer to you. Be respectful to your elders, you young'un!" Greg joked, earning him a laugh that sounded genuine enough. He took a deep breath as he finished double-knotting his second shoe. Then he stood, grabbed his hiking backpack, and closed the hatch on the SUV. Shouldering his pack, he turned to Allen, who reached out his hand.

"Ready?" Allen asked.

Greg didn't want to hesitate, so he took Allen's hand. But he held his husband's gaze for an extra second before answering, his voice rough. "I'm ready, but I want to be sure you're really okay. If something's bothering you, I'd rather we talk about it now, before we go."

A flicker of something in Allen's eyes sent a wave of unease through him, but then Allen smiled softly and nodded. "I'm okay, really. I want to do this. I want us to do this together. Come on, Mr. Old Geezer."

"Alright, alright," Greg finally agreed. "But you promise to tell me if we need to turn back?"

"Yeah," Allen said gently.

And with another nod, Greg motioned toward the trail. "Alright, let's go, then."

They started out at what Greg would consider a decent pace, even for him. Allen's steps seemed confident, and they held hands as they walked. The trail, initially wide enough for vehicle traffic, narrowed after about a quarter mile until it wasn't much more than an overgrown single-track path of partially flattened grass. Greg moved behind Allen, letting Allen take the lead so he could set the pace, and they followed along as the trail skirted the top edge of the low hills overlooking the water. It was peaceful, and he began to relax as they continued on, occasionally stopping to take in the view.

It wasn't until they'd gone maybe a half mile or so that Greg noticed it. And it was subtle at first. Just their pace slowing down slightly and an occasional tight shrug of Allen's shoulders. Then it became a little more obvious as Allen stopped chatting quite as much, his responses becoming slower and less articulate, their easy banter becoming stilted. The next time they paused to admire the view was when Greg really knew something was wrong.

Allen's hands were shoved in his pockets, and his face was pale, except for his cheeks, which were flushed and red. And he was visibly shaking, his breathing heavy and his expression taut.

Greg stepped closer and was just about to ask if Allen was okay, when Allen suddenly dropped his chin to his chest and let out a shallow, shuddering breath, his whole body swaying.

"Greg? Greg, I think I—"

He reacted quickly, lunging forward to catch Allen as Allen turned to him and nearly collapsed with some sort of strangled gasp. Allen's legs seemed to have given out completely, and he felt cold and weak in Greg's arms.

"Greg, you—you can't. I thought you could. I-I wanted you to. But—but you can't," Allen mumbled incoherently, his voice wavering as he clung tighter to Greg. "P-please don't. Please don't."

"Please don't? Please don't what?" Greg's heart began to race as he struggled to hold Allen upright, and he quickly glanced around them. The ground was flat enough, grassy. "Allen? Allen, let's sit, okay?"

"Yeah. Y-yeah. I—I'm not okay."

"I know, darling. I've got you, though. Here."

Slowly, Greg managed to lower them to the ground, and then he held Allen, his heart now hammering so hard his chest hurt, as Allen's shaking worsened and he began mumbling nonsense words, clinging to the front of Greg's shirt and taking short, uneven breaths.

It seemed like . . . something akin to a panic attack. Maybe?

God, Greg didn't really know. All he knew was how much he hoped his husband could still hear him.

He pressed a kiss to Allen's temple and started countering Allen's words with his own quiet affirmations of love, like he always had when Allen was struggling.

And he held onto his husband tighter, tears now slipping down his cheeks.

Chapter Twenty-Two
Allen

WRONG. HE'D BEEN SO, so wrong.

And now—now his heart was pounding hard in his chest and unevenly and skipping beats here and there, and he had to be having a heart attack. Also, he couldn't breathe right.

He had to be dying. Right here, in the middle of the trail, in his husband's arms.

All because he'd been wrong.

"Shh, shh. You're okay, Allen. Listen to my voice now. I'm here, and I love you, and you're okay. Breathe now, darling. Slow and steady."

Greg's voice was his only anchor, but he knew it wouldn't help in the end. Already, he felt detached from his body. Like he didn't belong. Like he was on his way somewhere else.

He gasped for air and managed to say something, but the words sounded incoherent even to him. "Greg, I can't do it. Please don't go. Please. I was wrong, and—and—and—"

His words didn't even make sense. What was he even trying to say? Something about a mountain. And how he'd wanted Greg to—to go. But now . . . but now he didn't? Now he needed Greg to stay? Maybe?

God, if he didn't even know what he meant, how would Greg have any idea?

A sensation like sharp pinpricks rippled through his hands and up his arms, and then his chest tightened again, uncomfortable and painful. And Allen whimpered and screwed his eyes shut harder.

"I'm not going anywhere, Allen." Lips pressed lightly against his temple. "I'm here now, and I'll be here with you always. I'm not going anywhere." A warm breath ruffled his hair. "I love you. You are loved and worthy and always will be. And I'm here. I'm here." A hand caressed his back. "Breathe with me, darling. Please."

Desperation.

He could feel it inside of him, and he could hear it in Greg's voice. He nodded weakly, barely able to respond, but then he tried. He tried his absolute best.

He flattened one hand against Greg's chest so he could feel as it rose and fell, keeping a slow, controlled rhythm.

"That's it, darling."

In and out. Slowly. There was a shudder and a hitch to his inhale, and the exhale was too fast, all wrong.

"You can do it. Slow and steady. I love you. I'm here."

"I was going to tell you to go, though. I was—but you shouldn't—god, I can't—"

"Shh, shh. I'm here. I'm not going. I'm staying right here with you. Breathe now, Allen. Please."

Greg's hand covered Allen's and squeezed gently, and Allen tried again. In and out. And then again. And when he managed some sort of a rhythm, he heard Greg again, counting for him this time. "Breathe in, two, three; out, two, three. There you go. Good.

I love you. I'm here with you. Let's try again. Breathe in, two, three; out, two three."

Gradually, the sharp pinpricks dulled, and the pain in his chest—the weight crushing his lungs—lessened. Gradually, awareness came back to him. He could feel the soft material of Greg's shirt against his palm, the reassuring and light caresses of Greg's hand up and down his forearm, the wetness of the tears on his cheeks. And there was a slight chill in the air as a stiff breeze blew in from the water. He shivered and closed his eyes tighter.

God, what had just happened? One minute, he'd been thinking about . . . about . . .

"I'm sorry. I-I'm sorry. I—" All of his energy was gone, and he took one more deep breath in and then exhaled on a sob. "I'm sorry, Greg. But I need you."

"You have me, Allen. I'm here. I'm here. You're okay. You'll be okay. Stay with me, okay?"

He heard it again—a desperation in his husband's voice—and he nodded against Greg's chest.

"Good, good. It's okay. We're here together, okay, Allen?"

They stayed that way for another few moments, and then Greg started talking again, quietly and reassuringly, his voice kind and gentle and resonant. "Do you remember, darling, on our first date, when I left my wallet at the restaurant? Ah, I thought you must have imagined me to be the most scatterbrained idiot in the world. I'd never done anything like that before, ever, and . . ."

Greg continued, and Allen listened as Greg recounted much of that night—how they'd had to backtrack to the restaurant to find Greg's wallet and then missed the first half hour of the movie; how Greg had been secretly overjoyed when the only seats left in the theater had been all the way in the top back corner, giving them just a little bit of privacy; how he'd felt so happy when Allen had leaned his head on Greg's shoulder midway through the film; how he had wanted to kiss Allen at the end of the evening but had been just a little too nervous; and how he'd absolutely *loved* when Allen had kissed him instead.

And the whole time Greg was speaking, Allen kept his hand solidly on Greg's chest, feeling it rise and fall, anchoring him there.

Finally, the fogginess cleared around him enough that he felt connected with his body again. Connected and present.

Greg was still talking. Something about the day they'd adopted Beans from the local animal shelter, and Allen smiled, even as another tear slipped down his cheek.

"Stubborn little thing, still," Greg said, and he seemed to maybe lower his cheek to rest against the top of Allen's head.

Allen sniffled and nodded into Greg's chest. "They warned us."

There was a half-second pause and then a quiet huff of laughter. "They did. I think the lady's exact words were, 'He's sweet, but . . . well, you know.'"

"I love the little stinker."

"Me too."

There was silence then, and Allen could hear the water down on the beach below them, lapping gently at the shore, and a low rustling of the grass in the breeze. He blinked his eyes open for the first time in however long, and though he'd *known*, for some reason, he was surprised that they were sitting. They were sitting there, right in the middle of the trail, right on the grass, Greg holding him with one arm around his shoulders. And . . . and he hadn't died. He hadn't been having a heart attack.

But he'd nearly collapsed, right there on the trail. Or maybe he *had* actually collapsed, and Greg had caught him. That seemed more like it, he thought, piecing together the bits of memories from the last . . . however long.

How far out were they? And would he be able to make it back to the trailhead?

And . . .

"I'm sorry," he mumbled, and then he swallowed hard as he felt Greg's breath hitch.

"We should talk about . . . whatever just happened," Greg said quietly, his hand stilling on top of Allen's, which now rested on Greg's thigh. "But maybe when we're back at the cabin, and when you're feeling okay."

That seemed logical, although Allen's brain wasn't feeling super logical right now, and he wasn't sure he could wait that long. He shook his head slightly, closed his eyes, and took a slow, measured breath.

"No?"

"No, I don't know if . . ."

"It's okay. I'll help you. We'll walk slowly, and—"

"I meant, I should tell you now. Before we go anywhere. And I don't think I can walk yet anyway. I feel so weak. I . . . I'm so sorry."

Greg kissed the top of Allen's head again and tightened his arm around Allen's shoulders. "We can take our time, darling. And I, um, I'm listening if you want to talk now."

The uncertainty in Greg's response hit him hard, and if he hadn't already been sitting, he might have swayed on his feet. He pressed his hand into Greg's thigh and took a long, slow breath. "Whatever just happened," he started, his voice low and shaky, "i-it was because I'd planned to make one last argument to—to . . . convince you."

"Convince me of what, darling?"

"That you shouldn't skip Jack Mountain," Allen said, and some deep shame tugged at his gut. It was actually physically painful. He shuddered and gulped in a lungful of air. "I didn't—I *don't*—want you to miss out on it because of me, even though—even though you already told me . . ."

"Oh, Allen," Greg breathed, and Allen felt him shake his head. "Darling, I . . ."

Greg trailed off, and Allen nodded into him. "I remember everything you told me, and everything you said. But I was feeling so much better last night and this morning, and then when you asked if I wanted to go out, I heard it in your voice, and—"

"That was my mistake," Greg interrupted. "I shouldn't have suggested anything. And I would have been perfectly happy staying at the cabin all day. Earlier this morning, in fact, I—I had been thinking how it was so wonderful." Greg's voice cracked on the last word, and Allen pulled back just a little and tilted his head to look up at his husband. Greg had his eyes screwed shut, and a tear fell silently down his cheek.

God, this was all so messed up. Allen was so messed up.

Broken.

Unlovable.

A burden.

Greg's eyes opened as though he could hear Allen's thoughts, and he began to shake his head lightly as he bit his lower lip. "This morning, Allen, I was so happy. I wish you could know what I was feeling." A small smile inched across Greg's face, and he reached up to cup Allen's cheek. "I told you already that I'm not going to Jack Mountain. And I had already decided something else too, and I needed to tell you, to talk about it. But you have to understand something first, and you have to hear me and believe me, my love."

There was a weak pulse of some unpleasant sensation in Allen's stomach, but when Greg bent down to kiss Allen's cheek and then whispered a soft "I love you" into Allen's ear, the sensation faded.

"I-I'm listening," Allen stuttered.

Greg didn't move except to pull Allen a little tighter up against him. "It's long overdue of me, I think," Greg started, his voice gentle but filled with something so deep Allen's chest almost ached just hearing it. Greg kissed Allen's cheek again, then dropped his hand back down to cover Allen's. "I'm going to cut back. On work. On hiking. On those solo traveling trips. I don't want all that anymore. And it's because I want to be with you more."

There was a short pause, and Allen realized he'd been holding his breath. He inhaled sharply as Greg continued.

"I told you already that I wasn't going to Jack Mountain, and I—god, Allen, I love you so much for wanting me to be happy. I love you for wanting that for me. But I realized in the last few days that I really actually don't even *want* to go."

Allen swallowed hard. "You . . . don't?"

"No. No, I don't want to go because you couldn't be there with me," Greg said. "And—and what I want—what I want *more than anything else*—is to just be *with you*. To be wherever you are, so I can take care of you, so I can love you, so I can be present with you. I want to cook you breakfast and cuddle in bed. I want to walk you to work. I want to go hiking, yes—but when you're healthy and feeling good so we can do it together. I don't *want* to be away from you anymore."

Greg blew out a short breath and slid his hand up Allen's arm until he was cupping Allen's cheek again. Allen tried to duck his chin and look away, so overwhelmed with emotion, but Greg shook his head slightly.

"Allen, darling, please look at me. Please, please hear me. Hear this."

So he did. With tears rolling down his cheeks and his lower lip trembling, Allen forced himself to hold Greg's gaze. And he saw regret and worry in his husband's eyes. But there was also love and a strong, powerful resolve.

"Allen, you are the single most important thing in my life, and I will be happy just knowing that you're happy. I will be happy just being with you. I *will* be happy, Allen. I *am* happy. What we have together is so, so special, and I love it, and I love you. I want this—*us*—and that's all. That's enough. You're enough for me, Allen. You always have been, and you always will be."

Allen closed his eyes as a wave of some huge relief crashed over him, pulling a sob from somewhere deep in his chest. God. He didn't even know how it happened, but Greg's lips were suddenly on his, caressing them softly with a quiet reassurance. When they parted, he sighed deeply and slowly and let his tired body lean up against Greg, exhaustion mixing with relief mixing with love.

And for the first time since breakfast, his mind was also quiet, and he could think without every thought being drenched in the intrusive, overbearing, negative self-talk. He opened his eyes and turned his head just enough to look out toward the water.

It was beautiful here. It would have been so peaceful. A peaceful, short walk along the coastline. And actually, in that moment right then, it was peaceful.

He reached up and wiped the tears from his cheeks, then rested his head against Greg's chest again. When he spoke, his words were quiet and careful, since he needed to finish explaining what he hadn't earlier.

"It means more than you know to hear you say all of that. Because . . . because what I think made me panic, or whatever that was just now, um, was that I was sort of gearing up to try to convince you to go on that trip, and—and I-I realized that I was terrified of you actually leaving." He paused to take a breath and turned slightly to bury his head against Greg's chest. "I've been trying to convince myself that I'm okay and that I'll be fine, but every time I try to *make* myself be okay and fine when I'm really not, something happens. Like—like when I pushed myself to go to work because Christopher and Owen would be there, and that drove me to have thoughts of—of—that I wished I weren't alive anymore. And then we had that fight, and I hated that so much.

And then I fainted. And now—and now—as we were walking here, and I was trying to figure out what to say, and I realized, no, you—"

He stopped and closed his eyes and shook his head to reset himself, and Greg's arm tightened around him reassuringly, lovingly. He blinked back more tears. "And . . . I realized that you couldn't go," he continued, "because I still need you here, especially right now, just as—just as you've been saying. But that thought—that I would be keeping you from doing something you really wanted or, um, something *I thought* you really wanted—the thought that I'd be making you miss out, it . . . started to—to amplify all those other voices in my head."

". . . Those ones I already know about?"

"Yeah. Those ones from when I was a kid . . . Those ones telling me . . ." He trailed off, not wanting to say the words now. Not wanting to repeat them or give them any space in this conversation. They'd already done enough harm.

Greg must have agreed with him, because Allen felt another kiss press against the top of his head, and then Greg whispered quietly, "I love you, Allen."

"I love you too."

It was several long minutes before either of them said anything again, and then it was Greg, making some joke about his foot falling asleep because of his "elderly man status." Allen managed a laugh, and they agreed to try to walk back to the trailhead. He felt dizzy and lightheaded when he stood, even with Greg helping him and even when they were slow and careful, but after a moment, he seemed to regain his equilibrium, at least enough for them to start back.

They walked slowly, Greg's arm staying wrapped around his waist the whole way. By the time they finally reached the SUV maybe close to twenty minutes later, he was exhausted and done.

Greg directed him to sit sideways in the passenger seat and then removed his hiking boots and slipped his tennis shoes back on for him.

And another few minutes after that, they were on the road, headed toward the cabin. Allen closed his eyes and rested his head back against the headrest, and when Greg reached over and took his hand, he felt that same deep, aching relief that he'd felt earlier.

He was loved—really, truly loved—for all that he was. He'd known that already, but he'd needed to hear it again. And he'd needed to know all those other things too—that Greg really, truly was okay with not going on that trip and that Greg really, truly was and would be happy.

He was still a mess—a tired, broken mess. Today had only proven just how much he needed to let his mind and body rest so he could heal. And even then, he would probably always still struggle, always still be a mess. But . . .

Allen glanced sideways at Greg, and his heart felt so full in that moment. As though he'd known he was being watched, Greg turned his head to meet Allen's eyes briefly before looking back to the road ahead. Then he brought Allen's hand up to his lips and brushed a light kiss along his knuckles.

And Allen's heart fluttered in his chest as he closed his eyes again and let himself rest.

Chapter Twenty-Three

Greg

ALLEN WAS BEYOND TIRED, which was expected, Greg supposed, after what had happened out at South Beach. When they'd arrived back at the cabin, Allen had barely had enough energy to stand, and Greg had had to support him on the walk inside and into the bedroom. He'd helped Allen wash up and change into a clean set of clothes, and then he'd brought him a small plate of fruit and a glass of water. And they'd lounged together in the bed with some documentary playing on the TV that neither of them really watched.

It hadn't been long before Allen had fallen asleep, the plate of fruit half-eaten and his glass of water still mostly full. So Greg had cleaned up, changed his own clothes, and taken a seat in a cushy armchair right by the window.

That had been nearly two hours ago. And Greg still hadn't moved.

Outside, the sunny skies persisted—gorgeous weather that would normally have him itching to get moving. Today, however, he was content to be inside, looking out. The window was still open, and the light breeze felt good and refreshing, smelling of forest and ocean.

He shifted in the chair to watch Allen sleep again, as he had been doing for the last couple of hours. His mind was still trying to wrap itself around everything that had happened, everything Allen had told him this morning, and everything yet to come.

The one constant thought that was—thankfully—louder than all others was how grateful he was. Grateful for Allen and their life together. Grateful for their community and the support they had. Grateful for the last thirty-plus years and whatever the future would bring.

Allen turned over onto his side with a quiet groan and blinked his eyes open, and when he found Greg, he smiled weakly. "Hey."

Greg didn't answer, but he pushed himself up out of the chair and shuffled over to the bed, not taking his eyes off his husband. He sat on the edge, just next to Allen, and reached out to smooth Allen's hair back off his forehead. "How are you feeling?" he asked quietly, and he bent down to press a gentle kiss to Allen's lips.

"Mmm, better when you do that," Allen replied when Greg straightened back up.

"Good, good. I've got an unlimited supply of kisses just for you, so any time you need one . . ." Greg smiled softly and continued gentle caresses with his thumb along Allen's forehead as Allen closed his eyes again.

"Any time, huh?" Allen chuckled lightly and set his hand on Greg's thigh. "You know I'm going to hold you to that."

"Oh, I'm counting on it," Greg said as he suppressed a laugh of his own. He bent down again and kissed Allen's lips, then his cheek, then his forehead, each kiss a little slower than the last, lingering. When he sat back up, he watched Allen's smile grow just a little more, and his heart stuttered. He caressed Allen's forehead one more time, that same sense of gratitude filling him.

Allen's eyes opened about halfway, and his chest rose and fell with a long, deep breath. "I've been asleep for . . . a while?"

"Yeah, a couple hours almost, but don't even worry about that," Greg said, bringing his hand down to cover Allen's. "You should keep resting if your body needs it or if your mind needs it. And I'll be right here when you wake up. And when you're ready to get up, I'm here to help you. Whatever you need."

He hoped he'd said the right words—the words that would let Allen know he had no expectations, no need to go anywhere or do anything except to be here, if and when Allen needed him. Out on the trail earlier, he'd told Allen everything he'd wanted to and needed to. He'd repeated again how he had no intention of going on that work trip, and he'd also finally broached the topic of cutting back on everything else as well. But those moments had been so emotionally charged, so tenuous and fragile, he was fully prepared to say everything again if he needed to. And he was fully prepared to do everything in his power to show Allen, every moment of every day, just how much all those words meant.

For now, though, Allen didn't question him. He just blinked his eyes closed again and nodded slightly. Then he pulled his hand away and set both hands by his sides to push himself into a sitting position. Greg scooted over a little to give him room and helped support him as he settled. Then, they both leaned in together in another embrace, Greg's arms wrapping around Allen and Allen resting his head on Greg's shoulder.

It was comfortable and comforting, and Greg was hit with another wave of gratitude for this moment. And for all the moments just like this that they'd shared. He turned his head and kissed Allen's hair, and he let his hand rub up and down Allen's back. Allen seemed to tremble slightly, and Greg felt him release a shuddering breath.

"I . . . might need another one of those kisses pretty soon," Allen said, his voice shaky and muffled against Greg's shoulder.

"Happy to oblige, darling," Greg murmured, and he tightened his arms around Allen for a brief second before pulling back, bringing one hand around to cup Allen's cheek, and then leaning in for another kiss, this one longer, deeper. And when they parted, there was moisture on Allen's cheeks. "Allen?"

But Allen just shook his head, reached up to wipe the tears away, and cleared his throat. "Um, I'm just . . . feeling a lot right now. Um, can we—can we talk a little more, maybe?"

"Of course," Greg answered right away, and he leaned back in again and kissed Allen's lips lightly. "I'd been thinking the same, actually."

There was a quiet laugh, though Greg didn't hear any humor in it, and he watched as Allen closed his eyes and took another deep breath. Something tugged at his heart—maybe it was the thought that Allen seemed so uncertain—and Greg wanted nothing more in that moment than to take away all of Allen's doubts and anxieties.

It wasn't in his power to do that, though. The best he could do was to be there, be what Allen needed, and be *present* and available and loving. And that he *could* do.

He kissed his husband's forehead again. "If you're up for eating, I can make us some lunch. We've got stuff for sandwiches. And we can talk about whatever you want," he suggested.

Allen nodded and gave Greg a small smile. "I think I could eat."

"Good."

Together, they got up and headed out to the kitchen, Greg supporting Allen the whole way since he was still unsteady. He helped Allen settle at the table and then got out all of the ingredients to make sandwiches, sending a silent thanks to Darryl for grabbing mustard and mayonnaise even though Greg hadn't added them to the list. A few minutes later, Greg set their two plates on the table, brought over a bowl of fresh strawberries, and got both of them glasses of water. Then he took his seat next to Allen, who was staring off toward the back slider door with a distant expression.

Greg reached over and ran his fingertips lightly down Allen's forearm to his hand. "Did you want to sit outside on the patio, darling?" he asked quietly, squeezing Allen's hand. But Allen shook his head.

"No, this is fine right here. Um, I just . . ." Allen trailed off, biting his lower lip as he dropped his eyes to his plate. "This looks wonderful, and I'm actually hungry," he said with a light laugh. He started to pick up his sandwich, but then froze and frowned. "What you said earlier about . . . cutting back . . . Greg, I-I don't want you to—" Allen shook his head and screwed his eyes shut, and when he spoke again, his voice was small and uncertain, like he was really having to force the words out. "I mean, did you . . . mean everything you said?"

Greg's heart clenched, and he turned his chair to face his husband, then reached out and took Allen's hand in both of his, brought it to his lips, and placed a gentle kiss on Allen's knuckles. "Every single word."

They leaned in toward each other, and their foreheads touched as Greg let go of Allen's hand and framed his face.

"Every. Single. Word." He pressed his lips to Allen's in a brief kiss. "You are the most important thing in my life. And I want"—something rattled inside his chest, and he sucked in a deep breath before continuing—"to spend my time with you, not away from you. I want to be with you, take care of you, go places with you or stay home with you. I just want . . . more time with you, my love. And I mean that—all of it."

"I-I . . . I want all of that too," Allen said hesitantly, pulling back slightly. His eyes met Greg's, and they looked stormy and troubled but clear. "But—but you can't . . . just because I'm a mess, and . . ."

Greg shook his head, letting his hands slip back down to take Allen's again. "No, no. You're not a mess, Allen. You're beautiful. And kind. And brilliant. And you're also complex and you feel deeply and love unconditionally. It's true that all the, uh, circumstances in the last few weeks have made me realize just how much I've been missing. But, Allen, I mean every word. And—and I—"

A shaky breath escaped him, and he blinked several times and looked down. He wasn't sure what else to say right then, except maybe the most obvious thing. He swallowed hard and lifted his eyes again. Allen was watching him, his eyes glistening with unshed tears and his lips pursed in a tight frown.

Another kiss. And this time, Greg was the one who needed it.

Greg closed the distance between them, tilting his head slightly, and captured his husband's lips in a tender kiss that was deep and loving and that he hoped conveyed everything he needed it to. When they parted, his heart stuttered. Allen had closed his eyes and had a small smile on his lips, and in that moment, it felt like everything.

"And I love you, and I'm so, so incredibly grateful you're here and we're together," Greg continued.

Allen's smile grew even a little more, though he still had his chin lowered, and he sniffled and nodded with an acceptance Greg hadn't entirely expected. "I love you too," Allen whispered, his voice rough with emotion. "And . . . and me too. I'm so grateful for you and for us . . . I've never wanted anything else."

There was a pause, and when Allen finally looked up at Greg, his eyes so full of love, the biggest flutter of hope Greg had felt in a long while spread through his chest—hope and relief and some bright warmth all at once. He inhaled deeply and touched Allen's cheek again. "You're all I want and all I need, Allen. And I just want to spend the rest of our forever with you, my love. That's all."

More tears fell from both of them, but Greg wiped Allen's away with gentle fingers, and then they kissed again, another long, deep kiss that seemed to hold all the promises and reassurance of three decades of love.

Chapter Twenty-Four

Allen

"THERE WE GO!" GREG climbed into the driver's seat of the SUV and gave Allen a wide grin that was much too eager for how early it was. "The trailer's all hitched up and ready to go."

Allen yawned and glanced at his watch. "Ugh, not even five," he complained with an exaggerated groan. "I'm getting too old for this, you know." His tease was an echo of the easy banter they'd had the last time they were leaving Friday Harbor, and he tried for a silly smile as well. But it really was much too early—even if he wasn't actually too old—so he was pretty sure whatever smile he managed probably missed the mark by a bit.

Greg didn't seem to mind, however, and he laughed lightly and played along. "If you're old, what does that make me?"

"Definitely an old geezer," Allen joked, and he leaned his head back against the headrest and tilted it slightly to look at his husband. Greg's expression was soft now, his small smile full of love and some other emotion that Allen was too sleepy to interpret.

With a nod, Greg reached over and touched Allen's cheek, then he straightened again and started up the SUV. "As long as we don't miss the early ferry, we should be home on time for you to go to work. If you still wanted to, that is."

Allen yawned again but nodded at the same time. "I do. Although I . . ." He shook his head to push away the guilt he felt and let out a short breath.

They'd talked about this already; in fact, it had come up several times in the last three days. He didn't need to feel guilty about asking Greg for support. It was normal and expected that he'd still feel unsafe at the library alone after everything that had happened. And most importantly, Greg did not and would not ever feel inconvenienced or irritated or unhappy to accompany Allen to work and stick around until Casey or Annabeth showed up.

So Allen took a breath and restarted. "I'd like to make it on time, so before ten. And if I'm remembering the schedule correctly, Casey will be in at eleven and Annabeth at one. So I'll just need you there with me for the first hour or so."

"Of course, darling," Greg said. "Whatever you need."

Allen's heart did something funny in his chest, and it wasn't that uncomfortable tightening and heaviness that he'd gotten so used to the last few weeks. There wasn't an immediate sense of guilt or shame like he'd usually have, and he wasn't silently wondering whether Greg would be happier spending his time some other way.

He wasn't silently wondering whether Greg would be better off without him there.

No, he was happy to have Greg there, and he was ready to let Greg support him. And mostly, he was so incredibly grateful that he was loved.

God, he felt so much more like . . . himself.

It had been hard—all the talking they'd done in the last three days. And he knew there would still be more to talk about as they continued to work things out and figure out what all was going to be changing. Greg's work and travel and . . . maybe Allen's work too.

That had been something unexpected that had come up over the weekend—whether Allen might consider retiring or cutting back on his hours. He still wasn't entirely sure. He did know that no matter what, he needed to be involved, a part of the community. But he had acknowledged, with Greg's help and gentle support, that he needed to take care of himself as well. So they'd talked about whether he should maybe step down as the head librarian, focus his time on the community outreach programs at the library that he'd helped to develop, continue to mentor Casey and the other interns.

It would be a huge change. He'd worked at the North Bend Public Library in one capacity or another for over thirty years now, and the library had been his safe space, his home, his passion. But just as Greg had acknowledged about his own career and hobbies, it might be time to step back and focus on different things. Himself. His health. Their relationship.

And regardless of what they decided, they'd move forward together, as they always had. That was one thing that would always be true, and this weekend had only shown him—again—just how much he really was loved and just how much his happiness meant to his husband.

"What's that smile for, darling?" Greg's voice was low and held more than a trace of hope, and that made Allen smile again.

"It's nothing. Just . . ." He paused and closed his eyes. How could he even articulate what he was feeling? That hadn't ever really been easy for him, but he supposed he could sum it up with something that might also make Greg happy to hear. He blinked his eyes back open, and Greg was watching him with a kind expression, so full of love and understanding. Allen nodded gently.

"I'm just feeling a little better. A little more like I maybe have a handle on things, at least for now, I mean. A little more . . . me?"

Greg's eyes brightened. "Ah, I love to hear that."

Allen nodded again, because he felt the same, and as though with some silent accord, they leaned in together and kissed softly, briefly, slowly. His heart felt even more full and happy.

"Let's get going?" Greg asked as he pulled away and straightened up. Allen murmured some sort of agreement, and a few minutes later, they were on the road, heading into town toward the ferry terminal.

The whole trip—from the cabin to the ferry, across the Puget Sound to the mainland, and then from where they disembarked in Anacortes down to North Bend—was relatively quiet and uneventful, and Allen found himself dozing off several times. When they pulled up at home, Allen stayed with Greg while he parked and unhitched the trailer.

They'd just started grabbing their stuff out of the back of the SUV to head inside when a burst of loud, rambunctious barking sounded off from their right. Beans suddenly seemed to materialize from out of nowhere, launching himself up into the hatch of the SUV and then jumping up to set his paws on Allen's chest. The dog's tail wagged furiously, and he barked again and bounced up on his hind legs to lick Allen's face.

"Beans! You stinker. Ah, I missed you, though," Allen said, laughing as he pushed the dog off of him and then scratched behind his ear. Beans barked again and then sat, his tongue lolling out the side of his mouth and his tail still going.

Joe jogged up, shaking his head. "Ah, sorry about that, Allen! He must've heard you two get home, and when I opened the door, he took off."

Greg laughed and reached out to shake Joe's hand. "Thanks for taking care of him for us. He's a stubborn one. I hope he didn't give you much trouble."

"No trouble at all, man, really. I'm glad to help. How was the trip? You both doing okay?" Joe asked the question of the two of them but glanced at Allen as he did.

And Allen let out a sharp breath and then nodded as Greg moved a little closer, his arm slipping up around Allen's shoulders. "Yeah, yeah, we're . . . we're doing okay. Apparently, I, uh, needed the break more than I'd realized."

He could say more; Joe was a wonderful neighbor and a great friend, and he'd been nothing but supportive and understanding, just like the rest of the community. But he also knew he didn't need to—what he'd said was plenty for now. Greg seemed to agree, giving Allen's shoulder a squeeze. And Joe just nodded.

"Yeah, we all need to get away every now and then," Joe said, and he smiled and hooked his thumb back toward his house. "Well, I've gotta run—got a meeting in a few minutes. Glad you're back, and let me know if you need anything, alright?"

"Thanks, Joe. We really appreciate it," Greg answered for both of them.

Joe gave one more nod and then headed toward his house, and Allen turned back to Beans, who had plopped down in the open hatch of the SUV next to the single duffle bag Greg had purchased in Friday Harbor to pack all their stuff up in. He shook his head and then scratched Beans behind his ear again before reaching out to lift the small dog up. "Come on, you little stinker."

Greg grabbed the duffle bag and shut the hatch, and together, they headed inside. Beans barked and bounded up the stairs as soon as Allen set him down, and Allen started to follow, but Greg shook his head, took Allen's hand with a gentle squeeze, and started leading them toward the kitchen.

"I know you need to get ready for work," Greg said, glancing back at Allen with a broad smile, "but this'll only take a few minutes."

"O-okay, I suppose I can—" Allen stopped abruptly in the entryway to the kitchen, and Greg shifted back a step to be at his side. His heart skipped a beat, and he leaned against his husband as he shook his head. "What . . . Greg, what is . . . ?"

Their small kitchen table was covered with an elegant white table cloth, and in the center sat a single lit candle, its flame flickering and illuminating the otherwise dim room. On either side of the table, among scattered rose petals in deep red and white, were two plates, each containing a single, large . . . donut.

Allen laughed loudly and turned to Greg, immediately reaching up to frame his face. He tugged Greg down to him, and their lips met in a brief but joyful kiss. "You . . . are so . . ." He couldn't even speak to finish his sentence, and he just shook his head and pulled Greg down again for another kiss, laughing. When they parted, he glanced at the table again. "They're Bavarian cream, right? Otherwise, this whole thing is a fail."

"Oh god, I hope so," Greg said with another laugh. "I was pretty specific when I talked to Joe last night."

"Joe helped set this up?"

Greg nodded and pulled Allen up against him again, dipping down to kiss Allen's cheeks and forehead and then his lips. When he straightened up again, he was grinning down at Allen with a twinkle in his eye. "He *did* make me explain before he would agree, though."

"I can't believe . . ." Allen pulled away from Greg and stepped over toward the table, blinking back tears as he remembered a very, very similar setup from over thirty years ago. "It meant so, so much to me that day. It was silly, just like this, but . . ."

Greg stepped up behind him and slipped his arms around Allen's waist, and Allen leaned back into him, closing his eyes as he let his husband's warmth surround him. Greg's lips brushed his cheek. "That day—when you first told me about your parents—Allen, I . . . had no idea what to do or how to handle anything, how to help you feel better. All I knew was that I needed to take care of you, because I already knew that I loved you."

"I remember that you stayed with me and held me and listened to me tell you all of that . . . stuff. And we couldn't go out because—because I wasn't doing well." Allen sniffled and reached up to wipe a tear from his cheek. "And when I woke up in the morning and came out to the kitchen, and—"

He laughed and shook his head. It had been just like this—flower petals, candle light, and donuts. Bavarian cream. It had been both silly and probably the kindest, most romantic thing anyone had ever done for him. He wiped another tear from his cheek. "You said—you said you owed me a romantic dinner out, but since it was breakfast time and we both needed to eat . . ."

With Greg's gentle encouragement, Allen turned back around in Greg's arms. The smile on Greg's face was soft, but also filled with some sort of deep, deep love. Greg's hand came up to cup Allen's cheek, and Allen leaned into the touch and closed his eyes.

"And I also told you then," Greg started, his voice low and rough with emotion, "that I was so happy to be there with you and that you meant the world to me." Greg kissed his forehead, and Allen inhaled a shaky breath.

He remembered that too. He remembered Greg holding him, hugging him, kissing him oh so gently on the forehead, telling him how important he was. It had been huge and had meant so much. Just like this did now.

"That's still true now. You mean the world to me, Allen Westin. We've been through so much together, and I love you more every single day. I'm so grateful for you, Allen. So grateful, and I know—"

Allen pulled back out of their embrace slightly as Greg's voice faltered, and when he looked up at his husband, Greg was smiling but with tears in his eyes. Allen stretched up as Greg bent down, and they shared another sweet, gentle kiss. Then Allen rested his head against Greg's chest as Greg continued.

"And I know that whatever this next phase of our life brings—whether it's harder days, easier days, more ups and downs, rain or shine—whatever it is, darling, we'll face everything together. Just like we have since that day."

Allen's heart clenched, and he nodded against Greg with a small smile. "That day when you stayed," he said.

"Yes. That day when I stayed."

". . . And brought me Bavarian cream donuts."

Greg huffed a laugh and shook his head. "God, these better be Bavarian cream. Did you check? I—"

Allen stopped him with a kiss that deepened and lingered and had some safe, comforting warmth to it. And when they parted, he closed his eyes and rested his forehead against Greg's with a long sigh. "Thank you, Greg. I love you."

"Ah, I love you, too, darling." Greg's arms slid around his waist and pulled him closer. "So," he whispered in Allen's ear, "you don't care if they're Bavarian cream or not?"

Allen chuckled and blinked back tears as he shook his head. "They are. I checked."

"Okay, okay, good. Otherwise, you know, I'd go get some. Whatever you want."

"I just want you," Allen breathed, "for the rest of forever."

Epilogue
Greg

One Year Later...

"Alright, Beans is asleep—poor guy is tuckered out—and the dishes are done, and it's just you and me and that big huge moon up there, lighting up the sky and blocking all the stars from view," Greg said with a chuckle as he settled down next to Allen on the two-person sleeping pad he'd set up just outside their camper.

"All that planning you did, and you forgot to check the moon phase, huh?" Allen scooted over next to Greg and curled up in his spot, with his head resting on Greg's shoulder.

Greg laughed as he stared up at the moon through the clearing in the trees above them. "At least it's clear, and the weather has been pretty perfect. I hope you've had a good time, darling."

"I have. I've had a great time. And the camper—it was an excellent idea."

Allen was right. It had been an excellent idea. And this, their inaugural trip in their new camper, had been everything he'd hoped, even with the moon being out and sort of ruining Greg's plans for stargazing.

They'd chosen a secluded camping spot at a small campground along Methow River in the Okanagan-Wenatchee National Forest in northern Washington, and despite the mild late-summer weather, the campground had remained quiet; for the last three days, they'd been the only ones there, save for day hikers using the campground as their trailhead. Together, they'd enjoyed light hiking along the nearby trails that ran along the river and Robinson Creek to the north, with stunning views of the surrounding rocky mountain peaks. They'd seen tumbling waterfalls, colorful wildflowers, and plenty of wildlife. And when it had gotten too warm or when Allen had gotten tired, they'd retreated back to the camper to relax and rest, read, or sit outside in their lounge chairs, talking and enjoying each other's company, as always.

It had been exactly what Greg had wanted it to be when he'd suggested they get a camper earlier in the year. And when Allen had finally decided to officially step down as head librarian, they'd timed this trip as sort of a celebration.

Greg turned his head and pressed a kiss into Allen's hair. "That makes me happy to hear," he said softly, "even if all we're seeing tonight is the moon."

"It's gorgeous and full and bright. I dunno, I kinda like it," Allen said, and Greg closed his eyes and inhaled deeply as Allen's hand ran a slow path up and down his chest. "And I'm really happy to be here with you."

Allen's lips brushed along his jawline, and Greg hummed contentedly. "Mmm, me too. Me too."

It was true, of course. The night really was beautiful, and . . .

He opened his eyes again and tilted his head to look at his husband, who was watching him with a smile full of joy and contentment, his eyes sparkling in the moonlight.

The night was beautiful, and so was Allen. Beautiful and kind and loving. And there was a joy and vibrance in Allen's smile that ignited something in him.

Slowly, Greg shifted to prop himself up on one elbow, settling slightly over Allen. He bent down, closing the distance between them, and captured Allen's lips in a deep, tender kiss. When they parted, he lowered his head to Allen's shoulder with a shuddering breath.

A year ago. A year ago, they'd been tried and tested and ultimately come out stronger. But a year ago, he'd been closer to losing this—to losing Allen—than he wanted to even think about.

God, depression and anxiety were monsters. And it had taken so much effort from both of them to overcome that bump in their journey. Ultimately, it had shown Greg what was important, and for the last year, he'd focused hard on reprioritizing. He'd cut back on work, like he'd said he would. He'd stopped going on solo, multiday backpacking trips altogether. He'd started spending more time at home and less time out on the trail. And it was all better.

He didn't regret any of it. In fact, he thought maybe he'd waited a bit too long to make the change. Because now—now, every day, he got to spend more time with his husband.

Allen's hand rubbed Greg's back lightly. "Are you okay? You know, if you're really set on seeing the stars, we can come back when the moon won't be out. We have time in our schedule now, since I'll only be working three days a week. Though it'll need to be soon, won't it? Because otherwise it'll be cold, and I'm not sure this would be so much fun if we were both freezing."

Greg laughed and nodded into Allen's shoulder, then pushed himself back up onto his elbow again. "I'm okay, darling. It wasn't that. The stars will always be here. We can come back whenever."

"We can." Allen's smile softened, and his hand came around to cup Greg's cheek. Then he drew Greg back to him with a gentle pressure, and their lips met again, softly, briefly. "You'll just have to be a bit more thorough with your planning," Allen teased when they parted.

With a quiet chuckle, Greg nodded again. "More thorough. Yep. I can definitely be more thorough," he said, and he dipped back down to capture Allen's lips. An addicting warmth coursed through him, and he deepened the kiss, slanting his mouth against his husband's as his tongue sought entrance. Allen gladly complied, and his quiet, low moan sent a jolt of arousal through Greg as he tasted remnants of chocolate and strawberries from their dessert less than an hour ago. It was an intoxicating mixture, and Greg quickly let himself get lost, his heart racing more with each passing second.

He finally broke the kiss minutes later when he heard a quiet whine from the camper. Glancing up with a sigh, Greg saw Beans through the closed screen door, standing with his front paws up on the mesh and his tail up in the air and wagging. Beans whined again, then let out a low bark and scratched at the screen door with one paw.

"Sorry, darling, I thought he was down for the night," Greg grumbled, shaking his head.

Allen twisted a bit to look back toward the camper and then grinned as his hand slipped down to Greg's chest. "I think he's just reminding us how much more comfortable the bed inside is than this camping pad, dear."

"Oh?"

"Mm-hmm," Allen hummed, and he stretched up and placed a kiss on Greg's jaw and then his neck. Allen's hand slid down more, stopping low on Greg's stomach. "Much more comfortable."

Greg groaned quietly and closed his eyes. "You know, I'm comfortable wherever you are."

"And I'd be most comfortable in the camper, in our bed."

"With fewer clothes on?" Greg murmured suggestively, his lips now only a hair's breadth away from Allen's.

"Mm-hmm. Or none."

"Ahh, yeah. That would be best, probably."

Beans whined again, and Greg huffed a light laugh. "He's relentless, isn't he?"

"Yup," Allen agreed, and his hand slid out to Greg's hip and then around to Greg's back. "But he's just trying to make sure we're most comfortable."

"Mmm." The pressure of Allen's hand on Greg's lower back sent another rush through him, and Greg lowered his mouth to cover Allen's again. It was a brief kiss this time, but no less tender or sweet, and when he pulled back, Allen smiled gently.

"I am really happy, you know," Allen said, and he held Greg's gaze for an extra moment before dipping his chin. "And this—"

Another bark, this time much louder and more insistent, cut Allen off, and he and Greg both groaned together.

"Yeah, yeah, Beans. We're coming," Greg huffed, giving Allen an apologetic look. "I want to know what you were going to say, but after we get inside and appease our little whiner in there."

Allen nodded in understanding, and together, they stood, rolled up the sleeping pad, and packed it back up in its bag. Then they headed inside the camper, where Beans greeted them both with more whiny yips and a wagging tail. Allen headed to the bathroom to wash up and get ready for bed while Greg snapped on Beans's leash and took him out to do his business. When they returned to the camper a few minutes later, Allen was just exiting the bathroom, now dressed comfortably in plaid pajama pants and a plain white T-shirt.

Greg unclipped Beans's leash, and the pup bounded over to Allen and hopped up to put his front paws on Allen's thigh. A soft smile graced Allen's lips, and he knelt down slowly and murmured some quiet words to Beans while scratching behind the dog's ear. Greg set the leash on the counter near the door and then stepped up the last step into the camper just as Allen straightened back up.

"Go on to bed now, silly dog," Allen said, the affection in his voice clear, and Beans—being the very, very good, very, very obedient pooch he was—did some sort of whole body shake and then trotted happily off to the bedroom area and hopped up on *their* bed rather than curling up on *his own* bed, which they'd put on the floor just at the foot of their bed. Greg rolled his eyes, and Allen sighed. Beans turned around to look at both of them, wagged his tail, and then circled twice before lying down at the end of the bed, right in one corner, his head resting on his paws.

"Well, at least he doesn't take up much space?" Greg offered, closing the rest of the distance between him and Allen. He reached out and set his hand at the small of Allen's back, and his husband leaned into the touch with a hum of agreement. Or maybe contentment? Greg dipped his head and touched his lips to Allen's neck as he wrapped his arms around Allen's midsection. "I can still make him get off, though, if you want."

"Hmm."

Greg kissed Allen's neck again and let one hand drift lower, under the hem of Allen's T-shirt and then along his stomach, gently pressing himself up against Allen's back. "Just . . . whatever you want."

With another quiet hum, Allen turned in Greg's arms until they were facing each other, and his hands slid up Greg's chest. "I just want you."

Allen's soft smile was everything. It *meant* everything, and it filled Greg's chest with love and happiness and joy. He bent down again and brushed his lips lightly against Allen's.

"You have me, darling. Now and forever."

The End

Note From the Author

I hope you enjoyed reading Greg and Allen's story! As with a lot of my stories, it took on a bit of a life of its own as I wrote, and both of the characters surprised me in ways I hadn't expected when I first started writing. Allen's journey with childhood trauma and mental health is one that is much too common, and much of it was difficult to write because I connected with Allen on many levels. My favorite part of writing this story, though, was being able to write that Greg was there with Allen at every step. I loved how they had each other and how the love and trust they'd cultivated for decades helped them both through the challenges they faced.

I wanted to expand for just a moment on one of the content warnings at the beginning of the book: refusal of medication for mental illness. In this story, Allen refuses to take medication for mental illness. This choice of his is related to his backstory—comments and remarks from his parents that he'd internalized when he was younger and that he's still been unable to move past. However, I want to be clear that *this is not meant to be a statement against medication in any way*. Medication is a very *valuable and lifesaving tool* in the mental health field, and there is no shame or weakness in needing or wanting to have medication for any mental illness.

As with my first two novels, *More Than Words* and *Tell Me Again*, I am committing to donating all of the proceeds from this book to a charity. For *More Than Words*, I chose RAINN, an anti-sexual violence organization, since Sam and Ollie's journey in that story focused on Ollie's healing in the years after he was assaulted. For *Tell Me Again*, I chose True Colors United, an organization that supports LGBTQ+ youth facing homelessness, because of the challenges Coop faced after his mother passed away.

For Greg and Allen's story, given the particular mental health challenges Allen faced, I've decided to donate all of the proceeds to the American Foundation for Suicide Prevention (AFSP) and The Trevor Project. Suicide is the eleventh leading cause of death in the US, and nearly four times more men die by suicide than women.[1] Additionally, middle-aged and older adults have higher suicide rates than younger adults and youth.[1] Despite that, suicide is the second leading cause of death among youth ages ten to fourteen and the third leading cause of death among young people ages fifteen to twenty-four.[2] Furthermore, LGBTQ+ youth are more than four times more likely to attempt suicide than their peers.[2] Both the AFSP and The Trevor Project provide resources, tools, and support to help prevent suicide nationwide.

For more information, or to find out how you can help, visit AFSP at http://afsp.org and The Trevor Project at https://www.thetrevorproject.org/.

[1]American Foundation for Suicide Prevention. Suicide Statistics. https://afsp.org/suicide-statistics/. Accessed August 31, 2024.

[2]The Trevor Project. Facts About Suicide Among LGBTQ+ Young People. https://www.thetrevorproject.org/resources/article/facts-about-lgbtq-youth-suicide/. Accessed August 31, 2024.

And just in case you were still wondering about the crossword clue in Chapter Fifteen . . .

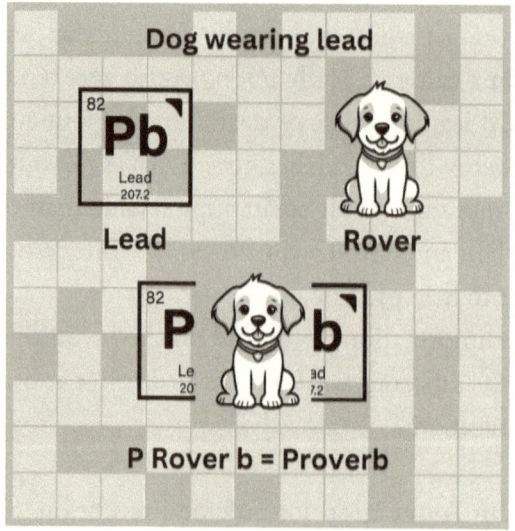

Acknowledgements

This story wouldn't have been finished without the constant support and reassurance of two very good friends (you know who you are, I'm sure!). I cannot thank both of you enough for everything, especially all the late night and early morning chats (and all our shared tears, smiles, and laughs) that reassured me this story was worth telling. I hope you both know how much I appreciate you. Thank you from the bottom of my heart.

Also, to my daughter, who once again (although metaphorically this time!) held my hand throughout the whole process and helped name Beans—I love you SO much. You are so much of the brightness in my life, and I can't thank you enough for all the happiness and joy you've brought to me and everyone around you. Keep shining, girlie.

About the Author

Becca Neil writes contemporary romance, heavy on the hurt/comfort and angst but always with plenty of fluff and swoons and an uplifting happily-ever-after. She enjoys crafting character-centered stories of love and healing and forever. When she's not writing or thinking about writing, she might be off hiking somewhere or lost in the beauty of a sunset.

To find out more about Becca and her upcoming projects, visit www.beccaneil.com or connect with her on the following social media platforms:

Facebook (Becca Neil and Becca and KC's Book Nook)
Instagram (@beccaneilauthor)
TikTok (@beccaneilauthor)

Be sure to check out her other novels, *More Than Words* and *Tell Me Again*.

www.ingramcontent.com/pod-product-compliance
Lightning Source LLC
Chambersburg PA
CBHW031939240626
47153CB00003B/792